Protection

By GJ Moffat and available from Headline

Daisychain
Fallout
Blindside
Protection

Protection

GJ Moffat

<u>headline</u>

Copyright © 2012 GJ Moffat

The right of GJ Moffat to be identified as the Author of
the Work has been asserted by him in accordance with the
Copyright, Designs and Patents Act 1988.

First published in 2012 by
HEADLINE PUBLISHING GROUP

1

Cataloguing in Publication Data is available from the British Library

ISBN 978 0 7553 6079 6 (Trade Paperback)

Typeset in Fournier by Palimpsest Book Production Limited, Falkirk, Stirlingshire

Printed and bound by CPI Group (UK) Ltd, Croydon CR0 4YY

Headline's policy is to use papers that are natural, renewable and recyclable products and
made from wood grown in sustainable forests. The logging and manufacturing processes
are expected to conform to the environmental regulations of the country of origin.

HEADLINE PUBLISHING GROUP
An Hachette UK Company
338 Euston Road
London NW1 3BH

www.headline.co.uk
www.hachette.co.uk

This one is just for Kay — because she's
got a thing for serial killers

Acknowledgements

First, huge thanks to Bob McDevitt who started me down this road and has always helped make the books better. Best of luck with everything you do from here on.

Thanks also to the people who volunteered their time selflessly and contributed to the creation of this story: Sergeant Larry Subia of the Denver Police Department; and Colorado native Karen Rinehart of Los Angeles law firm O'Melveny & Myers.

Finally, the professionals who help get to the finished product – my editor Ali Hope and my agent Simon Trewin of United Agents.

I carry a photograph everywhere I go. It's a picture of me when I was four. It was taken with a Polaroid camera and has faded with age and exposure to sunlight.

In the photograph I'm sitting on the floor and the carpet is heavily patterned. Behind me is a large chair in a style from that time. It looks like a comfortable chair. I think it was, though I don't have a strong memory of it. I'm not sure I even remember exactly where the photograph was taken. We moved around a lot, my mum and me.

It's not a typical photograph of a child, which is why I like it. I think.

I'm not looking directly at the camera but at my hand, which is raised in front of me. It looks like there's some food at the corner of my mouth; chocolate maybe. I seem to be staring at my hand, but there's no apparent trace of chocolate on it. I don't remember why I was looking at my hand.

I don't look happy. I don't look sad. It's just me, staring at my hand in a house that I don't remember.

I like to use my hands when I kill someone. Get right up close and personal.

It's not like I get off on it or anything. But I am fascinated by the final moments. I'll often sit and watch as the last breath hitches and leaves the body. I imagine that I look like my four-year-old self in those moments. The look in the photograph.

I'm not happy. I'm not sad. I just . . . am.

I took a Polaroid of myself once after the event. I sat in front of a mirror in the house of the dead and tried to replicate the pose from the photograph. It's not exactly the same, and you can see the body on the bed behind me — a reflection of a life that used to be.

There's no food on my mouth in this new photograph. The hand that I'm holding up is covered in blood and it looks like I'm staring at the blood, fascinated.

I'm not.

Blood holds no interest for me.

Funny thing about the old photograph — the one of me as a child: there are punch holes seemingly at random on each of the four corners. Not neat, single holes like it was once kept in a folder. There are four or five holes at each corner. I don't know how they got there.

Sometimes I put the two photographs side by side and I stare at them. I lost three hours doing that one time.

When I do that, I wonder what it would taste like if the new picture came to life and I licked the blood from my fingers. I've never done that, you understand.

I'm not a monster.

Part One
Double Jeopardy

1

Denver, Colorado

He sees them when he closes his eyes.

The light bars on the patrol cars outside the house pop and flash, bathing the interior alternately in blue and red.

For some reason he always remembers the dog first — not the kids. He doesn't know why. It's been eviscerated: cut open from the neck to the belly. The floor in the entrance hall is slick with its blood.

The Crime Lab techs are there already. He saw the van outside and hears the hushed murmur of voices up the stairs. Usually there's black humour to lighten the mood. It's how cops handle the horror of what they see.

Not this time. Everyone is real quiet this time.

He nods at the two uniformed officers shuffling from foot to foot in the hall — the first to respond to the call. Then he heads upstairs.

* * *

Detective Jake Hunter pinched the skin at the bridge of his nose, hoping to squeeze the memories until they were gone. A child's face floated in a red haze. Hunter opened his eyes and the after-image of the face remained for a second before fading in the hot sun.

Hunter was sitting on a bench in a tastefully landscaped plaza outside the Alfred A. Arraj Courthouse on the north-west edge of Downtown Denver. Two raised areas planted with shrubbery that seemed to stay green all year round flanked a narrow, winding river of water cut out of the stone in the centre of the plaza. The artificial river burbled slowly down to a pool at the steps leading up to the plaza. Hunter had always felt that the pleasant space was at odds with the business ordinarily transacted inside.

Especially today.

The courthouse was a modern building with a two-storey glass-fronted pavilion that formed the public entrance and also housed the Special Proceedings Courtroom. The main ten-storey building, clad in glass and stone, stretched into the air behind Hunter.

It was just before 10 a.m. and the plaza was crowded with journalists, photographers, uniformed cops and lawyers in dark suits. The uniforms had taped off the steps leading up to the plaza to keep the massed hordes of the general public back and to maintain some kind of order. There was a constant, loud hum of noise.

Hunter squinted as a photographer hunkered down in front of him and shot a few frames, the flash popping even in the stark February sun. He'd been sitting there for ten minutes and had ignored the journalists who had tried to engage him in conversation. They had all given up as he stared back blankly. It was a mild day given the time of year, but Hunter still wore his wool overcoat.

A man five years younger than thirty-four-year-old Hunter ducked under the tape, patted one of the uniforms on a shoulder and mounted the steps lightly, taking two at a time. Danny Collins, Hunter's partner in the Denver PD Homicide Unit, was a full two inches shorter than Hunter at five-ten and had a mop of blond hair that he was constantly tousling with his hands. Collins, unlike Hunter, was still very much single with looks good enough to exploit his status: something he was never slow to talk about. Sometimes Hunter thought that his partner, the youngest detective in the Unit, still believed he was seventeen and living it large in high school.

Collins stopped in front of Hunter and put his hands in his pockets. He was dressed in a grey suit with a blue shirt and brown tie. No overcoat. Hunter's coat felt too warm in the sun. He pulled at the collar of his shirt, feeling like it was too tight and wanting to loosen the top button. Department regulations would not allow it. Ordinarily, he was a man who lived by rules. There wasn't much else if you didn't, was how he looked at it. If the cops don't follow the rules, what hope for the rest?

'Mornin', chief,' Collins said.

Hunter nodded.

'Not in the mood for idle banter?'

'What do you think?' Hunter asked, standing and walking towards the court entrance.

* * *

The title given to the Special Proceedings Courtroom described succinctly what it was used for. It was the last place Hunter wanted to be today. He and Collins walked along a bright corridor with light streaming in from floor-to-ceiling windows. The *clack-clack* of their footfalls echoed from the tiled floor.

Ed Bowman, the detective sergeant in charge of the team of six detectives that Hunter and Collins belonged to, was standing at the door to the courtroom beside a smaller black man. Both of them were neatly dressed in suits with white shirts and plain ties. Bowman was a tall man, light of foot and with a bushy moustache. The other man, the Unit's administrative head, Lieutenant Art Morris, was of medium height, about five-nine, and slim, but his reputation as a man not to mess with, mentally and physically, had followed him throughout his career from uniformed patrol to his current position. He was a good boss, working his detectives hard but protecting them from the worst excesses of his own superiors.

'You don't need to be here today, Jake,' Morris said, shaking Hunter's hand.

'I'll see it through to the end.' Hunter shrugged.

'If it is the end.'

'Everyone knows what's going to happen. Chase Black will be a free man today.'

Bowman huffed out a breath – his way of showing displeasure. He was an overly officious man who always looked over the shoulders of his detectives rather than trusting their instincts. The Homicide Unit was the best in the Detective Bureau – it was where all the good detectives wanted to work. The elite. Which meant that the cops in it were mostly good enough to be allowed to investigate cases with minimal supervision. Bowman saw it differently.

Hunter stared at Bowman but said nothing.

'Let's get inside and find a seat,' Collins said, pulling at the heavy wooden entrance door to the public gallery of the courtroom.

Hunter felt an immense weight settle on his shoulders and it was all he could do to stay upright. He looked out of the window behind Bowman and saw a bird land next to a flower bed. It stooped, paused and burrowed into the earth before pulling out a worm and flying off again with breakfast still dangling from its beak.

Collins held the door open, waiting for his partner. Hunter looked past him into the carpeted hush of the court. He glanced at Morris.

'Let's go watch a serial killer let loose again in our city,' he said.

2

The courtroom was wider than it was long with a raised podium and an imposing wooden desk for the panel of three judges who would preside over the appeal. The room was double height and a square skylight in the centre of the ceiling allowed natural light to flood the space. Two tables faced the judges' bench at floor level, one each for the prosecution and defence teams. Behind them, five rows of seats made up the public gallery. A woman in the front row of the gallery turned her head at the sound of the door being opened and her eyes locked on Hunter. She stood and walked to the end of the line of seats before turning towards him.

Alice Dale was attractive in a cultured kind of way: high cheekbones and short, dark hair framing a narrow face. She had done her best with make-up this morning but had been unable to completely hide the bruised crescents beneath her eyes and the hollowed-out look of her cheeks. Hunter thought that she must have lost a lot of weight during the course of the three-week appeal hearing. She looked worn out.

'Mrs Dale,' he said, nodding at her.

Her bottom lip trembled and a vertical crease formed in the skin between her eyes. Hunter wondered if she was going to break down, but she drew in a long breath and held it together.

'He's getting out, isn't he?' she asked. 'The man who killed my babies.'

Hunter tried to remember seeing the photographs of her two children around the living room of her house in Cherry Creek. He and Collins had gone to see her there before the appeal started. Instead, images of their lifeless bodies from the scene of their murder scratched at the edge of his consciousness.

Hunter blinked hard.

'Yes, I think he's going to win,' he told Alice Dale.

He didn't see any point in sugar-coating it for her.

She swallowed and a tear slipped from her left eye and down her cheek. She must have felt it but made no move to wipe it away. Hunter was aware of others in the public gallery turning to watch them. He felt like a child again, lost and helpless in an adult world; unable to function properly.

'I watched him on the TV this morning,' she said. 'Black, I mean. He walked out of the jail in that orange jumpsuit and handcuffs so confident, like he always knew it was only temporary. Laughing and smiling with the reporters. It never touched his eyes, though. The emotion, I mean. Did you notice that? I don't think he's capable of a genuine emotion. Except maybe when he's . . .'

A group of three lawyers led by a thirty-something man came into the court from a side entrance and started laying out papers on the defence table. Hunter knew this meant that the judges were about to come on to the bench and start the day's proceedings. It meant that Chase Black would be here soon as well.

Wiping the tear from her cheek and smudging her make-up, Alice Dale turned and looked at the defence lawyers. The dark circles under her eyes became more pronounced and Hunter felt a surge of anger course through his blood-stream, the air thickening around him.

Alice Dale shook her head at Hunter as if physically unable to speak any more. She walked back to her seat without saying anything further and Hunter thought that he saw her stride falter as she turned the corner. He was in awe of her strength.

Morris and Bowman passed Hunter to find seats that had been kept free for them by the Sheriff's deputies who handled security in the court. A tall, broad-shouldered man came into the court and sat alone at the prosecution table in front of the judges' bench. The man nodded at Morris. Robert Angel was the senior Assistant District Attorney who had handled both the original prosecution and now the appeal in the Chase Black case. He was nearing forty and had no intention of seeking better-paying work in the private sector. He loved his job. Loved putting the bad guys away. He was Hunter's favourite lawyer.

Hunter remembered the first time he'd met Angel: on a gang-related attempted murder. A sixteen-year-old boy had been caught in the middle of a turf war and had been badly injured – stabbed five times in the back and neck. He was lucky to have survived.

The attacker, a seventeen-year-old, had hired an inexperienced lawyer. Hunter was in the hallway outside the court when Angel, all six feet five, and two hundred and twenty pounds of him, came barrelling down the hall looking for a fight. The other lawyer never had a chance. Angel literally cornered the guy by a window, stepped right into his personal space and loomed over him until a very favourable plea bargain (for the prosecution anyway) was agreed.

Angel looked from Morris to Hunter and set his lips in a thin line before turning back to the pile of papers on the desk.

'Take it easy, partner,' Collins whispered, sensing Hunter's fury. 'I don't want to have to pull you off of that bastard.'

A loud *clunk* sounded as the door from the cells beneath the courtroom was unlocked. Another deputy sheriff walked in leading a man in a linen suit with an open-necked white shirt. Chase Black had been allowed to change from his prison-issue jumpsuit to attend court.

He looked like a man who was about to know freedom again.

3

Black looked as casually powerful as always – wide shoulders tapering to a narrow waist. He had dark hair that was short enough to require no real styling and green eyes. He had a face like a big cat. The camera loved him. Hunter had read somewhere that he'd received close to a thousand letters from female fans during his two-year stay in jail. This man convicted of the murder of five families over a six-week span of time. It made no sense to Hunter.

Black saw Hunter standing beside the public gallery and inclined his head in greeting before walking to the defence table and shaking hands with his main lawyer, John Preston. The other two members of the legal team were young associates not long out of law school. Preston, on the other hand, was fast gaining a reputation as one of the best criminal lawyers in town.

Hunter followed his partner to spare seats at the far end

of the second row in the gallery. A man sitting three seats along in the front row turned and looked at Hunter before quickly facing the front again. Hunter recognised him. Jay Drayton was the husband and father of two more of Black's victims.

The Drayton family lived in London, England and had been vacationing in Colorado when Black went on his killing spree. They had rented an apartment in the town of Dillon – a short drive west across the Continental Divide through the Eisenhower Tunnel. Jay Drayton's wife had driven into Denver for some shopping with their teenage daughter and they had got cut off from making the return journey the same day by a heavy snowstorm.

Their bodies were found the next day in a motel on I-70.

Like most of the surviving family members, Drayton was a shadow of the man he used to be. He was still a big man with a face that looked like it had seen action on the rugby field or in the boxing ring – a broken nose with thick ears – but had become a near recluse. A property developer who got out before the market crashed, he was wealthy enough not to have to work again if he didn't want to.

But the look Drayton had given Hunter was not that of a defeated man. He looked agitated, his neck flushing red under the collar of his shirt.

'Keep an eye on Drayton,' he said in a low voice, nudging Collins. 'He looks ready for something.'

Collins glanced at the back of Drayton's head and nodded.

Black pulled out a chair from the table and looked back at Hunter, something like a smile passing across his face.

Hunter thought about the dog again, how he had found it gutted in the hallway. Images from that night flooded into his head.

He was upstairs in the house. Steve Ames, the lead Crime Lab investigator, was standing in the hallway with his second in command, Molly August. They wore thin, blue windcheaters with department badges. Both looked shaken. Ames was a stocky, twenty-year-veteran detective sergeant. Fifteen of those years had been spent with the Crime Lab and the lines on his face spoke of a thousand crime scenes. Molly was taller than Steve and still fairly new to the department. She was sometimes brusque but maybe she felt she had to be tough to make it. Whatever, Hunter liked her. You had to be tough in a male-dominated world.

Flashbulbs popped in two of the bedrooms off the hall.

Ames turned to look at Hunter as he came up the stairs.

'I'm guessing the dog is the least of our concerns,' Hunter said, looking back down the stairs.

Ames nodded.

'Two kids and the father up here,' August said, her voice sounding thick.

'No mother?'

'Separated. She's at her sister's house.'

'Someone will have to go over there. Tell her.'

August looked at Hunter — knew that it was his responsibility.

'Want to show me the bodies?' Hunter asked.

'Not really.'

Hunter smiled grimly and followed August as she went into the first bedroom. It was decorated in pale blues and greys, a sophisticated room in a big house. The parents' room.

Correction — the father's room.

No one's room now.

A man lay on the bed. Blood had soaked through the covers underneath the body, turning them almost entirely red.

Hunter did his best to suppress his gag reflex.

'The photographer done in here?'

'No,' August said, tying her dark hair back in a ponytail and putting on a pair of safety glasses. 'He's in the other room right now. The kids' room.'

'But somebody checked for a pulse?'

She turned her head to look at him. Couldn't tell if he was serious.

'Yeah, we did that, Jake.'

'I didn't mean . . .'

Two Crime Lab team techs waited inside the room in full body overalls, leaning against the wall and trying not to look at the man's body. They would have to wait until the room was shot on video and photographed before kneeling in the blood and picking over the place for trace evidence. Paper masks covered the lower half of their faces.

He heard Danny's voice out in the hallway, talking to Ames.

'What about the kids?' Hunter asked August.

She inclined her head.

'Next room over. Want me to show you?'

Hunter wondered, not for the first time, if Chase Black deliberately chose families where he could leave some of them alive. Certainly that was one of the patterns common to all five families. Perhaps that was part of Black's methodology: somehow gaining gratification from seeing the pain he inflicted on the survivors.

Hunter wasn't religious, but he figured he now knew what true evil was; seeing it in the ruined bodies of Black's victims.

4

The hearing didn't last long. The lead judge on the panel, Judge Painter, raised his hand to cut off Bob Angel before he had even fully stood. Angel's shoulders slumped, though he had known at the close of the proceedings the previous afternoon that John Preston had irretrievably swayed the judges with his argument.

Angel had warned them about Judge Painter weeks ago; he was an appellant's judge. The selection process for the three judges to hear an appeal was a random one – three being picked out of twenty-two eligible judges. Local attorneys referred to it as 'the Wheel'. You never knew where it would stop spinning. This time, they were out of luck.

After his conviction, Chase Black had sacked his original legal team and hired Preston to work on the appeal. The new firm put a big team on it. One of the young lawyers at the defence table had been given the task of reviewing all the Crime Lab records from the five scenes. He had spotted an anomaly at the last scene. A technician was seen in the video of the room where the single most incriminating evidence against Black had been found – a drop of blood that was ultimately matched to Black. The only real piece of evidence they had ever been able to link to him. But that technician had not signed in on the log sheet. Without any official record of him at the scene, all the evidence gathered was tainted and inadmissible.

That was the killer blow Preston had delivered in court yesterday.

Everyone in the Homicide Unit and the Crime Lab knew it had been coming. Preston had filed written arguments highlighting it. But it still felt like being punched in the gut.

It was amazing what a good lawyer could do with something so basic.

Hunter listened with no emotion showing on his face as the judge effectively told Angel that he had no option but to concede the appeal on the grounds that the original conviction was unsafe. They would not even entertain Angel's argument that the case should be sent back to the trial judge to be re-heard without that tainted evidence.

'Doesn't mean he's innocent,' Hunter whispered to Collins.

Angel did the only thing that he could – he withdrew the State's opposition to the appeal. Black turned in his seat and grinned, thumping Preston on the back and shaking his hand.

Game over.

Jay Drayton moved fast for a big man. He roared and pushed up from his seat, the sound unlike anything Hunter had ever heard a human utter before. A woman screamed as he ran to the barrier between the gallery and the main part of the court. Drayton placed a hand on top of the four-foot-high barrier and vaulted over it.

Hunter stood, put a hand on the shoulders of the people sitting in front of him in the first row and jumped forward over the seats. He saw Black stand and turn to face Drayton, saw a dark shadow pass across Black's eyes and wondered who was more in danger – Drayton or Black.

One of the deputies who had ushered Black into the court sprinted from his seat outside the door to the cells. He must have been a football player in his youth because he dived full length and wrapped his arms around Drayton's legs when he was no more than six feet from Black. Hunter got there quickly and grabbed Drayton's arms, pinning him to the floor.

There was despair and fury in Jay Drayton's eyes. Hunter didn't think he'd seen anything so sad before. The deputy sat on Drayton's legs and shouted at him to be still or he would be arrested. Hunter felt immense strength in Drayton as he pushed his arms off the floor. Hunter realised that he would not be able to restrain him alone. Then Collins was beside him, grabbing one arm with both hands and pushing it to the floor with his knees. Hunter did the same with Drayton's other arm.

Drayton screamed and made one last effort to push the three men off him, almost succeeding. After that, he gave up and sobbed like a child.

'He killed them,' he said, through phlegm and salty tears. 'He killed them all.'

Black had watched the whole thing: silent and unmoving while chaos raged around him. Hunter looked up at him, Black holding his gaze while Drayton's body heaved on the floor. Hunter looked for something, anything, to demonstrate that Black felt any emotion.

But his face was blank.

5

Hunter sat alone in his department-issue Ford sedan. It was three hours since he had left the courtroom and clouds darkened the sky. He looked up at the sound of a door slamming shut and saw two men walk out of the main prison building and pause. The taller man stopped and raised his face, closing his eyes and seeming to breathe in deeply. Hunter knew it was a show for the press goons packed ten deep at the perimeter fence, all of them screaming for the man to give them their photo opp.

Guy knows how to work an audience.

Hunter pulled the door handle and stepped out on to the tarmac of the parking lot at the Denver County Jail. The jail, located at 10500 East Smith Road, was a sprawling collection of stark concrete and brick buildings surrounded by arid brush land. Built in 1957, it had since been rebuilt and remodelled to cope with the increased inmate traffic down through the decades. It averaged around nineteen hundred prisoners in any given day.

There was one less today.

Hunter's breath misted in the air and he pulled his coat across his chest. The sun broke low through the cloud cover, shadows flitting across the ground.

Hunter put on a pair of vintage Ray-Bans — a birthday gift from his wife Ashley — pushed his hands into his trouser pockets and leaned back against his car, feeling the cold of the metal and glass through his clothes.

The two men walked towards the parking lot. The taller man gave no indication that he had seen Hunter yet. Behind him, Hunter heard the yells of the press pack grow in volume, shouting the man's name.

Chase Black.

The men reached their car and the shorter of them, Black's lawyer, John Preston, opened the rear door of his Cadillac. Black was about to duck inside the car when he saw Hunter. He started walking towards Hunter, leaving Preston at the car. Hunter waited, watching Black as his body seemed to phase in and out of existence as the shadows moved over him. A mild throb pulsed at Hunter's temple and he rubbed his fingers at the pain, trying to dislodge it.

Black stopped a few feet from Hunter.

'Detective,' Black said.

'Chase.'

'You look cold.'

Hunter looked up at the sun and back at Black, trying to ignore the pain in his head.

'It'll be spring soon,' Hunter said.

'Is that supposed to be profound?'

Hunter shrugged.

'My lawyer says that the case will have to be re-opened now. I bet that doesn't sit right with you, does it?'

'Cases.'

'What?' Black frowned.

'There are five cases. Five families.'

Black's head tilted to one side.

'They said I'm innocent.'

'No they didn't.'

Preston walked up to join his client, looked from one man to the other before fixing his gaze on Hunter.

'You know this could be seen as unwelcome attention on my client, detective.'

'You mean a cop being out here at the county jail?'

Preston did not look impressed by Hunter's response.

'I've spoken to your captain about the case already today. My client is no longer the focus of your investigation. I mean, you can't put him on trial again for the same crimes.'

'I know.'

'So why are you here?'

'Felt like taking a drive.'

'To the jail?'

'Each to their own, right?'

Preston turned to Black and put a hand on his arm.

'Let's go, Chase. Don't let him drag you into saying something that you'll regret.'

Black smiled at Hunter.

'I hope you catch him.'

'Who?'

'Whoever killed all those people.'

'Right.'

Hunter watched the two men walk away, hearing the incessant clicking of cameras behind him. He got into his car and turned the heat all the way up. The throbbing in his head moved to a spot behind his eyes.

Preston's car swept past him. He looked over and saw Black staring at him; the face of the man that Hunter was certain had killed all those people.

6

Hunter drove from the jail to police headquarters at 1331 Cherokee Street, arriving around three-thirty. He felt hollow as he walked past the red granite Fallen Officer Memorial in the plaza. He stopped at the memorial and looked down the list of names and at the inscription:

> *'When duty called there was no thought but answer*
> *No question but the task that must be done'*

He went into the Administration Building and nodded at the desk sergeant behind the bullet-proof glass in the ground-floor entrance before heading to the bank of four elevators.

The Homicide Unit squad room was on the third floor along with the rest of the Detective Bureau: Assault, Vice, Sex Offences, Domestic Violence and Robbery. Hunter came out of the elevator and walked along an inner corridor until he reached the door to the squad room at the south side of the building.

There were three cellular offices located to Hunter's right as he came in through the door. They were occupied by the squad's two sergeants and the head of the unit, Lieutenant Art Morris. Past those offices were a holding cell and an interview room.

The desks for the twelve detectives in the unit were in an open-plan area that took up the rest of the room. Each two-man team was separated from the next team by shoulder-high partitions. It was not luxurious, but it worked. Hunter walked to the desk he shared with Danny Collins. Collins leaned back from his computer screen and made a big show of looking at his watch.

'I was out at the jail,' Hunter said, taking his suit jacket off and placing it over the back of his chair.

Collins's smile faded.

'You didn't . . .'

'No.'

'Good.'

'Not really, anyway.'

Hunter sat down and switched on his PC. The murder books on the five families killed in the Chase Black case were stacked on and under his desk: fifteen binders filled with internal paperwork, photographs and Crime Lab reports. He put his hand on top of the pile on his desk.

'Where did these come from?' he asked, looking at Collins.

Collins's eyes looked past Hunter at the man approaching their desk.

'The Lieutenant's room, you two.'

Hunter turned when he heard Ed Bowman's voice. 'Now.'

Morris was leaning back in the chair behind his desk when Hunter followed Bowman into the room. Morris wasn't fond of official displays of valour and so there were no commendations or other awards on his walls. There were a couple of pictures of his wife and even more of his only son, mainly in football uniform. Hunter had heard that he was on the verge of a scholarship to Stanford's football programme.

Morris pushed heavy glasses up on his nose and looked at Collins as he closed the door to the office.

Hunter waited to be asked to sit. It didn't happen so he stood with Collins behind him. Bowman sat in one of the two free chairs.

'We had this discussion last night, Jake,' Morris said, looking from Hunter to Bowman. 'We all knew what was going to happen in court.'

Bowman nodded, aiming to look wise. Looked more like he was constipated, Hunter thought. The detectives in Bowman's charge were not his biggest fans. Hunter didn't respond to Morris's statement. Figured he hadn't been asked a question.

'You were out at the jail today after court,' Bowman said. 'For Black's release.'

'Yes,' Hunter replied, not looking at him.

'I got a call from the Captain ten minutes ago,' Morris said, shifting in his seat. 'After the Captain got a call from Black's lawyer. John Preston is not your average scumbag lawyer and so he didn't make idle threats. But he made it clear that any overly heavy-handed treatment of his client would lead to an inevitable claim against this department.'

'Black's a killer,' Hunter said.

Bowman leaned forward in his chair to speak but Morris held up a hand, cutting him off. Morris took his glasses off, placed them carefully on his desk and rubbed his hands over his face. Collins shifted his weight from one foot to the other and glanced at Bowman.

'We are not the judge and jury, detective,' Morris said. 'No matter what you, or I, may think, the appellate court decided that the conviction of Black was unsafe. Technically, he's innocent of those crimes.'

'Technically,' Hunter said, his voice rising a little. 'Sir, everyone in this room knows that Black is guilty.'

Morris pursed his lips and clasped his hands on the desk.

'Actually,' Bowman said, unable to hold his tongue, 'I don't know that.'

'Figures,' Hunter said, immediately regretting it.

'I don't know it either,' Morris said loudly. 'Not for sure. None of us can.'

Hunter was surprised by the anger he heard in his boss's voice.

'What I *do* know,' Morris went on, 'is that you are convinced that he's a killer. It's not the same thing. Not even close.'

'So what do you want me . . . us to do?'

'The case is open. Go work it.'

'I did that already. We caught the guy.'

'You are a stubborn bastard, Jake,' Bowman said, shaking his head. 'I'll give you that.'

Morris smiled, but no humour showed in his eyes. 'Go work it,' he repeated.

Hunter turned, pushed past Collins and pulled the door open.

'Jake,' Morris said sharply.

Hunter stopped and turned to his boss.

'Leave Chase Black alone.'

Hunter stared at him.

'I mean, I want you to concentrate all of your efforts on other avenues of inquiry. Do we understand each other?'

Hunter barely nodded before leaving the room.

Bowman followed Hunter and Collins back to their cubicle. He made a point of slowly surveying the binders from the five cases. Hunter waited for him to speak.

'You want me to re-assign this to someone else?' Bowman asked.

Hunter looked up at Bowman. He saw food crumbs caught in his moustache.

'No, sergeant. We'll do fine.' Hunter smiled at him. It was not genuine.

Bowman looked at Collins, stuffing his hands in his pockets.

'Keep me updated,' he said to Hunter, turning to go back to his office.

'Where do you want to start?' Collins asked Hunter when Bowman's door was closed.

Hunter sifted the binders on his desk till he found the one he wanted. He slid it out of the pile and opened it at his own initial report from the first crime scene. Behind the report were photographs that Hunter thought – hoped – he would never have to look at again. The Dale children had been eight and ten years old. A boy and a girl.

Hunter followed Molly August out of the father's room and into the hallway. Danny Collins was there with Steve Ames.

'Hey, Jake.'

Hunter nodded at his partner.

'Molly's going to show us the kids' room,' Hunter said. 'Let's go.'

Collins nodded and walked down the hall after Hunter. White light strobed out of the doorway of the kids' room at the end of the hall as the crime scene photographer recorded the carnage.

Hunter always smiled at the movies where the sound of the flash was amped up. It never sounded like that. But when he walked into the room after August and the flash popped, he would always remember it like the beat of a bass drum. It started in his feet and shook his body all the way up through his chest and into his head.

The children were together on the bed, their hands and feet bound to the metal frame. It didn't look real to Hunter. He'd seen plenty of murder scenes in his time on the force: witnessed violent death up close and personal. But this was something different. His mind had difficulty processing the level of violence inflicted on those children.

The flash popped again and his vision blurred.

'Jesus,' Collins whispered behind him.

Hunter stared at the bodies as August described their injuries in clinical forensic language. It didn't seem adequate. Not by a long way.

'Jesus,' Collins repeated.

August looked at Hunter.

'You seen enough?' she asked.

He turned and brushed past Collins to get out of that place, leaned back against the wall outside the room and sucked in a deep breath.

Steve Ames walked over to Hunter and put a hand on his shoulder.

'We do our job, Jake. We do our job and we catch this guy, you know. That's all there is to it.'

Hunter nodded, unable to erase the things he'd seen from his brain.

'Jake?' Collins said.

Hunter looked over at his partner.

'I said where do you want to start on this?'

'At the beginning.'

Part Two
Rules of Engagement

Memorandum

From: Agent Franck Zimmer
To: Interpol Section Chief
Re: Project Eden

Interpol Ref: 735F-27

Sir,

The suspected assassin designated subject 'Eve' has been located again after some months with no fresh leads. Her last known location was Denmark where she is implicated in the murder of the industrialist Arend Rasmussen. He was on bail awaiting trial for sexual offences relating to minors. The operation to track, trace and apprehend subject 'Eve' ('Project Eden') has been re-activated.

Echelon Listening Station B-12 was triggered last night in regards to subject 'Eve' at 20.14 hours. The attached transcript was relayed to me at 01.37. It is regrettable that such a delay occurred and I have requested a report from the station head.

Subject 'Eve' was mentioned in a telephone conversation. Trace was incomplete except that: (1) the outgoing male caller (unknown subject, now designated 'Mamba') was engaging from the public telephone network within the United Kingdom; and (2) subject 'Eve' received the call via a mobile network connection in France.

Call duration was not long enough to otherwise narrow the location of either subject. The mobile telephone number used by subject 'Eve' was cloned. Domestic officers in the French police force have already interviewed the original owner of the number. It has been determined that he is not connected to subject 'Eve'.

The transcript discloses that subject 'Eve' is to be engaged by subject 'Mamba'. Target of the engagement is unknown. Field of operation is the United Kingdom. SOCA (UK's domestic Serious Organised Crime Agency) has been notified and border controls are in effect. Further reports to follow.

Call Transcript

(Echelon connection made)

Subject Mamba: [three seconds of silence] That's an awful lot. I mean, more than I was told it would be.

Subject Eve: Does this strike you as a negotiation?

Subject Mamba: [five seconds of silence] It's just, you know...

Subject Eve: Because it's not. If you want me, it's on my terms. That should have been made clear to you.

Subject Mamba: It was.

Subject Eve: Then let's move on.

Subject Mamba: How does it work?

Subject Eve: We meet. You arrange to transfer the funds. When I have confirmation of the transaction we are good to go.

Subject Mamba: That's it? I mean, how do you know who—

Subject Eve: Don't say any more. That part has to be done face to face. You understand?

Subject Mamba: This is all...new for me.

Subject Eve: I know. Otherwise we would not be talking. I'm a one-time only engagement. Always.

Subject Mamba: I can see how that would be safest.

Subject Eve: What's the timing?

Subject Mamba: Within the next few weeks.

Subject Eve: That's kind of imprecise. I'm used to getting more than that. These things need to be properly planned.

Subject Mamba: Can you still do it?

Subject Eve: Of course.

Subject Mamba: So, how do we progress it from here? Do I text you or call again or...?

Subject Eve: No. I won't use this number after tonight. I'll contact you when I'm ready.

Subject Mamba: What if the timing changes and it becomes more urgent? I mean, how will I contact you then?

Subject Eve: We'll work something out.

Subject Mamba: Like I said, this is all new.

Subject Eve: I'll be in touch soon.

Subject Mamba: He deserves to die. [four seconds of silence] I need you to know that.

(Call ends)

1

Monday: Glasgow, Scotland
Six months later

Logan Finch reached across his chest with his right hand
and slid a nine-millimetre pistol into the holster fixed under
his left arm. He pushed the gun down until it was firmly in
place and pulled on his suit jacket. Carrie Richardson stood
eight feet from Logan and mirrored his actions with her own
weapon.

Logan looked around the small room. Almost every spare
inch of wall space was taken up by weapons of some sort.
He saw handguns, rifles, knives and a number of solid wood
cabinets and drawer units. There were no external windows
and the floor was bare concrete. It was inside an old warehouse building on Scotland Street in Glasgow – a commer-
cial district south of the River Clyde. The building was

owned by CPO – a company run by Logan's best friend, Alex Cahill. The name 'CPO' was something of a private joke: it stood for Close Protection Operatives. Cahill ran a team of professional bodyguards.

The door behind Logan pushed open. Tom Hardy walked into the room with Bailey Judd. Hardy was Cahill's oldest friend and his second in command at CPO. They had served together in both the US Army and Secret Service. And 'some other stuff', as Cahill was fond of describing it. At six feet four, Hardy was a good four inches taller than Logan.

'Y'all ready for this?' Hardy asked in his Texas drawl, smiling at Logan.

Judd walked past Logan, clapping a hand on his shoulder as he passed.

'Don't mind him, Logan,' Judd said. 'He's looking to get a rise out of you.'

Logan put his hand over his jacket, feeling the holster underneath and thinking that it would be far too obvious that he was armed.

'You get used to that,' Judd told him, opening one of the cabinets on the wall and taking out his own holster.

'First time always feels weird,' Carrie added.

Logan looked at his watch as Hardy and Judd got ready. It was not long past eight in the morning.

'Where's Alex?' he asked Hardy.

'In the office. He sends his best.'

'He's not coming down here?'

'No. Why should he? I mean, he's not part of this detail.'

'I just thought . . .'

Cahill was more than Logan's boss. They were friends.

And Logan had been through a lot with Cahill in the last few years, starting with the murder of Logan's old girlfriend and the kidnap and rescue of the daughter they had together, Ellie. Logan had started out as Cahill's lawyer before training to become one of the company's bodyguards. He thought that Cahill might have been here to see him off on his first real protection job.

Hardy pulled his jacket on and came to stand in front of Logan.

'Listen,' Hardy told him. 'You wouldn't be going with us if Alex didn't think you were ready. Hell, you wouldn't be with us if *I* didn't think you were up to it.'

Logan nodded and took a breath.

'We ready to roll?' Judd asked. 'Got to be at the airport over in Edinburgh in no more than three hours. Get briefed by Special Branch before the Minister arrives.'

Judd was about an inch shorter than Logan with his fair hair cut close to his scalp. The suit jacket he wore was tight across his muscular shoulders.

'Don't want to be late for Special Branch,' Hardy said as he opened the door. 'Let's get moving.'

There were two cars parked outside in the inner courtyard of the warehouse – behind a heavy-duty metal gate that was operated electronically. Logan followed Carrie to a silver Ford saloon while Hardy and Judd got in a similarly plain-looking Toyota. The engines of both vehicles had been completely reworked so that they bore no resemblance to the cars that had rolled off the production line. They would be able to keep close to, or get away from, anything except a high-end sports car.

Carrie got in the driver's seat and Logan sat beside her. They put small radio earpieces in one ear and clipped microphones to the lapels of their jackets.

'Test, test,' Carrie said.

Her voice was clear and sharp in Logan's earpiece.

'Copy,' Hardy's voice sounded next.

They each spoke in turn to check the equipment was working.

Carrie started the car and the powerful engine rumbled to life. Logan lifted a remote control device and pressed a button to open the gate.

He looked across at Hardy in the second car, glad that the big man was with them.

'Relax,' Carrie said. 'It's an adventure.'

She pressed the accelerator and the car lurched out into the road.

Logan couldn't help but feel the excitement buzzing in his bloodstream.

2

Logan was the junior man on this detail. Everyone else had years of experience – Hardy more than anyone. Judd was a former soldier, an army Ranger, and had served in Iraq.

Carrie was something of a mystery to Logan and he still thought that she looked nothing like a bodyguard – five feet five and slim with brown eyes and dark hair. She was thirty-three but looked years younger. Good genes. He knew that she could handle herself, that her slim figure was lean and muscular, but she was the one team member he knew the least about. He was aware that she had been a police officer very briefly, for about six months. Other than that, she was very vocal about her love of Mexican food and she kept a low profile.

Carrie was quiet as she drove east on the motorway. Logan flipped through a file of papers – going over their briefing materials again. Their client today was the British Defence

Minister, Drew Jones, a man who had ended his military career as a high-ranking naval officer. The fact that he had served in the armed forces at all marked him out as unique in his government post.

Jones had seen action in the Gulf as an Apache helicopter pilot and had distinguished himself. He was a blunt speaker and while that had served him well in the military, it was not usually a characteristic that led to a long political life. He had already had to survive one media frenzy when he'd referred to a certain foreign politician as a terrorist.

Logan got the feeling that the man shared many characteristics with Cahill. No bad thing, so far as he was concerned.

The official purpose of the minister's visit to Scotland today was to brief the Scottish politicians at the Parliament in Edinburgh on the current status of the plans to close an RAF base in the north of the country. In reality, it was more of a PR exercise for the minister to show face in a country where he was not well liked. A lot of people were going to lose their jobs when the base closed. The fact that he had served in the Navy and not the Air Force added to the bad feeling.

Logan looked at the photograph of Jones in the file. He was a stocky man – powerfully built but with a developing belly. Life in political office was rarely good for your health; too many briefings over big lunches and late nights with bad food choices. He had thinning grey hair and a wide face. Dark eyes peered out from under a heavy brow.

'Wouldn't want to come up against him in a one-to-one situation,' Logan said to Carrie, tilting the photograph for her to see as she glanced over.

'I suspect he'll be the first one to wade into the crowd if it kicks off,' she said, smiling.

Logan put the file of papers on the floor, opened up his laptop and found the Facebook campaign against the minister that had started the concerns about his security for this trip. Special Branch had identified around fifty linked individuals from the campaign: all of whom looked to be largely harmless. Then again, it was always the quiet ones you had to be most careful of – the lone gunman.

Logan lifted his mobile phone from the pocket in his door and dialled Rebecca Irvine. She was a detective constable in Strathclyde Police CID – based in Glasgow. They had been together for a while, but had not yet committed themselves to living together.

'Hey, Becky,' he said when she answered.

Beside him, faint frown lines appeared on Carrie's face. Logan didn't notice, oblivious to the growing feelings that she had for him.

Logan heard Connor, Irvine's young son, screeching in the background.

'Sounds like you've got your hands full,' he said.

'Like you wouldn't believe,' Irvine replied. 'Don't know what's wrong with him today.'

Logan had not seen Irvine for a couple of days and realised when he heard her voice that the space in his life when she wasn't around was perhaps bigger than he was willing to admit.

'Anything special on today?' he asked.

'Nope. Usual stuff, you know.'

'Death and destruction?'

She laughed. 'That about sums it up.'

Connor screamed again.

'Anyway,' Logan said. 'I was just—'

'Damn, I forgot, didn't I? It's your first thing today.'

'Yeah.'

'How you feeling?'

He glanced at Carrie.

'A little bit excited. And a lot scared. The gun helps.'

'You got a gun?' she sounded wary, her voice dropping lower. 'Be careful, okay?'

'I will.'

'Listen, I have to go. Stay safe. Love you.'

'Me too.'

'You still all loved up,' Carrie asked, trying to keep her voice light as they passed a sign telling them that they were ten miles from the capital.

'Something like that,' Logan said, uncomfortable speaking too openly about his feelings.

Carrie went back to frowning in silence.

Logan shifted in his seat, the gun feeling too big again. He looked at the world passing by outside at seventy miles per hour and tried to remember how his life had got him to this point.

It didn't seem all that long ago that he spent his days as a corporate lawyer across boardroom tables negotiating deals where the only thing he needed to win his client's argument was a pen or a computer.

Now it was a nine-millimetre handgun.

Times change.

3

'Tom, good to see you again,' Lawrence Ryder said, extending a hand to greet Hardy.

Ryder was the chief Special Branch officer responsible for the security arrangements for the whole British Cabinet. His voice had been made gravelly by years of smoking French cigarettes and he was almost as tall as Hardy.

They were in an aircraft hangar in a private section of Edinburgh Airport where the minister's plane would come to rest in around an hour's time. The hangar inventory: four plain-clothes policemen; Lawrence Ryder; and two black Jaguar cars with darkened windows.

'You too, Lawrence,' Hardy replied before introducing the CPO team to Ryder.

Everyone nodded in greeting.

'I haven't forgotten the last time we saw each other,' Ryder said to Hardy, shaking his head.

'I think I've still got a lingering headache,' Hardy replied. 'It was legendary.'

Ryder laughed and invited everyone to sit at a makeshift command post comprising a picnic table and folding chairs located in the middle of the cavernous hangar. Logan had expected something a little more glamorous for his first job.

Logan hadn't met Ryder before, but he liked what he had heard about him: a career cop who joined straight out of school when he was eighteen, working up through the ranks on ability alone.

'You've all had a chance to go through the briefing materials, I take it?' Ryder asked.

'Yes,' Hardy replied.

Logan wanted to be seen to be involved, even though this was his first detail.

'Can you tell us if there is any specific threat against the minister that you're aware of?' he asked.

'He's had a lot of standard-type stuff about the RAF base closure. Nothing that makes us think there is likely to be a targeted attack of any nature.'

'He was the Minister for Northern Ireland before this?'

'Yes.'

'Any hold-overs from that?'

'Again, nothing out of the ordinary that I'm aware of.'

'This is his first trip north of the border since the base closure was announced?' Carrie asked.

'Correct, yes. So we didn't really know what the level of opposition was likely to be. I'm told there's a crowd of around two hundred protesters marching from Edinburgh

Castle, down the Royal Mile and then to the parliament building.'

'What's the official threat level?' Bailey Judd asked.

'Elevated, but we're not at red or anything like it.'

'That's because of the lack of a direct threat?'

'Right.'

'Any last-minute changes likely to the itinerary?' Hardy asked.

'You know me, Tom. There's always a last-minute change. I like to keep that stuff to myself until it happens.'

'Be spontaneous,' Hardy said.

'Best defence, I find.'

'Any chance we get a decoy car this time? You know, take the guy in the back while a dummy car pulls up at the front door.'

Ryder laughed.

'Thought I'd ask, you know,' Hardy said.

'Keep asking, Tom. One of these days I'll be able to convince someone that it's in their best interests to keep their faces *off* the TV.'

'I'll not hold my breath.'

'Okay. Listen, let's go over everything before the minister touches down.'

Logan had kind of hoped that his first job might be little more than a walk-through. Not that he would have approached it with anything less than complete commitment, but he knew from his legal training that being thrown into a major piece of work on your debut was not a pleasant experience. His first boss had handed him the papers for a criminal trial the day before it was due to start, giving him a long, sleepless night of preparation. The fact that he won the trial was of little comfort after the event.

'The basic plan,' Ryder said, 'is we take our man from here, drive with him to the Parliament, make sure no one kicks his head in, and bring him back again.'

Logan liked Ryder's straightforward approach.

'We take four cars,' Ryder said. 'My men will drive the two Jags in the middle of the convoy – with the minister's car third in line. CPO will cover front and back and walk the fence line at the Parliament once he's inside.'

Ryder pointed to the laptop on the table in front of him showing a plan of the route from the airport to the parliament building at Holyrood and back. The routes were different for each leg of the journey – a standard tactic, Logan knew.

'Looks good to me,' Hardy said. 'Fixed and known start and finish points but that can't be avoided. Varying the travel routes is the best we can hope for.'

Ryder nodded.

'Biggest point of risk will be at the Parliament,' Logan said. 'Not on the car journey.'

'I agree,' Ryder replied. 'But if something does happen while we're in the cars, the lead CPO car engages up front if there is a head-on attack. The rear car covers off anything at the back – any pursuit – and helps engage up front if need be.'

'And the minister's driver gets him the hell out of there,' Judd added.

'Carrie, I think it's your choice this time,' Hardy said. 'Front or back?'

'You always say the nicest things.' She smiled at him.

'Cute,' Hardy said. 'Front or back?'

'Front.'

'Right,' Ryder said. 'Let's do our jobs and keep the man safe.'

4

Monday: Denver

Jake Hunter and Danny Collins stood uncomfortably on the steps of Alice Dale's house listening to her footsteps as she approached the door.

Hunter tried to hide the shock on his face when she opened the door. She had lost more weight since the appeal hearing six months ago, her face was gaunt and heavily lined. She lifted a hand to one cheek, self-conscious about her fading looks, and stepped back to allow them inside. Hunter regretted not having been to see her before now. Truth was, he had been avoiding her. He knew how she would feel about the investigation focusing on any suspect other than Chase Black.

Hunter and Collins sat quietly on a couch in the living room while Alice Dale made some coffee. The hiss and burble of the machine going to work sounded from the kitchen. Photographs of her lost children were hung on the wall; portraits of what was and could have been.

She came into the room and handed them a cup of coffee each. Hunter sipped at his, to delay what he was going to tell her.

'You don't have anything, do you?' she said, standing in the middle of the room. 'I watch the news, you know.'

'No,' Hunter told her.

'We're doing all that we can to bring whoever did it to justice,' Danny Collins said.

She stared at him as though he had slapped her. Hunter said nothing, turning the coffee cup in his hands.

'We all know who did it,' Alice said. 'And that there's not a damn thing anyone can do to get him behind bars.'

Collins's mouth opened but she cut him off before he could speak.

'What's the official police department position on this now, Jake? That someone else did it, is that what you're telling me?'

Her voice hitched, tears welling in her eyes. She put a finger under her eye to hold back the tide – the way a woman will to preserve her make-up.

She looked from Collins to Hunter.

'I'm sorry,' was all Hunter could muster.

He felt the same anger she did.

'The investigation is open,' Collins said. 'All possibilities are being considered. We're on this full time.'

'Do those possibilities include the one where Chase Black is the murdering son of a bitch who butchered my babies?'

Her voice rose and this time there was nothing she could do to stop the tears.

'He's free of it now, isn't he?' she said, her anger now all-consuming. 'I mean, I'm not a complete idiot. I've seen enough movies to know how it works.'

'He can't be tried again for those matters,' Collins said. 'That's correct.'

'So he can do as he pleases. And then what? You wait till he kills again. Until another family is ripped apart by that man. Because he will. That's what men like him do. They can't help themselves, can they? *Then* you lock him up.'

'It's beyond my control, Alice,' Hunter said, opening his hands.

He felt helpless and ashamed; angry at Bowman and Morris having tied his hands for the last six months.

She stood and straightened her skirt, tear-soaked make-up smudging her cheeks. She wiped her face but only succeeded in making it look worse.

'I don't want to hear about this any more,' she said. 'There's nothing you can tell me that will make it better.'

Hunter nodded and stood to leave. She followed them to the door and touched Hunter's forearm as he left. He turned to face her.

'I don't blame you, Jake. You know that?'

Her face softened and he almost saw the woman she used to be – before her life was stolen from her.

He nodded, unable to form any words that would be adequate in the circumstances.

5

Hunter dropped Collins off back at the department and told him that he was going home for lunch. It wasn't true but Collins believed him. Hunter's wife Ashley – an ER physician – was three months pregnant and starting to show more significantly now. Collins assumed that Hunter was going home to see her. He wasn't.

Sun slanted into the car through the windscreen as he pulled up outside Quest Tower in downtown Denver. The offices of the law firm that represented Chase Black – Baker, Philp and Adam – were on the fifteenth floor. The firm had called a press conference for Chase Black at two-thirty and a couple of news vans were already in place. Hunter wasn't sure what it was all about, but he wanted to find out.

Hunter stopped the car and switched the engine off, rubbing at the long scar on his right forearm, thinking about how he had got it. It had been hot that day, when he went to the diner for breakfast in his crisp, blue uniform. So proud to be a cop on his first day and savouring the beautiful morning.

Before the gunfire started.

Before he ran across the blistering tarmac and held the hand of a dying FBI agent.

The man gurgling blood as his throat filled from the bullet wound in his neck.

Hunter running into the bank.

Before he got shot.

But amid the blood and the death of that day he had made a friend. Special Agent Dean Graves was now a big noise in the Bureau's Critical Incident Response Group based at the FBI Academy in Quantico, Virginia. He hadn't seen Graves for a while, but his friend had been on his mind more and more in the last couple of weeks as their investigation stalled and an idea began to gestate in his brain – that maybe there *was* a way to get to Chase Black.

He knew that the idea was not one that Morris would sanction. Not yet anyway. He needed something to take to Morris to get him on board.

Hunter scrolled through the contacts database on his phone, found the entry for Graves and pressed the button to dial his number.

'You still alive, son?' Graves said when he answered the phone, his bass voice booming all the way from Virginia.

Graves had been a naval aviator, a fighter pilot, before joining the Bureau, and had spent his last tour of duty on the USS *Eisenhower*. The crew called it the 'Ike' and he had a tattoo of the name on his right bicep. Most people who met him didn't forget him.

Hunter smiled thinly.

'I'm doing fine, Dean.'

'Why don't you call your old man any more? I haven't seen you guys for months.'

'Ash misses you too.'

'So what's up?'

'You still got profilers over there?'

'Sure. Except we call them behavioural analysts now, why?'

'You heard of Chase Black?'

'I heard of him. You need help with a profile now that the case is open again?'

'Kind of.'

'No need to be coy with me, Jake.'

'I still like Black for those murders, you know, and I need a way back in to him.'

'Not sure how that relates to what we can do for you, but go on.'

'I mean, if Black is our guy, and I think he is, maybe it didn't start with these families.'

'You think he killed before?'

'Isn't that the conventional thinking on serial killers? I mean, the Black case was my first but in my limited experience with the research on serial killers they don't just go off like he did – slaughtering whole families.'

'So you're looking at his past? For an unsolved case you can put on him?'

'I don't know. Maybe. If there even is such a thing.'

'Don't get your hopes up, Jake. I mean, who knows. But I'll help you if I can. You know I will.'

'Thanks, Dean.'

'You want me to route this through official inter-agency channels?'

Hunter didn't answer, hoping that Graves would understand what his silence meant. He did.

'It's like that, is it?' Graves said after a few moments.

'Let's say I'm interested in the profiling process and would appreciate a general background chat with one of your guys. Think you can help out?'

'Leave it with me.'

Hunter ended the call and looked across the street as increased activity caught his eye. Chase Black stood up from a Black Lincoln Town Car followed by a slender, sharply dressed woman. Photographers and TV cameramen jostled for position as Black and the woman walked from the car to the main entrance of the building.

Hunter watched from his car, feeling a mild pain throb at his temples. He pressed his hands there to relieve the pressure, but it didn't work. His mind filled again with the Dale house. He squeezed his eyes shut to wipe it away.

Hunter opened his car, stepped out on to the road and walked towards the door where Black had been moments before. He looked up as he crossed the street, his eyes going up the face of the building, trying to see through the brickwork. Trying to find Chase Black. Like the essence of the man was too strong to be hidden by mere physical things.

But there was nothing. It was just a building.

And Black was just a man.

6

Hunter pushed through the packed journalists, holding his detective's shield up to cut off any complaints. He took a few hard shoulders and sharp elbows but ignored them, tapping his shield against the glass door to attract the attention of the two security guards inside the building.

The floor inside was covered by dark, marble tiles and the heels of his shoes clicked on the hard surface as he walked to the main reception desk. The wallpaper on the walls looked expensive – copper coloured and roughly textured. Two women in matching black suits and white blouses sat behind the reception desk, bleached teeth shining brightly behind red lipstick. Even their blond hair matched.

There were two doors on the opposite wall; his and hers washrooms. The place smelled faintly of cleaning fluids and more strongly of the scent of flowers sitting in a tall vase on the desk. One of the women smiled at him as he placed his hands on the desk.

'Can I help you?'

Hunter held his shield up again. He liked the impact it made.

'Detective?'

He looked at the list of company names on the wall above the desk, pointing at Baker, Philp and Adam. The firm that represented Chase Black.

'They're having a press conference today,' Hunter said, not as a question.

'Yes.'

'Where?'

The woman glanced at the near twin sitting beside her.

Hunter heard a door open behind him. It swung shut with a quiet thud. Even the washroom doors here were expensive, he thought, as he turned around.

Chase Black tugged at his shirt cuffs until he was happy that they showed an even length beyond the sleeves of his jacket. He looked up and saw Hunter. Outside, the massed ranks of the press started to make noise as they saw Black through the doors, camera shutters clicking like a thousand crickets.

Black glanced towards the doors. He turned back to Hunter and walked forward, holding his hand out. The shutters went into overdrive.

He's doing it for the press. Wants me to look bad if I don't shake his hand.

Hunter looked down at Black's hand as the man he still thought of as the worst serial killer in Denver's history stopped in front of him. He wasn't prepared to play nice. Instead, he slowly pushed back his suit jacket and put his hands in his trouser pockets.

click-click-click-click-click-click-click-click

The crickets chirped.

Black dropped his hand. The woman that Hunter had seen exit the car with Black came out of the women's washroom. She had blond hair and a physique that spoke of every free hour spent in the gym – sinewy and tight. She smoothed her skirt and the front of her suit jacket as she walked forward, freezing in place when she saw Hunter. Her eyes flicked to the two women at reception.

'You here for my press conference?' Black asked Hunter, his face neutral.

Hunter nodded.

'What's it all about?' he asked. 'I mean, the book's not doing so good, is it?'

Hunter smiled, trying to needle Black into a reaction. The book was Black's autobiography of sorts – entitled *Inside Out*; a first-hand account of his arrest, trial, conviction and appeal. He had written most of it while in prison and signed a publishing deal the day after his release. Published to much fanfare in the US, the book had not even broken into the *New York Times* top 100 bestsellers.

'That's a narrow view of success,' Black said, smiling now. 'It's going down a storm in foreign markets.'

Hunter had not heard. He wondered if Black was telling the truth or trying to hide behind a lie.

'That's right,' the woman said, finding her voice now and striding towards them. 'Mr Black is an international bestseller. He's doing particularly well in the UK, as it happens. He's been serialised in a major newspaper over there.'

'Interesting choice of words,' Hunter said. 'Serial, I mean.'

Black laughed.

'Still can't give it up, eh, detective?'

'I never give up.'

The woman stopped beside Black.

'I'm Kate Marlow, Mr Black's attorney.'

'What happened to Preston?'

'John handles criminal matters in my firm. I'm a media and entertainment lawyer so Chase is my client now.'

Hunter saw how close she stood to 'Chase'. Maybe they were together in more ways than one.

'I'll be accompanying him on his tour of the European countries where he's selling well. Starting in England. That's what we're announcing today.'

'Jay Drayton may not be happy with those plans,' Hunter said, looking at Black.

Black shrugged and ran a hand through his dark hair. Hunter wondered if it was a hand that had once been deep in the entrails of the Dale children. He could feel anger building, coursing through him; knew he had to leave the building before anything happened.

'I stopped him from killing you at the appeal. I won't be there next time.'

'I can handle myself,' Black said, turning and heading for the elevators.

'It's probably not a good idea for you to come to the press conference,' Marlow said.

'Don't worry, now that I know what it's about I won't waste my time. I've seen and heard enough of that man for today.'

Marlow turned to follow Black and looked back at Hunter.

'He's innocent of those crimes,' she said.

'Keep telling yourself that.'

Hunter left her staring after him as he pushed through the glass doors and out into the fresh air.

7

I was thirteen the first time I killed someone.

It was messy and violent and he took a long time to die. I sat on a wooden chair and watched him squirming on the floor in his own blood as it leaked out of him. I had stabbed him sixteen times with a big butcher's knife. That kind of activity creates a lot of blood.

He made such a noise. I remember that. It got kind of annoying after a while.

Then he died.

I didn't bother cleaning up the mess before my mother arrived home. She made even more noise until I told her that if she didn't shut it I'd stab her in the neck as well.

Should've seen the look on her face. It was a picture.

She called him her husband. I never called him my father.

He said I should call him Daddy. When he had his hands on me.

'How do you like that, Daddy?' I asked when I stabbed him.

The first one was the best; a real deep slice into the side of his neck. I came into the kitchen and he was sitting there drinking a cup of coffee and reading a newspaper. I know he heard me but he didn't turn around. I'd been in the shower for more than twenty minutes trying to scrub his stink off me.

The therapist said I was disturbed. That I had no recollection of the attack. He prescribed some drug that made my brain numb. I stopped taking it after a while.

He was wrong. The therapist, I mean. I remember the attack vividly.

The knife went into his neck real smooth. My mother was a great cook and she always kept the knives sharp as hell. It was much easier than I had imagined.

It was when I saw him sitting in the chair. I had gone into the kitchen for a glass of water and I opened the door to see him there. I thought he'd gone out. He usually did after.

So, I went to the drawer where the knives were and opened it. He ignored me the whole time. I picked a nice, big one. The blade was a good ten inches long. I grabbed it and felt the weight, getting used to the heft of it. Sometimes I helped my mother when she cooked, but she never let me touch the knives.

When I was good and ready I walked over and stood behind him. I reached around and put my left hand on his forehead to steady him and stuck the knife in hard. He made a sort of choking sound, like he had a piece of meat stuck in his throat. When I pulled the knife out of his neck there was a brief instant when all that I could see was the gash in his skin. I could see right down through the layers of fat and muscle.

Then the blood came.

Boy, did it come. In a gush of claret.

He reached up and grabbed at the wound, like he could shove all the blood back in.

I stabbed him again in almost exactly the same place. He didn't like that. Started shouting and tried to grab my hand. Idiot only managed to grasp the blade of the knife. I pulled it back quick and took one of his fingers right off. It dropped on to the floor.

After that, I put the knife in again.

When I was done with that, there wasn't any fight left in him.

I walked round till I was standing in front of him, so he could look into my eyes. I often wonder what he saw there – when I look again at that photograph of myself as a four-year-old.

I stabbed him in the face and then in the chest. He lurched at me and fell on to the floor. He never got back up.

Sometimes I tell people about him – before I kill them. Not to shock them in that unique moment of stress, but to help them understand the truth.

My truth.

There are some people in the world that deserve to die.

Correction – that deserve to be killed.

It's not a difficult concept to get your mind around, really. The difficulty is in the implementation of this truth. In the killing.

I came upon the knowledge of my true self early in life. I like to kill people. And I'm good at it.

But how to judge who deserves it?

That's easy.

I'm the judge. And I'm always right.

8

Hunter pulled into the narrow driveway of his home in the Washington Park neighbourhood close to six that night. They had moved there before Ash fell pregnant, attracted to the area's older, brick-built properties and its location within a five-minute drive of downtown Denver. The house they had bought was smaller than some of the more substantial properties in the area, but they were in the middle of a minor renovation project to add what would be the nursery room at the top of the house. The plastic sheeting visible outside showed that there was still work to be done.

Ash was in the kitchen, leaning over a pot of bubbling water with the steam enveloping her head. She turned as he came into the room and he slipped his arms around her waist and pulled her tight to him. She kissed his cheek and gently pushed him back.

'Dinner's almost done,' she said.

Her face was flushed from the heat of the kitchen and the child she was carrying. Hunter pressed a hand gently to his wife's belly and felt the weight of the day fall from him. She put a hand on top of his and smiled.

'Things are going to be different around here soon,' she told him. 'Big changes.'

'Yeah, maybe we can get the builders to finish off the nursery before then.'

He took his jacket off and hung it over the back of one of the chairs at their dining table. Ash frowned when she saw that he still had his gun holstered on his belt.

'Sorry,' he said, when he saw her face. 'I didn't get back to the office to drop it off.'

'Can't have that thing around when there's a baby. Not like now anyway.'

'I'll get a safe for it.'

'You'd better.'

Ash turned back to the pot and he walked into the hall and then through to the living room, slumping on the couch and rubbing at his eyes. He grabbed the TV remote and clicked on to a local news channel. Chase Black's face grinned out from the screen: freeze-framed at the end of the afternoon press conference.

Hunter switched the TV off. The last thing he wanted now was to see that face again. Not here, in his home. He went back to the kitchen.

'Did you see the news?' he asked Ash. 'About him.'

She sighed. She'd lived with Hunter's mood since Black had been released — knew all too well how much it was affecting him.

'He's a free man now, baby,' Ash told him. 'I know you hate it, but there's nothing you can do.'

'I don't have to like it.'

'Were you there today?'

'I think you know that I was.'

She sighed again.

'I do. Danny called three times this afternoon looking for you. He said he hadn't seen you since before lunch.'

He didn't say anything.

'Are you trying to get yourself fired?'

'No. I went for a drive. To clear my head.'

'Jake . . .' exasperation sounding in her voice.

'You know I can't let this go, Ash. There's no new evidence. No new suspects. We've been at it for months now and it's going nowhere. This man is—'

'Not guilty. That's what the court said.'

'No. That's just the name for the verdict. What they really said was that the evidence was unsafe and could no longer be relied upon. Which is so much bullshit. I know our lab guys and—'

'Jake, you've got to stop this.'

'We'll be a family soon, Ash. You weren't there. You didn't see what he did.'

She walked over to him and put her arms around his waist, her swollen belly pushing against his.

'Be with me tonight and start again tomorrow.'

'It's not that easy.'

'I know, Jake. I deal with the dead and the dying every day. Every damn day. So don't you go on acting like you're the only one who cares. Because you're not.'

'I didn't mean it like that. You know I didn't.'

'So stop it.'

'I'll try.'

After dinner, Hunter went upstairs to the study. It was mainly used by Ash and was filled with medical books and research that she had printed off — stacked in unruly bundles on the floor.

He switched on the laptop and checked his e-mail account. There was a message from an address that he did not immediately recognise — ending with '.co.uk'. He opened the message. There was a single sentence.

How could this happen?

Underneath that was a hyperlink to a website. Hunter leaned forward and clicked through to the website. It was a report about Chase Black and his plans to embark on a signing tour for his book in the UK. According to an online book retailer it had been in the the UK top ten bestseller list for the last five weeks.

The public's appetite for tales of the worst excesses of human behaviour could, it seemed, never be sated.

He looked again at the e-mail address of the sender. It started 'JD' before the @ symbol.

It hit Hunter who it was from — Jay Drayton.

He clicked to reply to Drayton's message. Sat staring at the screen for five minutes, not sure of what he could say. Everything that occurred to him sounded like meaningless platitudes: we're working hard; doing what we can. He deleted the blank message and closed the laptop.

He sat in the quiet of the room staring at his own reflection in the window as the sun sank in the sky.

Blue bleeding to orange.

Bleeding to red.

9

Monday: Glasgow

The Defence Minister, Drew Jones, was exactly as advertised. He carried himself like a naval officer, upright and poised. It looked to Logan as though he had lost some weight. His belly was not quite as pronounced as in his picture in the file.

Logan stood beside the silver Ford, feeling the heat of the autumn sun on his head as it broke through the light cloud cover. The tarmac was still damp from a rain shower earlier in the day and he had to squint in the glare reflecting off the wet surface.

Lawrence Ryder greeted Jones warmly as he came down the steps of the plane and they shook hands like old friends. Jones clapped a hand on Ryder's upper arm and it looked to Logan as if the bigger man was actually rocked by the blow.

Jones laughed loudly at something Ryder said and then followed him towards the second of the black Jaguar cars beside the plane.

Jones's entourage consisted of two women and a man and they followed behind their boss, each of them with a mobile phone glued to an ear. They all talked loudly, each one trying desperately to appear more important than the others.

Logan looked along the line of cars to Tom Hardy at the rear. He waited for Hardy's signal to get in the car beside Carrie. The Ford's engine was idling and Logan tasted exhaust fumes on his tongue. The smell of tyre rubber and jet fuel filled his nose. Nothing else quite smelled like an airport.

Ryder waited outside until all of his charges were settled in the Jaguars and then gestured with his hand to Hardy who, in turn, nodded at Logan.

Logan opened the door of the Ford and slid into the passenger seat.

'We all set?' Carrie asked.

Logan didn't reply, knew that she was talking into her radio mike rather than at him.

'Lawrence,' Hardy's voice sounded. 'Are we good to go?'

'Hold for now. I'm getting an update on the situation on site.'

Carrie depressed the accelerator a few times and revved the car engine. She raised her eyebrows in time with the noise from the car when Logan looked at her. Logan was genuinely lost for words. He covered his mike with his hand.

'You're weird, you know that?'

Carrie nodded.

Ryder's voice came back on line.

'Okay, team. We're good to go.'

'Let's look after each other,' Hardy said.

Carrie covered her mike this time.

'He always says that. It's so cheesy.' She rolled her eyes.

Logan kind of liked it.

10

En route to the Parliament, Ryder got a message that there was a sit-down protest at the public entrance to the front of the building. He immediately ordered a change to the route – taking access to the underground car park at the rear, via Holyrood Road.

Fifteen minutes later, Logan heard the chants of the crowd before they turned on to the road. They were making an awful lot of noise for what was supposed to be no more than two hundred people. Carrie turned the car left and he saw the crowd behind the police lines.

It was difficult to judge exactly how many people were lining the street to the entrance gates, but it was certainly north of three hundred. Clearly someone had guessed that Jones would come along this route.

'Crowd is much bigger than we were told,' Logan said into his radio mike.

He glanced at Carrie and saw that her jaw muscles were tensed and her hands gripped the steering wheel tightly.

Logan quickly assessed the situation, looking left and right at the massed crowd.

The first thing he noticed was that the police presence would not be enough to hold the crowd if there was a real push to break ranks.

Then he saw a small group of men at the back of the crowd on the right, moving along the pavement and watching the convoy intently. The lead man raised his hand to his face and spoke into a mobile phone.

'On the right,' Logan said into his mike. 'Possible problem. Looks like someone might be organising a concerted effort from the rear of the crowd.'

Carrie kept her eyes on the road ahead and the police officers waving her forward from the entrance gates. The heavy bollards sunk into the tarmac had been lowered electronically to allow the cars in.

'Someone should have told us about this,' Lawrence Ryder's voice sounded in Logan's earpiece.

'Pick up speed?' Hardy asked from the rear car.

'No,' Ryder replied. 'We can't risk someone running in front of a car. The last thing we need is a photograph in the tabloids with the minister running over a protester. Unless we absolutely cannot avoid it.'

'Keep the cars close,' Hardy said. 'Maintain your speed.'

Logan looked left, his eyes sweeping the crowd. He saw nothing out of the ordinary. He looked back to his right and locked on the group of men still moving along the rear of the crowd. The car was fifty yards now from the entrance.

The man whom Logan considered the leader of the group was still speaking on his phone.

'We've got a break.' Bailey Judd's voice sounded urgent.

'On the left,' Ryder said. 'Behind the lead car.'

Logan whipped his head round and strained to look behind his car. He heard raised voices outside, rising in volume and number.

'Police line breached,' Ryder said.

'Punch it,' Hardy's voice sounded loudly.

Carrie pressed her foot down on the accelerator and the car sped forward as the engine's turbo kicked in. Logan looked at the Jaguar behind him as they pulled away from it. He saw three men break free from the crowd, running at the car immediately behind them. They must have assumed that was the minister's car. The police driver accelerated to follow Carrie's lead and the men were left grasping at air. One of them stumbled and fell in the road, blocking the path of the second Jaguar.

Another group of men spilled into the road from the same position as the first three and Logan knew that it was only a matter of seconds before the police were overrun and the road filled with civilians.

'Go through or over them,' Ryder shouted. 'Do it now.'

The driver of the minister's car swerved to his right and floored it.

The front of his car narrowly missed the head of the man lying in the road. Bailey Judd followed in the last car.

The crowd burst out from the police line on both sides of the road.

Carrie put her foot flat to the floor and the car sped through the entrance gates, followed by the first Jaguar.

A number of people reached the minister's car but simply bounced off it and fell heavily as it rapidly increased in speed.

Judd had no choice but to keep going and hope that no one got in his way. He watched with relief as the car ahead of him pushed on through the gates and was almost there himself when a man ran in front of his car. Judd held his nerve, pulled the wheel right and heard the fleshy thud as the front quarter panel of his car collided with the man and sent him spinning in the air.

Then they were through the gates and into the gloom of the car park.

11

Carrie pulled the car to the rear of the car park and braked hard to bring it to a standstill. She and Logan got out fast and ran back as the rest of the convoy came in behind them. The metal gates were securely closed and Logan could see the police skirmishing with protesters out on the street.

'Check the building,' Carrie shouted at him, pointing to the entrance door. 'Make sure it's clear.'

Logan walked quickly to the entrance and held up the security pass that hung on a lanyard around his neck. One of the Parliament's own security team put a hand up and leaned down to look at the pass from inside the building. Logan waited till the man had finished examining his credentials and stepped inside when the door was opened.

'What happened out there?' the guard asked.

'Crowd broke the police lines. We had to plough through.'

The guard's eyes widened. 'Literally?'

'I think we clipped at least one guy.'

Logan looked around the narrow hall. There were two lifts and a secure door beyond them.

'Are the press upstairs?' Logan asked.

The guard nodded.

'Somebody checked their credentials?'

The guard said yes as a woman dressed in an identical outfit to the guard came through the secure door. Logan glanced at her pass and saw that she was head of security.

'What happened?' she asked.

'Trouble outside. Don't worry, we got the minister here.'

Ryder's voice sounded in Logan's ear. 'We're bringing the minister in. Are we cleared inside?'

'Clear,' Logan answered.

He went to the door and pulled it open as Ryder bundled the minister in, followed by two of his own men. Carrie came in behind them. Hardy, Judd and the rest of the security team stayed in the car park, spreading out in front of the door.

Logan closed the door after Carrie and nodded at the guard to secure it. It was tight with all of them in the hall.

'Some mess,' he heard Ryder say behind him.

Logan took a breath and tried to clear his head. Not quite the easy ride he had hoped for. He reached across his body and felt the handgun secured there.

Focus.

He and Carrie left the minister with Ryder and his two men and went into one of the lifts. They got out one floor up and stepped into another narrow hall. They moved from there into the main foyer through another secure door.

Logan scanned the area quickly and more slowly on a second pass.

Carrie stood with her back to the door and looked at everyone in the building foyer. A large group of press photographers stood snapping away at the protest outside, visible through the glass entrance doors.

The secure door behind them opened and Ryder came into the foyer followed by Jones and another Special Branch officer.

Logan walked towards the press group and held his hands up.

'Okay, guys,' he said loudly. 'No photographs for now.'

He positioned himself between the group and the minister so that they would not have a clear shot of him.

'How are things inside, Logan?' Hardy asked over the radio.

Logan turned his back to the press pack.

'Under control, Tom. How's it looking out there?'

'More cops just showed up. They're getting stuck into the crowd. I think the worst of it is over.'

'Hey, you.'

Logan looked up at the new voice. The minister, Drew Jones, was motioning for Logan to come over to him.

'Yeah, you,' Jones said, nodding.

Logan walked to him and Jones held his hand out. Logan shook his hand.

'Thanks,' Jones said. 'I liked how your team handled things out there. No hesitation and no bullshit.'

Logan nodded but said nothing. Jones held on to his hand.

'Did you serve, son? I mean, in the army.'

'No, sir.'

'Police?'

'Ah, no. I used to be a lawyer.'

Jones's head tilted slightly to the side. Logan shrugged.

'Well, I don't know what firm you worked for but they trained you well for this kind of thing.'

He winked and Logan smiled.

'I've been through some stuff,' Logan told him. 'Forced me to learn fast.'

Jones looked at Logan for a moment and released his hand. He turned to Ryder.

'Right, Lawrence. Let's have a quick chat with the jackals and then get to the debating chamber.'

He said it loud enough for the reporters and photographers to hear him. A few of them laughed and a couple rolled their eyes. Logan figured they'd heard it before from Jones.

Carrie moved to join them and Jones walked forward to meet the press. Ryder stayed where he was, talking to the head of security. Logan was conscious that Jones should always have one member of the protection detail close by him at all times – no matter what the circumstances.

As he turned to follow Jones he saw the man move from the corner of his eye. He was short and wide and partially hidden behind one of the photographers.

Logan felt a jolt as a current passed through his muscles.

The man moved past the photographer quickly and brought his right hand up as he closed in on Jones.

'Knife!' Logan shouted.

The shout served two purposes: to alert the security

team that there was imminent danger; and to freeze the bad guy.

The first part worked. Ryder's head snapped around and Carrie sprinted forward. But she was too far away.

Logan wasn't.

He moved fast, Jones staring at him after the shouted warning – not seeing the danger in front of him.

Make it.

The man jumped forward and thrust his hand out.

Logan made it.

He grabbed the man's wrist with his left hand, brought his right arm up sharply and smashed his forearm into the man's face. He felt the nose break and saw blood splash.

The man's head snapped back. Logan released the grip he had on the man's wrist and kicked his legs out from under him. Logan bent his knees, following the man down to the floor. He pushed his hand under the man's chin as his head was about to impact on the tiled floor.

There was an audible crack of bone and the man's eyelids fluttered as he lost consciousness.

Carrie got there and grabbed the knife.

'Cuff him,' Ryder shouted at his men.

Logan stood, feeling unsteady on his legs.

'And can somebody tell me how a guy with a fucking knife got past security,' Ryder roared.

12

It was six hours later when Rebecca Irvine handed Logan a beer and sat beside him on the couch in the living room of his flat in the Shawlands area of Glasgow, a few miles south of the city centre. The bottle was ice cold, condensation making it slick in his hand. He said thanks and took a long pull on it, feeling the stress of the day easing with every mouthful. He stopped with half of the bottle drained.

'I guess you needed that,' Irvine said, kissing him on the cheek and sipping from a glass of white wine.

'Jesus, what a day,' Logan said. 'I feel like I ran a marathon or something.'

'That's the adrenalin.'

'Not sure I'm cut out for this stuff.'

'You looked fine to me.'

Logan turned his face to hers and kissed her mouth, her warmth exaggerated by the cold of the beer.

'Kids asleep yet?' he asked.

Irvine laughed.

'What?' Logan asked. 'I missed you.'

'Connor's out like a light. But not Ellie.'

Logan's daughter was fourteen and at over five feet four was maturing quickly into the young woman that she would become. She was already taller than her mother had been, but otherwise shared her delicate features and dark hair.

She was also a hard worker – a trait she shared with her father – and was studying for both music and other exams. She was becoming an accomplished pianist, but still wanted to achieve a certain level of academic success.

'I'll go see her,' Logan said, setting his beer on the floor and getting up from the couch.

The flat was a modest, two-bedroom affair on the first floor of a Victorian sandstone building. When he had moved in with Ellie, they had stripped and polished the original oak floorboards themselves. He loved the sound of their creaks and groans as he walked through the hall to Ellie's bedroom.

She had her back to him with headphones on while she played an electric piano, her fingers moving with what looked to Logan like impossible speed. He watched her, leaning against the door frame and hearing the soft clicking sounds the keys made as she worked them.

She must have sensed his presence, stopping and turning her head. She smiled and pulled the headphones off.

'Hey, Logan. What's up?'

She used his first name more now than 'Dad' – a product of their only having come together as a family after her mother was killed when she was eleven years old. He had let their relationship find its own level and there was a sense of comfort now that he enjoyed.

'Nothing much.'

She gave him a look.

'Watching some TV with Becky.'

The look stayed on her face.

'How come she's not been around as much lately?'

Logan wasn't surprised that Ellie had noticed. While her relationship with Irvine had started off rocky – Ellie fearing that Logan was replacing her mother with her – they, too, had settled into something more comfortable.

'She's working hard like you. Going for a promotion.'

'Nothing's up, is it? I mean, nothing bad.'

Logan frowned and shook his head, though a doubt nagged in his mind. It was true that Irvine was pushing for promotion to Detective Sergeant, but they had not been seeing as much of one another for some weeks.

'We've both been busy,' he told Ellie.

He turned to leave.

'I saw you on the TV,' she said, biting her bottom lip. 'In that fight.'

Logan had been there when Ellie had been rescued from kidnappers by Cahill and the others at CPO. She knew what Logan's job was all about, though some things he kept from her.

'Are you okay with that?' he asked.

She shrugged. 'I suppose. But it looked scary, you know.'

He went to her and kissed the top of her head. 'I'll be safe, don't worry.'

She smiled tentatively.

'I'm not going anywhere, Ellie. And if you don't like what I'm doing, I'll stop.'

She shook her head. 'I don't want you to stop. You and Alex keep people safe. Like you did for me. That's a good thing.'

'I think so too.'

He left the room, the clicking of piano keys starting up again before he closed her door.

'Are we okay?' he asked Irvine when he was back in the living room. 'I mean, we don't get as much time together any more.'

She put her wine glass down.

'Where did that come from?'

'I don't know. Something Ellie said.'

Irvine pulled her legs up on to the couch and straddled him, kissing him deeply.

'What do you think?' she asked when she pulled back from him.

13

Tuesday: Denver

Jake Hunter arrived at his desk early. Two detectives on the other sergeant's squad were in, having caught a call last night – a depressingly familiar gang-related shooting. They had a suspect locked up in the holding cell and were talking through their interview strategy. Hunter saw that his squad sergeant, Ed Bowman, was also in his office. Bowman looked up and stared at Hunter for a moment before returning to the paperwork on his desk.

There was a flashing sign on the screen of Hunter's desk phone. He picked up the receiver and dialled into his voicemail to listen to the message.

'This is Special Agent Nick Levine. I'm in the behavioural analysis unit at Quantico. The FBI. SAC Graves asked me to give you a call about a case. Said it was an unusual situation and that I was to help you as best I could.'

The message ended with Levine reciting his phone number. Hunter looked at his watch, trying to work out the time difference between Denver and the FBI academy in Virginia. He dialled the number that Levine had given. It rang twice before Levine answered.

Hunter glanced over at Bowman. He was still engrossed in whatever was on his desk.

'This is Detective Hunter, Denver PD. You left a message for me?'

'Yes. How are you, detective?'

'I'm good.'

'I had a look on our system here, but couldn't find any active cases with your department. Is this something new?'

'Dean didn't tell you what this was about?'

'I only had a brief talk with SAC Graves. He was heading out.'

Hunter had hoped that Levine would know the unofficial nature of the inquiry.

'Listen,' Levine said. 'When the SAC says he wants me to help in any way I can, it means I do exactly that. No questions asked.'

Hunter relaxed a little.

'This isn't a department inquiry. More of a personal one.'

'Don't sweat it. We're used to the sensitive stuff.'

Hunter looked over at Bowman again.

'There *is* an active investigation,' Hunter said. 'But I don't have authority to bring you guys in on it.'

'Okay. Can you send me the case files?'

'No.'

Levine didn't say anything in response.

'I could probably scan some stuff and e-mail it to you, if you needed it. But I can't copy the files.'

'Let's start at the beginning. Tell me the basics and then we can see if I can help you out.'

'You heard of Chase Black?'

'Of course. Is that what this is about? I mean, wasn't he released a while back?'

'He was. Which means that my investigation into the murder of five families is open again.'

Levine was quiet for a moment.

'Do I take it', Levine said finally, 'that you are not totally convinced of his innocence?'

'Correct.'

'I didn't really follow the case too closely. How did he win the appeal?'

This was still the part of the whole thing that Hunter found hard to accept: that a man like Chase Black was free because of something that his department did. Or, to be more accurate, did not do.

'He won because the evidence we recovered to lead us to him in the first place was tainted.'

'What happened?'

'We didn't have anything on the killer until the last family. The fifth. No leads and clean crime scenes. Nothing that the Crime Lab could work with.'

'That's unusual.'

'We figured that either he got careless—'

'Unlikely,' Levine interrupted. 'I mean, from what I

understand of the murders he was a very organised individual. More likely that he became increasingly frenzied in his attacks.'

'That's what we think. We found a blood sample at the last scene. A single drop.'

'He used a knife, right? To kill, I mean.'

'Yes.'

'It happens a lot, I'm sure you know. Anyone who uses a knife can end up getting cut themselves.'

'Anyway, pretty much the entire conviction rested on that single drop of blood. We got enough for blood typing and DNA comparison.'

'How did you get a comparison from Black? Was he in the system somewhere already? An earlier crime?'

'No. He volunteered to give us a sample.'

'What?' Levine was unable to disguise the surprise in his voice.

'You have to realise that Black is a . . . unique individual.'

'That's an understatement. I've rarely seen a suspect volunteer a sample without a warrant.'

'Oh, he wasn't a suspect when he gave us the sample. He was a potential witness.'

14

Hunter still remembered the interview with Black after the first attack at the Dale house. They had arranged a canvass of the homes in the area and expanded it after the initial sweep to a radius of a mile around the house. Black lived about a half-mile south in an apartment in a modern condominium.

He was a successful businessman: CEO of a small chain of sporting goods stores in Colorado. His salary was north of $150,000 per year and his lifestyle as a single man was suitably comfortable. In fact, his status as a potential loner was the only reason that they asked him to come into the department for an interview at all. They were really just covering all bases because he didn't fit anyone's idea of a killer – never mind one capable of the level of violence seen inside the Dale house.

Hunter had planned to take the interview himself, but

Ed Bowman had stepped in. Hunter didn't know why – other than that Bowman was ultimately in charge of the squad.

Black had been put into the interview room on the Homicide unit floor of the police Administration Building. He sat in an uncomfortable, folding plastic chair. Hunter was outside, looking into the room through the one-way security glass.

It was a Friday afternoon and Black was dressed for work in what looked like a bespoke suit. His pale blue shirt was open at the neck and Hunter could see the muscle cords in his neck as Black looked around the sparse room.

Black's gaze turned to the window into the room. It felt to Hunter as though he was looking directly into his eyes: seeing right through the security glass.

Bowman clapped a hand on Hunter's shoulder.

'I'll take this one, Jake,' he said. 'You can watch if you like.'

Bowman walked past him and opened the door to the room without waiting for Hunter's reply. Hunter felt a surge of anger, but swallowed it down and followed Bowman into the room. He looked back at Danny Collins who was standing by their desk. The look in Collins's eyes said – what the hell? Hunter shrugged at his partner and walked into the room.

'Mr Black,' Bowman said. 'Thank you for coming in today to assist with our investigation.'

'Happy to help.'

Hunter watched Black carefully, examining his body language, looking for any 'tells': the signs that someone is lying. It was a cop instinct kind of thing. You learned some of it on the job – getting lied to all the time by criminals. But part of it could not be taught. It was one of the reasons that Hunter had moved quickly up the ranks from uniform patrol to the Detective Bureau to the Homicide Unit. He had a knack for picking out the bad guys.

Now, in the interview room, Hunter stood in the corner leaning against the wall while Bowman sat opposite Black. Bowman introduced them both. Black's green eyes moved to Hunter, looking him up and down carefully. He had the polished ease of a successful man.

He does it because he likes it.

If he's the guy.

That was what Hunter thought, standing in that room with Black for the first time. Watching him. Sure, he'll have suffered some kind of trauma, some trigger, for what he does. But deep down, he's not compelled to do it by some chemical imbalance in his brain. He *wants* to do it.

Black smiled at Hunter and nodded in greeting.

'Detective,' he said, 'I don't know if I can help, but I'll try to tell you what I can.'

That was another thing he probably had learned in his business career. People want you to be interested in them, in what they do. Give them your full attention and they will like you more for it.

Black sat straight in the chair, not shifting to get comfortable. He'd obviously worked out early on that he would never be comfortable in the chair and accepted it. His movements were slow and deliberate: a nod of the head; turning his hands palms up.

Hunter got the impression that the man could endure anything that they would throw at him. Standard interview techniques would never break him down.

'You ever meet the Dales?' Bowman asked Black. 'I mean, socially or . . .'

'No. But I'd seen them around.'

'Around where?'

'You know, at the local store or whatever.'

Hunter remembered the Dale family from their photographs. A strikingly good-looking family. Cute kids. Alice Dale was noticeable if you were a man. She'd be around the kids even though she was separated from their father.

He wondered if Black, who lived half a mile away, had the same 'local' store as the Dales. He took a small notebook from his jacket pocket and made a note to check that out. He did it partially to remind himself, but also to watch Black's reaction.

Black looked up at Hunter for the first time since he had been introduced. His face registered no emotion. His green eyes were flat.

Hunter finished the note and put the pad back in his pocket.

'Do you see your father much any more?' Hunter asked.

He had not had the opportunity to discuss the interview strategy with Bowman before the meeting. Decided his sergeant was making it too comfortable for Black. The question was not connected to anything that Bowman had asked. The fact that it followed immediately on from Hunter making notes was designed to throw Black further off balance.

Bowman, to his credit, did not react. For all his faults, he wasn't a bad detective.

Black cleared his throat. Hunter thought that it looked like a move to gain him thinking time.

'Could I have some water?' he asked.

Hunter left the room and went to the water cooler down the hall. He came back and put the cardboard cup in front of Black then resumed his position in the corner of the room.

'Thanks,' Black said after taking a drink.

He put the cup back on the table.

'No,' Black said. 'My father died when I was a kid. So I haven't seen him in a while.'

'Did your mother remarry?' Hunter asked.

'She did. But what's this got to do with anything?'

'We like to get background on our witnesses,' Bowman added. 'So we get a full picture, you know.'

Black wrapped his hand around the cup.

'Oh, sure,' he said. 'I understand. You want to get it all.'

He took a sip of the water.

Hunter and Bowman said nothing.

'You want a blood sample or something?' Black asked when he put the cup down.

That took both of them by surprise.

Looking back on that moment later, after Black's arrest, Hunter had recalled Black's manner as one of arrogance. In reality, his face was as blank as it had been through the entire interview.

'Cause it's no problem to me if you do.'

'Why would we want that?' Hunter asked. 'I mean, you're not a suspect or anything, Mr Black.'

Black looked from Hunter to Bowman and back. 'Hey, I get it,' he said. 'I'm a single guy from a broken home. Sort of.'

He laughed at that. It was an odd thing to do in the situation. 'Let me do this for you. Put your mind at ease.'

15

Nick Levine listened to Hunter retelling the interview without interruption.

'Let me guess,' he said. 'After he gave you the sample he went off your radar as a suspect. No one looked at him again until you had the blood from the scene.'

'Yeah. I mean, there was something off about the guy but, after the sample and when you considered his business success and his social skills . . .'

'He didn't fit anyone's idea of a killer.'

'Right.'

'So how did the blood evidence get tainted?'

Hunter explained the screw-up with the Crime Lab technician at the scene – caught on video.

'What can I do?' Levine asked.

'I hope you can help me put this guy away where he belongs. For good this time.'

'You're convinced that he's still your guy?'

'Yes.'

'I mean, I ask because I've seen investigators get it wrong. You know, getting locked in on a suspect and losing sight of the real perpetrator.'

'Like I said. I have no doubt.'

'Did you have any profile work done as part of the original investigation?'

'No. We talked about it and maybe would have done it if we hadn't caught the break when we did.'

'So why now?'

'Let's just say that I want to consider all our options.'

Hunter finished the call and busied himself scanning some of the items Levine had asked to see: photographs of at least two of the scenes; notes of the interview with Black; and the arrest report. He wanted to see more, but Hunter had limited time before Bowman would start to wonder what he was doing at the scanner.

Funny how quickly the rules could be discarded when it suited, Hunter thought.

He finished before Danny Collins arrived and e-mailed it all to Levine. He wondered, as he pressed 'send', if Levine might be right – about having too narrow a focus and maybe missing something by only looking at Black. He'd known cases where that had happened, and he didn't want to be that kind of detective.

Part Three

Behavioural Analysis

Memorandum

From: Franck Zimmer
To: Section Chief
Re: Project Eden

Interpol Ref: 735F-27

Sir,

We now believe subject 'Eve' is en route to the assignment in the United Kingdom. A known alternative identity was used on a flight from Paris, France to Munich, Germany. However, the same identity was not used again on any flight departing Munich. In fact, no other known alias of subject 'Eve' was identified on any outbound flights.

With the assistance of German security personnel we obtained CCTV footage from the airport with a view to getting an image of all female passengers disembarking the Paris flight. Unfortunately, the footage proved unhelpful – with no recordings available from that gate due to a defective camera. Subject 'Eve' has experience in counter-intelligence techniques.

A painstaking search of all international flights departing the same day was undertaken to verify that passenger names were genuine. A flight to Dublin, Ireland from Munich three hours later turned up the name of an apparently British national but with no passport registered in the United Kingdom. We are 99 per cent certain this was subject 'Eve'.

The name has been added to our list of alternative identities for subject 'Eve'. Authorities in the United Kingdom have been alerted. Reports to follow.

1

Tuesday: Glasgow

Logan watched the video of the moment when he subdued the man who had tried to attack Drew Jones. That was the word that the reporters used – subdued. It was low-key. Logan liked it.

A news crew inside the parliament building had filmed the whole thing. The camera movements were sudden and jerky, but clear enough.

Alex Cahill came into Logan's room in the CPO office at 123 St Vincent Street. It was on the third floor of a converted Victorian building. Logan kept the place simply furnished with not much more than a walnut desk and a couple of chairs.

'You watching yourself again?' Cahill asked with a smile.

'Maybe,' Logan answered, closing the Internet browser on his computer.

'You know, we're supposed to be invisible. Unseen. I might have to pay a PR consultant to field all the calls we're getting for interviews with you.'

'What? I can't help that the guy came at us with a knife. You want me to let him kill our man?'

Cahill pulled a chair out from the other side of Logan's desk and sat down.

'On the plus side,' he said, 'we've also had a couple of enquiries for new jobs. Even some international stuff.'

Logan raised his eyebrows.

'You're famous,' Cahill told him. 'Welcome to the Z-list.'

'Maybe I should get a raise.'

Cahill leaned forward, resting his elbows on the desk.

'Actually, that's kind of the reason I came to see you.'

'How much do I get?'

Cahill looked at Logan for a moment without replying. 'How long have we known each other?' he finally asked, leaning back again in the chair.

'A while. So?'

'The company is doing well. We're making money and we'll probably make some more now that we're all over the news.'

'That's a good thing, right?'

'Sure is. I'm not complaining.'

'Did you have a point when you came in here to see me?'

'Do you like being a lawyer? I mean, in this company. Not before, when you were out in private practice.'

'I like it fine.'

'And how do you feel about the real stuff? Like what happened yesterday.'

'One of these days I'd like to get an easy job where no one tries to kill anyone else.'

'Yeah, you seem to be a magnet for that shit.'

Cahill saw ghosts of the past in Logan's eyes.

'Where is this going, Alex?'

'How would you feel about being an equal partner in this with me and Tom? A shareholder in CPO.'

That took Logan by surprise. 'Does Tom know about this?'

'I haven't spoken to him yet. And anyway, it's not going to happen right now. I wanted to see what you thought of it first.'

'You'd give me a share in the business that the two of you have grown?'

'Christ, no. You have to make an investment. Buy in.'

'I don't know, Alex. I don't have much money put away, what with Ellie's school fees and all.'

'I'd make you a director of the company as well. With a salary bump. And the bank would be up for a business loan for the buy-in.'

Logan rubbed at his chin. 'Sounds like you have it all planned out.'

Cahill stood and walked to the window, looking down on to the street three storeys below.

'You're, what, ten years younger than me, Logan, and I don't want to be doing this much after fifty-five. Neither does Tom. We need a successor.'

'What about Bailey and Carrie and the others?'

'They're operators. Grunts. And you know me, that's not an insult. I value their contribution. But you're got the business and legal acumen. I just wasn't sure until now whether the physical stuff would suit you.' He turned back to Logan and leaned against the window sill.

'It was one job, Alex. That's all.'

Logan wasn't sure he was ready yet to commit to being at the sharp end of their business on a regular basis.

'You'll be ready soon enough,' Cahill told him. He walked forward and held his hand out. 'Think about it, okay?'

Logan looked at his friend: this man who had been through real wars and come out the other side. He stood and shook Cahill's hand.

'I will. I appreciate the vote of confidence.'

'Yeah. Now, go bring in some more business and make us all some money.'

2

Logan finished early after lunch and went home to his flat in Shawlands, picking Ellie up from school on the way. She went straight to her room and was hard at work on her piano when Logan went in to see her half an hour later. She was scribbling notes on a piece of music. He asked what she was working on. She spoke absently about some concert that was planned for later in the year and then went back to making notes on her music.

'Sorry,' she said. 'I've got to get this finished tonight. It's my recital piece for tomorrow.'

'Let me hear it.'

'It's not finished.'

'Humour me.'

He sat on her bed while she played, startled by how good she was getting; there was real sensitivity and depth to her playing.

'That was great,' he told her when she finished.

'Yeah, it's okay,' she said, picking up her pen to make another note.

Logan stood and walked to the door of her room.

'Is Becky coming over again tonight?' she asked.

Logan stopped and turned to face her. 'I thought that I would ask her, if that's okay? We could have dinner together.'

'It's okay with me,' Ellie said.

'We'll order takeaway, if you like.'

'Chinese?'

'It's a deal.'

He went to the living room, not feeling guilty about bribing her with food that was likely to take a good session at the gym for him to work off. He sat down as the phone rang. It was Cahill.

'Did you watch the news?' Cahill asked.

'Hello to you.'

Cahill said nothing.

'Not since I left the office, no.'

'The guy that went after the minister is in a bad way.'

Logan sat forward.

'How bad?'

'Bleeding inside his skull. Lapsed into a coma.'

'I guess he hit the floor pretty hard, huh?'

'You guess right.'

Logan wasn't sure how he felt about it; he'd been too busy doing his job to realise how hard the man had fallen. Killing or seriously hurting another human being wasn't why he had agreed to become a CPO operative. He'd seen enough pain and loss in his life.

'Should I be worried? About going to jail, I mean.'

'Nah. Don't sweat it. I mean, Ryder will smooth it over. He won't let anyone come after you.'

'I was only saving the life of a member of our government, after all.'

'Fuck that guy. If you bring a knife to a fight, you'd better be prepared to get your ass handed to you, right?'

Cahill's past as a soldier gave him a different perspective on these things. Logan agreed with the sentiment, but it didn't make him feel any less conflicted about it.

'It'll be good for business. We'll be the hard cases that take no crap from anyone. Couldn't have paid for a better advert.'

He figured that Cahill was trying to make him feel better. In his own special way. 'I appreciate the effort, Alex.'

'All part of the service.'

Logan ended the call and stared at the blank TV screen. He had no desire to watch his endeavours again. He'd seen it enough.

Ellie's piano started up again. He replayed the attack in his mind to the soundtrack provided by his daughter, and decided there was nothing he would have done differently.

He wondered if he was going to like his new self.

3

Wednesday: Denver

'I'm sending you a very rough profile,' Nick Levine told Jake Hunter by phone. 'And I mean, rough. I don't have a lot to work on and this is not an exact science.'

'I understand. I'm only looking for pointers at this stage.'

'Good, because that's about as much as I can give you.'

'Can I call you after I've read it?' Hunter asked. 'I mean, if I have any questions.'

'Of course. I'll be at my desk all day.'

Hunter thanked him and hung up. He stared at his inbox until the e-mail message from Levine arrived, a little paperclip icon next to the message indicating that it had an attachment. Hunter clicked through the message and waited for a few seconds while the profile downloaded. He printed it off and then read it at his desk, underlining the passages that jumped out at him:

Subject will be physically strong but will not be a member of any public fitness facility. It's likely that the subject sees physical prowess as a tool only . . .

Subject is likely to be in secure, long-term employment – perhaps in a senior role. He will view the stress of a senior role as something that attracts him to the role. He will feed off the stress. He will take care over his appearance – perhaps to an extreme degree . . .

Subject will be socially adept. Victims are likely to be unthreatened by him on initial contact. He will be self-centred and materialistic but able to mask the worst excesses of those characteristics . . .

Killings indicate a high level of organisation and daring – a degree of thrill-seeking behaviour. Subject will contain his temper at most times but will have displayed bursts of extreme anger before . . .

It is unusual for a subject to start killing families in this manner. Subject is likely to have killed before – or displayed serious criminal tendencies . . .

Given the concentration on families, subject is likely to be from a broken home. Some sort of abuse – most likely violence – will have been present in the subject's early family life. It is possible that the subject deliberately identifies family units where he can leave survivors. He will view it as punishing them for perceived abandonment.

Hunter looked across at his partner. Collins was leaning back in his chair talking on the phone. Hunter held up the paper copy of the profile and pointed to it. He slid it across the desk they shared.

'I need to call you back, sir,' Collins said into the phone before hanging up.

He looked down at the profile and then at Hunter.

'Dean Graves help you with this?'

'Yes.'

Collins shook his head.

'Why didn't you clear it with Bowman? I mean, you could have gone through official channels.'

Hunter scratched his nose.

'Just read the damn thing and we'll call the profiler.'

Collins shrugged and started reading. Hunter twisted in his seat and looked at Bowman's office. It was empty. He got up and walked the short distance to Lieutenant Morris's office, knocking on the door before going in.

'What can I do for you, Jake?' Morris asked, taking his glasses off.

Hunter sat in the chair on the other side of the desk.

'I got a profile on our open cases from Special Agent Levine at the FBI. He's out at Quantico.'

Morris blinked twice slowly.

'I don't remember seeing any request for Bureau involvement passing across my desk. I mean, that kind of thing has to go through me.'

'I did this on my own, sir.'

Morris put his glasses back on and leaned forward. Hunter was gambling that after six months of no progress Morris might see the profile as a way of taking a fresh look at things.

'What kind of profile?'

'I sent Levine a bunch of stuff from the files. And I spoke to him.'

'I meant, is this a general profile of our killer or more specifically one of Chase Black?'

'The first kind.'

Morris looked down at his desk. After a moment he looked back at Hunter and nodded.

Hunter stood up to leave.

'I know how hard it's been since the appeal, Jake. And I don't mind that you went behind Bowman on this,' Morris said. 'But I do mind that you went around me.'

Hunter figured it was best to stay quiet.

'We're all chasing the same goal,' Morris said. 'You know that, right?'

'Actually, I'm not sure that we are.'

Morris's eyes narrowed. Hunter closed the door.

'What I mean', he said, 'is that I feel like you've been tying my hands. Not letting me do my job.'

'Explain.'

Hunter sighed. 'I understand that the case files are open again. I don't have a problem with that. But you have to let me work it. All of it. Including looking at Chase Black. Otherwise we're not doing our job properly.'

'We've been over this, Jake.'

'I know that. But what if he is our guy? What then?'

'We close the files.'

'That's unacceptable to me.'

It was Morris's time to sigh. 'We're going round in circles.'

'Look, maybe he killed before. Black, I mean. We can

still get him on any other untried cases. That's what I was going to tell you. It's why I got the profile.'

'And?'

'This profiler, Levine, he thinks whoever killed the five families didn't start there. He must have done something else before. Then escalated.'

'Show me.'

4

Hunter waited while Morris read the profile. He looked across the desk at Hunter when he finished, sucking on one arm of his glasses.

'It says he came from a broken home,' Hunter said. 'Black's from a single-parent family. He fits a lot of this stuff. The social skills, the strength, the high-level job.'

'Did you tell the profiler you were still looking at Black?'

'Yes. But I didn't ask him to lie. I wanted his honest opinion.'

'Have you spoken to him since you got this?' Morris put his hand on the piece of paper on the desk.

'No.'

'Get Collins in here.'

'Sir?'

'I want to be in on the call.'

Hunter walked to the door and stopped, turning back to Morris.

'What about Sergeant Bowman?'

'Get Collins. We'll talk about everything else after the call.'

'Special Agent Levine?' Morris asked when the phone was answered.

'Yes. Who is this?'

'My name is Lieutenant Arthur Morris. I'm head of the homicide division, Denver PD. I have Detectives Hunter and Collins with me.'

Hunter and Collins said hello. They were sitting at Morris's desk with his phone on speaker mode in the centre of the desk.

'What can I do for you, lieutenant?'

'Detective Hunter showed me your profile. I thought it would be useful to have a talk about it.'

'Of course. What more can I tell you? Other than that you're dealing with a classic psychopathic personality disorder.'

Morris looked at Hunter – inviting him to take the lead.

'Agent Levine, this is Detective Hunter. Your profile indicates that it's likely this killer didn't start with these crimes. That there would be something earlier in his life. Can you elaborate on that?'

'Well, the reason I reached that conclusion was the degree of organisation and, for want of a better word, skill involved in the attacks on the families. It's not impossible for him to have started there, but I'd say the better odds are that he did something else before this.'

'Like what? I mean, you say in your profile' – Hunter

looked down at the printed version to find the section he was looking for – 'that he probably killed before. Or was involved in some other serious crime.'

'I think, on reflection, and given the level of sophistication shown in the attacks in Denver, he probably has killed before.'

'Too much of a leap to go from something less than murder to this kind of slaughter?' Morris asked.

'That would be my assessment, sir, yes. I told Detective Hunter it was a rough profile.'

'I understand.'

'I can work it up now that it's, ah . . .'

'Official?'

'Right.'

Morris stared at Hunter.

'How much did you know about Chase Black before you wrote the profile?' Morris asked, still staring at Hunter.

'Not much. What I had read in the newspapers, you know. And the TV reports.'

'This fits him pretty well.'

'It may well fit other individuals also.'

A thought struck Hunter. 'There have been no further attacks like these five since Black's arrest and conviction,' he said. 'What do you make of that?'

Levine was quiet for a moment before he spoke again.

'Serial killers are normally driven by a compulsion to do what they do. It's very unusual for them to stop and never do it again.'

'But some do?'

'Yes. In rare cases. The norm would be for him to keep killing.'

'Could a killer like this control himself enough to stop after Black's arrest? So as to make sure it looked like Black did it.'

'I think the individual who did this would find it difficult to stop for this long. Black was arrested, what, two years ago?'

'Closer to three.'

'My own view is that he would have killed again by now.'

'He could have moved to a new location,' Collins said.

'Yes, that's possible.'

'Could he have changed his methodology?' Hunter asked. 'Started targeting individuals rather than families?'

'That's difficult to say. If he did, any new attacks would probably still exhibit similar characteristics.'

'You mean the use of a bladed weapon, the binding of victims? That kind of thing.'

'Yes. You should run a ViCAP search. See if you get any hits.'

ViCAP – Violent Criminals Apprehension Program. The FBI's nationwide database for collating and analysing crimes of violence, particularly murder. Any unsolved homicide suspected as being part of a series was likely to be registered. The only downside for ViCAP was the questionnaire – 186 questions.

'Thanks, Agent Levine,' Morris said. 'I'll ensure there's some proper paperwork for this today. An official request for Bureau assistance.'

'Yes, sir.'

5

'You go through the files and complete the ViCAP application,' Morris told Collins. 'I know those things are a pain but we need to do it right. I don't want any mistakes this time. Understand?'

Collins nodded. Hunter was impressed that his usually hot-headed partner had not jumped down Morris's throat at the condescension.

'What's your next move, Jake?' Morris asked.

'If it's okay with you, sir, I'd like to send Nick Levine a copy of everything that we have. That way he can work up a complete profile.'

Morris nodded.

'After that? Profiles can only take us so far.'

'I'm going to speak to Steve Ames and Molly August. Have them go through the forensics again. Check all the lab reports from each scene. See if there's anything new that jumps out.'

'Or anything that got missed?'

'Yes, sir.'

'And what about Chase Black?'

'There's not much I can do with him right now anyway.'

'What do you mean?'

'He's on his way to the UK for some big book tour.'

'Let's hope we don't have to try to extradite him. That can be a bitch.'

Morris waved his glasses at them, a sign that he considered the conversation finished.

'I got an e-mail from Jay Drayton,' Hunter said as Collins got up to leave.

'He's the Englishman?' Morris asked. 'The property developer?'

'That's him.'

'How is he taking the press junket to the UK? That can't sit well with him.'

'It doesn't. But there's nothing I can do about that.'

Morris looked down at a photograph of his son framed on his desk.

'Do you think Drayton would have killed Black? I mean at the appeal when you stopped him.'

Hunter thought for a moment. 'I think he was serious in his intent.'

'That sounds like an equivocal answer.'

'I don't know how that encounter would have ended up. It didn't look to me like Black was scared of Drayton.'

'Should we alert the police over in the UK? Give them a heads-up about possible trouble from Drayton?'

'The good thing about being a detective and not a boss

is that it's not my decision. If you don't mind, I'll leave the politics to you, sir.'

Morris leaned back in his seat and pushed his glasses up his nose.

'You're a difficult guy to read, Jake.'

'My wife says the same thing.'

6

There was a note on Hunter's desk telling him that Steve Ames from the Crime Lab was looking for him. Hunter left Collins at their desk searching online for the ViCAP form. He went to the bank of elevators and rode up to the top floor of the building where the Crime Lab was located. It was split into seven sections: blood serology/DNA, latent prints, analytical/chemistry, trace evidence, firearms, photo lab and questioned documents. Access to the technical sections of the Lab was restricted and non Crime Lab personnel had to be buzzed in through a secure door.

The detectives' offices were located outside the secure section down a hall to the right of the reception area. Hunter walked along the hall and saw Steve Ames leaning against the door frame of Molly August's office. She was sitting with her arms folded in front of her on the desktop. Neat little bundles of paper were spread out along one side of the desk. Molly August was big on systems. It was one of the things that propelled her so fast through the Crime Lab ranks to be Ames's deputy – methodology and analysis.

'What's up?' Hunter asked. 'I was just thinking about you guys.'

'Three guesses,' August said.

'Do I need that many?'

She smiled at him and shook her head.

'This is about the five families,' Hunter said.

'I noticed you didn't ask if it was about Chase Black,' August said.

'My shrink says I'm making progress.'

August laughed out loud.

'Good for you,' Ames said. 'Let's go to my office. I've got the files.'

Ames motioned with his head and the three of them walked the short distance to his office next door. If August was a neat-freak, Ames was clearly her mentor. He sorted, filed and labelled everything – to an extreme degree. He even had a system of using different coloured pens to make his notes. They were lined up in a neat row on his desk – green, blue, red, orange and a fetching shade of purple. No one in the Lab knew what the system was. Ames preferred to keep it to himself.

'Still got the pens, Steve,' Hunter said, sitting on a chair at Ames's desk.

Ames ignored him and crouched behind his desk where there were five perfect stacks of files and binders. He went to the first tab of the top binder on each stack and took out the post-mortem report for each of the victims from the five scenes. August sat in the chair next to Hunter and waited for her boss.

Ames took a pair of reading glasses out of the top drawer in his desk and perched them halfway up his nose, peering at the first page of the report on the father from the Dale house. Hunter wasn't sure if he was looking for something specific or going through a sort of ritual to get his mind focused on these cases above all others.

Ames flicked through to the end of the report on the father, leaned back in his chair and looked at Hunter.

'I've been over everything again in the last couple of weeks,' he said.

Hunter raised his eyebrows.

'You didn't get a request to do that from the homicide unit,' he said. 'It's not official policy down there.'

'I'm capable of independent thought, Jake. Just like you. How is the official search for new evidence going, anyway?'

'What's that phrase? Nowhere fast.'

Ames took the glasses off and folded them on top of the file he had been reading.

'I need to read them again. And review the other trace evidence we recovered.'

August was quiet, letting her boss deliver the news. She had better instincts than Ames, but he was the master technician. It made them a good team; kept the rest of the Lab squad on their toes too.

'You know these cases, Jake, don't you? As well as either of us.' He pointed his chin at August.

Hunter looked at her and back at Ames. 'Yes.'

'We always had some . . .' he waved his hands around

– 'stray pieces of evidence. Pieces of the puzzle that never fit.'

'You're talking about the hair fibres?'

Ames nodded slowly. 'Recovered at the Draytons' motel,' he said.

'Nothing unusual in that. Plenty of people used that room before the Draytons did. It's a motel.'

'That was certainly how we rationalised it at the time. I mean, after Black was arrested. After we found his blood at the last murder scene.'

'Rationalised,' Hunter repeated, leaning forward in his chair.

He held Ames's gaze for a long moment.

'What exactly are you saying, Steve? That we made a mistake – another one? That we overlooked something?'

'I'm not certain, but it's been eating at me since the appeal. I couldn't leave it any longer.'

'You found something?'

Ames's eyes flicked to August.

'We have,' she said.

Hunter looked at her.

'What is it?' Hunter asked.

August turned in her seat to face him. 'We didn't do anything with that piece of evidence at the time. Didn't go back and sift through all the evidence from the earlier scenes for anything that might match it.'

Hunter frowned.

'There wasn't anything. I mean, we didn't have any other hair samples that didn't fit.'

The corners of August's mouth turned down. Hunter looked back at Ames.

'Steve, are you telling me there is a match? From another of the murders?'

Ames shook his head. 'No. Not yet anyway.'

'Riddles, Steve.'

'We went back over the inventories from each scene. Checked everything again. Double checked it. You've got to understand that there were literally hundreds of individual items.'

'Actually not far off a thousand,' August added.

'Right,' Ames said. 'This was the biggest and most complex forensic case any of us had seen. The most brutal and emotional serial killings this city has ever suffered.'

'I agree with that,' Hunter said. 'But where are you going with this? You guys are the most organised people I know. I don't believe that you could have missed anything.'

Ames nodded. Hunter wasn't sure if he was agreeing with him.

'I did find something else,' Ames said.

'What?'

Ames fingered the Dale file on his desk.

'There's a hair sample we pulled from the father's bed at the Dale house. It was labelled and described in our inventory as "canine hair fibre". Which meant that we didn't pay much attention to it.'

'But it's not,' August added. 'Dog, I mean. It's human.'

'Who recovered it and wrote the label?'

Ames raised his eyebrows.

'The same technician who took Black's blood sample and didn't sign in at the last scene?' Hunter asked.

'Yes,' August said. 'He didn't find the hair at the scene,

but he was the last to handle it in the chain of custody. He labelled it and filed it in the system.'

'He quit after the appeal,' Ames said.

Hunter couldn't read Ames's face.

'Do you think this guy deliberately screwed our case?' he asked. 'I mean, right from the very start?'

'It's a theory I'm considering.'

'Where is he?'

'No one has seen him since he left.'

'You said you don't know if the fibre is a match for anything yet.'

'Analysis is due back from trace today.'

Hunter ran his hand up through his hair.

'Jesus. What if it matches the other hairs?'

'Then we have a second suspect.'

Hunter opened his mouth but said nothing.

7

Wednesday: Glasgow

Logan's desk phone at the CPO offices rang late in the afternoon as he was logging on to his computer after a meeting. He saw that it was a call from London, but not a number that he recognised.

'Logan Finch, CPO,' he said when he answered.

'Mr Finch, my name is Kate Marlow. We've not spoken previously.'

The woman spoke with an American accent.

'How can I help?' he asked her.

'I know this is kind of short notice, but I have a client who urgently requires a security detail. I was wondering if you would be able to help.'

Logan slid a pad in front of him and wrote the woman's name and the date on it. He put a question mark after her name.

'Can I ask how you got my name?'

She hesitated before she spoke. 'Uh, well, I saw you on the television yesterday.'

Logan drew a little square on the pad.

'And I asked around about your company. Spoke to the police. That kind of thing.'

'Okay.'

'You come highly recommended. And I know that a lot of your people are my fellow countrymen. Americans.'

'You said this was urgent. When do you need us to start?'

'This morning would have been good,' she said, and laughed.

Logan frowned. 'I don't understand,' he said.

'Sorry, that was inappropriate. A private joke. Let me explain where we're at.'

Logan highlighted an icon on his computer desktop and clicked on it, activating a recording device. It was standard procedure in the office now – record all sides of any conversation regarding an operation.

'I'm a lawyer with Baker, Philp and Adam in Denver, Colorado. A partner in the media team. My firm represents Chase Black.'

She paused. Logan figured he was supposed to know who Chase Black was. The name seemed vaguely familiar, but he couldn't remember from where.

'Do you know who my client is, Mr Finch?'

Logan balanced the phone between his shoulder and his ear and opened the Internet browser on his computer. He typed Black's name into a search engine.

'I've heard the name before,' he told the lawyer.

She huffed out a breath like he was an idiot for not knowing. He'd encountered lawyers like her before and knew the type.

The search engine returned hundreds of entries for Chase Black. He clicked through to a news report that had been written on the last day of Black's appeal. It described the Drayton family murder. There was a photo of Jay Drayton being pulled from the courthouse, his face twisted in grief and rage.

'Mr Black is a US citizen wrongly accused of murder and now enjoying his freedom after a successful appeal. An appeal that my firm handled for him. He's in London for a book signing tour. A book, I might add, that currently sits in the top ten bestseller lists in at least five countries. Including yours.'

Logan knew that he was supposed to be impressed. He kind of was.

'Go on,' he told her.

He continued reading some more of the stories the search engine had thrown up while the woman spoke. He saw Detective Jake Hunter's name mentioned as the lead investigator on the Black case. He knew Hunter from his time in Denver a while back, from an investigation into a rogue soldier. Knew that Hunter was a straight-shooter.

'My client was attacked outside his hotel this morning when we arrived from Heathrow Airport. We flew in overnight. I was with him and I can tell you that it was a traumatic experience. Not the kind of thing I expected in this country.'

'Can you tell me what happened?' Logan had been a little preoccupied with the assault on Drew Jones and its aftermath.

'It was on the news.'

'I was busy with other things.'

More huffing from the lawyer. She was not endearing herself to him, but Logan was conscious that if he was going to be a full partner in CPO he would be responsible for bringing business to the company on his own – not relying on Cahill and Hardy. And this was the first direct enquiry he'd had.

'Well,' Marlow went on, 'my firm took the view that we would not have a heavy security presence for Mr Black on this tour. After all, he's an innocent man and we wanted to avoid giving the impression that he had anything to hide. Or fear.'

'I can understand that.'

Logan read through another story on his computer screen – saw that Black had been accused of the murder of five families. The killings were described as the most notorious in Denver's history. There was a photo of Black in this report. He was staring straight at the camera with the Denver jail in the background – a tall, powerful-looking man.

'But I think we have to accept now that we underestimated the depth of feeling against my client. It's only a small minority of people that have this view, you understand. But they are very . . . active.'

'But if he's been acquitted . . .'

'The reporting of his appeal was not balanced.'

'What do you mean?'

'The media needed an angle. They chose to report that he won his appeal based on a technicality, as they are fond of calling any proper legal argument. And one of your tabloids took up a very unbalanced campaign to have my client excluded from entry to the UK. A campaign that was rightly ignored.'

'I see.'

'Don't be misled by the media, Mr Finch.'

'I wasn't expressing an opinion, Miss Marlow.'

'Good. I wouldn't want the security team to doubt my client's position.'

'I haven't said that we'll take the job yet. Can you tell me about the attack?'

'One of the families that suffered terribly at the hands of the killer in our city was British.'

'The Draytons?'

'Yes, I thought you didn't—'

'I'm looking at a story on it now.'

'Well, Mr Drayton has not seen fit to accept the court's verdict. He has spoken out very volubly to the press about matters. He also tried to attack my client at the appeal.'

'From the photos I've seen, it must have taken a lot to hold him back. I mean, he's a big man.'

'Yes, he is. One of the detectives subdued him.'

'Detective Hunter?'

'Yes.'

Logan decided it would be best not to tell her that he knew Hunter.

'Anyway, it seems that two sympathisers found out where we are staying and attempted to assault Mr Black.'

'Attempted?'

'Mr Black was able to defend himself against one of the

men. The hotel doorman then secured the doors, locking them both out on the street.'

'Are you expecting further attempts?'

'We can't be sure. But we want to prepare for that eventuality. Can you help? I'd like you to travel to London immediately to meet with my client and put the necessary arrangements in place. I wouldn't want any more than two of your people working on this. Keep it as low-key as we can.'

'Two is the bare minimum. And we're not cheap.'

'The publisher has undertaken to cover the cost so that's not an issue.'

'Give me your number and I'll call you back.'

'This is urgent.'

'I'll speak to my colleagues and call you in the next half-hour.'

Logan hung up and searched online for a story on the attack on Black that morning. He found one – confirming that the man Black had engaged with had suffered a broken jaw. Seemed like he could handle himself just fine.

8

The door to Cahill's office was open. Logan walked in and sat on the couch opposite the desk.

'I got an enquiry about a job,' Logan told Cahill. 'There's a Colorado connection.'

Cahill was a native of Colorado and his eyes widened a little. He swept a hand over his closely cropped hair.

'What's the story?' he asked.

'You heard of Chase Black?'

He nodded slowly.

'The serial killer?'

'Technically, he's not. He won his appeal.'

'Right.'

'He's in London this week. Some book tour he's doing. His lawyer wants us to provide a team to look after him while he's there.'

'They paying top rate?'

'Yep.'

Cahill shrugged. 'Then why not? Go for it.'

'No concerns about this guy?'

'Court says he's innocent now, right?'

'Yes.'

'So what's the problem?'

'Two things. First, it was a technical evidence thing that got him off. Second, Jake Hunter was the lead detective.'

Cahill was a fiercely principled man, Logan knew. It was one of the reasons that they were such close friends. That wasn't to say that everyone agreed with his view of the world and how to separate right from wrong. He had been a soldier after all. Had killed people in the line of duty without hesitation.

He was also one of the most patriotic men Logan knew – absolutely loyal to his country. He'd served in the Secret Service after the army. Had been willing to put his own life in danger to protect his nation's leaders.

Cahill leaned forward and pursed his lips. 'Did you speak to Jake?'

'No.'

Cahill looked at his watch, knowing that Denver was eight hours behind UK time. 'So do that now. Get it direct from the man himself.' He looked at Logan and spread his hands out on his desk. 'But ultimately it's your case, your call,' he told Logan.

'If we do accept it, I thought maybe I'd take Carrie. The lawyer wants a small team. Something unobtrusive. We could pass as a couple if need be, but still stay close.'

'Good thinking. If she's free it's okay with me. You want Ellie to stay at my place while you're gone?'

Logan nodded. Though she was older than Cahill's two daughters, Ellie had formed a close bond with them and frequently stayed over at the weekend.

'Hey,' Cahill called to him as he turned to leave. 'Good luck.'

9

Wednesday: Denver

Hunter got back to the homicide floor after the meeting with Ames and August and filled Danny Collins in on the new development.

'Holy shit,' Collins said.

'I think that's an appropriate reaction in the circumstances.'

'What's the story? I mean, do we have a rogue Crime Lab tech? And what's his motivation anyway?'

'All good questions that we don't have answers to right now.'

'What about the technician? I mean, we question him, right?'

'He's gone. Disappeared.'

'So what do we do?'

'Wait for the lab results on this other hair sample and take it from there.'

'It's going to match the other hairs, right?'

'That would be my guess.'

'That means we have matching hair samples from two of the crime scenes.'

'Yes. Hair samples that don't match any victim or Chase Black.'

'What's our working assumption? That the samples belong to the real killer?'

Hunter knew that it was a sensible assumption, but hesitated to go that far. He wondered if his hesitation was because he was too focused on Black.

'Let's not make assumptions about anything, Danny. We deal with the facts. Those facts are that the same person was at two different crime scenes and we need to speak to that person.'

'What does this do for the sample of Black's blood that was found at the last scene? I mean, it puts it in a whole new light.'

'It raises a doubt about its authenticity, that's for sure.'

'We bringing this guy in for questioning? The lab tech, I mean.'

'He's off the grid.'

'Want me to start looking?'

'Yes. Get his file from personnel and make a start there.'

'This comes ahead of the ViCAP search?'

'For us, yes. See if you can get someone else to do the ViCAP thing.'

'I'm on it.'

* * *

Collins had left the homicide office to go and speak to the personnel team when Hunter's phone rang.

'Jake Hunter?' a Scottish voice asked.

'Yes, this is Detective Hunter.'

'Jake, it's Logan Finch.'

The last time he had seen Logan had been in the aftermath of a gunfight on a quiet street in Denver in the early morning. They had stayed in touch by e-mail since then and had spoken by phone once or twice. They exchanged brief pleasantries about their families before Hunter asked what Logan was calling about.

'I got a call about a security assignment today for someone you know. Chase Black.'

Hunter hadn't thought that the day could have got any more interesting. Turned out he was wrong.

'What's the job?'

'He's in London for some publicity tour.'

'I know.'

'Some people over here aren't too friendly towards him. A couple of them decided to act on those feelings and attacked him at his hotel.'

Hunter hadn't heard.

'What happened?'

'Black came out of it okay. But his lawyer wants us to look out for him for the next week while he's here. Should I have any concerns about him?'

'If you'd asked me that yesterday I would have said yes, absolutely. He's a killer.'

'And now?'

'Now I don't know. In fact, I'm really not sure about anything on this case.'

'Your investigation is open again?'

'Wide open. And some new information I got today potentially points to Black being innocent.'

'You're not convinced?'

'I don't know what to think. But I'd be glad to have someone looking over his shoulder while he's in the UK.'

'Sounds like you think he's not the one who needs the security.'

'The jury's out.'

'Can you keep me posted on how your investigation is going? Nothing confidential, obviously. But it would be nice to know if it turns out my client is actually a killer.'

'Let's agree to keep each other in the loop, okay?'

'That's a deal.'

'Look after yourself, Logan.'

Hunter put the phone down and stared at it, shaking his head.

10

Wednesday: Glasgow

'We'll take the job,' Logan told Kate Marlow when he called her.

'Great. When can you get here?'

'How about we fly down first thing tomorrow? Meet at your hotel.'

'Perfect. Do you need anything else from me?'

'An itinerary for all of your client's movements while we are engaged by him.'

'How detailed do you want it?'

'You can stop short of bathroom visits, but let me have everything else.'

That was his best joke. She didn't laugh.

'Let me give you my contact details,' he added quickly.

They exchanged information and she promised to e-mail

him as much as she could on her client's plans for the days ahead.

'I assume that you've discussed this direct with Mr Black?' Logan asked. 'I mean, it works best if the subject is happy with the arrangements.'

'He's comfortable with it.'

'Good enough.'

'Can I ask . . .' Marlow started then paused.

It was obvious that she had an unanswered question.

'What is it?'

'It's just that, you know, in the US our bodyguards would be armed. With guns. I mean, how does that work over here?'

'We get special dispensation from the Government for certain assignments.'

'Like this one?'

'No. This wouldn't qualify.'

'So what do you use?'

'Contrary to what the movies show, it's our job to avoid confrontation where possible. I'd like to avoid a fight as much as you would.'

'But if it comes to it? I mean, what if an attacker has a knife?'

'We carry extendable batons. And we have extensive training in hand-to-hand combat.'

'Right.'

She sounded less than convinced. Logan decided on a different approach.

'You called me because of what you saw on the news, right? What happened at the Scottish Parliament.'

'Yes.'

'That man had a knife. It ended up with him unconscious on the floor and me with not a scratch. Good enough?'

She was quiet for a moment. 'When you put it like that . . .'

'We get paid to put ourselves in harm's way for our clients. We volunteer to do it and we get trained to ensure we are as good as we can be. You've seen that the UK Government uses our services. That's because they want the top operatives guarding our country's leaders.'

'Okay. I'm convinced.'

He sensed resentment in her voice – not used to being talked to quite that firmly.

'I don't mean to be aggressive, you know. And I am not boasting. But you need to be sure of our abilities because the only way you and Mr Black will be able to relax is if you trust in our abilities.'

'I didn't mean to doubt you. But I needed to make sure you were the right team for us.'

'Good. So long as we're on the same page.'

'We are. And I like your confidence. We'll see you tomorrow.'

Logan ended the call and left his office to find Carrie. She was working on some paperwork in the War Room – the largest of the CPO meeting rooms. She looked up and smiled when Logan came in.

'You up for another assignment?' he asked.

'Sure thing.' She beamed.

'We need to be in London first thing tomorrow. You got anything else on right now that will interfere?'

'Nope. Good to go.'

'Great. Let's go to my office and I'll fill you in.'

He turned to leave.

'Who's the client?' she asked.

'Just some serial killer.'

'Awesome.'

11

The human face is fascinating up close. I like to examine my own features. Sometimes, I sit on the floor in front of a mirror and lean in real close. Don't get me wrong. I'm not a narcissist. I'm more interested in imperfections: the open pores, blemishes and uneven distribution of hair follicles.

Nobody's perfect. I believe that.

Not me. Not anyone.

I tied a man up before I killed him one time. Well, more than one time, truth be told. Having control like that is useful. Otherwise it can get messy. Dangerous even. But there's one I remember more than the others.

He wasn't a big man, but you have to look them in the eye to judge if they'll fight it. And I could see that this one was wild as they come; would have killed me, given half the chance.

I did it quick. Hit him in the face three times with the butt *of my knife. He went down easy. Break a person's nose and it really messes them up.*

After that, I wrapped the rope around his throat and pulled until he passed out. Then I tied him up.

I sat in front of the mirror in his room. I thought I looked tired. I probably was.

When I heard him starting to stir I propped him up against the wall. Bastard kicked out at me and caught me high on the cheek. I didn't see it coming. Gave me a real shiner for a couple of weeks.

Then he's squirming against the wall, trying to push himself up with his legs. Might have been a problem if he'd managed it. Would've given him the chance to rush me, use his head to butt me. The head is pretty hard. Good weapon at times.

I didn't let him get all the way up. Cut one of his Achilles clean through with my knife.

Man, did that make him scream. Like you wouldn't believe.

I know what you're thinking — that I took my time with him. Made it last. Punished him for that.

Not my style.

He screamed real loud and fell on to the floor. I put my knife into his chest, sliced right through his heart.

That put a stop to the screaming.

All that noise can be a problem when there are people around. Can't have that. Might attract the wrong sort. The police.

I don't mind crowds. Not at all. Big cities are my favourite places.

12

Wednesday: Denver

Molly August walked to Hunter's desk and smiled wanly at Danny Collins who was coming back from the coffee machine.

'It's a match?' Hunter asked.

She nodded slowly.

Collins handed a paper cup to Hunter and sat on the edge of the desk, sipping at his own drink.

'Jake filled you in about this, Danny?'

'Yep. Sucks.'

'We need to track this guy down,' August said. 'The lab guy, I mean.'

'I'm all over it,' Danny told her. 'Personnel e-mailed me all they have on him but there's not much that helps. Did a credit search as well that turned up nothing since the last known address.'

'He's in the wind?'

'Looks that way.'

'What do you think, Jake? What's the story with this guy?'

Hunter put his hand on the armrests of his chair.

'Could be any number of things. I don't want to get stuck on one idea, you know. Keep an open mind. Keep digging.'

August was holding a sheet of paper with the test results printed on it. She held it up and placed it on Hunter's desk.

'For what it's worth,' she said. 'Good luck, guys.'

Hunter nodded and turned in his chair to look at the results. They were pretty meaningless unless you were a Crime Lab geek. Except the line that confirmed the match.

'Kinda feels like your world turned inside out, huh?' Collins told his partner.

Hunter said 'yeah', and told Collins about the call with Logan Finch. Collins laughed and it sounded like there was genuine humour in it. Hunter could've laughed. Could've put a fist through his computer screen. Ended up doing neither.

Collins stood and looked over the top of the partitions across the open-plan space.

'Yo, Choons,' he shouted. 'What's up with that ViCAP thing? You done yet?'

Hunter winced at the shout. 'Danny, he's just across the room. Think maybe you could go talk to him?'

A short man with a belly spilling over his trousers and straining the buttons of his shirt got up from his desk twenty feet from Hunter and shuffled over. He looked pissed off. Which was pretty much standard for Detective Arturo Sanchez.

'What I tell you about calling me that shit?' Sanchez told Collins, smoothing a hand over his bearded chin.

Hunter heard muffled laughter from the detective that Sanchez partnered with – Sally Kaminski. She was the only woman on Bowman's squad and had been the one to give Sanchez his nickname.

'But you sure do love them show tunes,' Collins said, still finding the joke funny after three months.

Kaminski had come in after lunch one day and found Sanchez listening to an iPod and singing quietly along to *Oklahoma!* In a homicide unit, you can't live that kind of thing down.

Ever.

Sanchez flipped Collins the bird and walked away.

'What about the ViCAP?' Collins asked.

'Last thing on my friggin' list, dickhead.'

Hunter shook his head.

'I'll do it,' he told Collins. 'Get him to send me what he's done so far and I'll do the rest. It's our case anyway.'

'Yo, Choons . . .' Collins shouted.

Hunter smiled in spite of himself.

13

Hunter spent an hour labouring through the ViCAP form.
It turned out that Sanchez hadn't made much of a start. It
took three attempts to log the form on the FBI's system
because he had forgotten to fill in some 'required fields'.

An acknowledgement e-mail pinged into his inbox.
Almost immediately after that an e-mail from Art Morris
followed. It was primarily addressed to Nick Levine but
Hunter and Collins had been copied in. There was a formal
letter from Morris as head of the unit requesting FBI assistance in the case of the five families.

Hunter picked up his phone and called Levine.

'I got the e-mail from your lieutenant,' Levine said.

'I'll arrange to get copies of everything made up and sent
to you.'

'Great, thanks. What can I do for you now?'

'I filed the ViCAP form. What's the process after that?'

'Someone, an agent, will be allocated the case and will run the data for you.'

'How long does that normally take?'

'I don't know. Weeks sometimes, I think.'

'Is there any way we can speed that up? I mean, can you or Dean help with that?'

'Sure we can. I'll speak to Special Agent Graves and get a rush put on it. Send me the acknowledgement e-mail. It'll have a unique reference number on it that I can use.'

'I appreciate that.'

Hunter was quiet.

'Anything else?' Levine asked.

'You'll see when we send the evidence over, but we got a fresh hit today. Matched up hair fibres from two of the scenes.'

'New evidence?'

'No. Long story, but we think that one of the Crime Lab guys was trying to hide it. Same guy that screwed up with Black's blood sample.'

'Any idea why?'

'None. Maybe you could factor that into your thinking. Somehow.'

'I'll see what I can do.'

Hunter ended the call and looked across the desk at Collins.

'You got that last known address for the lab guy?'

'Yeah. But that's not all.'

Hunter didn't like the look on his partner's face.

'What is it, Danny?'

'I think we should head over to his place right now.'

Collins drove out of the underground garage at the police headquarters Administration Building and headed southeast.

'South Grape Street,' Hunter told him, looking at the first sheet of a bundle of printed paper on his lap.

'You know it?'

'I know it's in Glendale. Beyond that . . .' Hunter flipped up the first sheet and traced the route from the city centre to the house on South Grape Street on the map underneath.

'Colorado Boulevard then Leetsdale Drive,' he said. 'East of Four Mile Park.'

They drove the short distance to Glendale in silence. Hunter looked through the rest of the printed sheets. It was all the information that Collins had managed to track down on the Crime Lab technician, Joel DeSanto. Trouble was, it mostly related to someone named Kurt Smith. The social security number DeSanto had given when he joined the department actually belonged to Smith, who died five years ago – at the age of seventy-three.

Collins turned on to South Grape Street. It was an unremarkable street with mainly single-storey houses that had small patches of grass for front yards and narrow driveways. It was neither poor nor affluent. It just was.

Collins pulled to the kerb outside a red-brick house that had a ranch-style porch and a small garage. The grass in the yard was growing high and a tree in the middle of the yard looked as if it had been neglected for months.

'How the hell did none of this show up when he applied to join the department?' Hunter asked, waving the sheaf of paper. 'I mean, did this guy just walk into a job in the Crime Lab and no one checked him out?'

'I spoke to personnel about that. No one could give me an answer. Seems like he passed the interview with flying colours and he was registered as living at this address. That's about as far as it went.'

Hunter shook his head.

'Let's go,' he said, stepping out of the car on to the sidewalk.

Collins got out and looked across the car at Hunter. They pushed their jackets behind the holsters on their belts and unsnapped the catches on the holsters. Hunter rested his hand on his handgun and started up the path to the front door of the house.

14

They stood either side of the front door. Hunter had one hand on his gun and his detective shield in the other. Collins pressed the button for the doorbell that was mounted on the wall. The bell chimed inside the house. A woman walking a dog passed by on the sidewalk. She looked at them and slowed when she saw the weapons exposed on their belts. Hunter flashed his shield at her and she quickened her pace.

Collins rang the bell again.

Hunter strained to listen for any movement inside the house. There was nothing. He reached out and pulled down on the door handle. It was locked. He looked at Collins and motioned with his head towards the back of the house. Collins turned and went around the right-hand corner of the house, pausing to look in the windows he passed on the way. The blinds were all closed so there was nothing to see. Hunter went in the opposite direction past the garage.

There was no fence or wall separating the house from the one next door. Hunter walked in the space between the two houses and stopped at the rear corner. He looked into the backyard and saw Collins at the far end of the house. He nodded and they both walked towards the door at the rear of the house, again looking in the windows they passed. All the blinds were down.

They stood either side of the door and Hunter banged on it with his fist. He waited for a few seconds and did it again. Collins tried the door. It was locked.

'No one's home,' Collins said. 'Want to break a window?'

Hunter said no and they walked around to the front again. Hunter tried the garage door handle as he passed and was surprised when it turned and the door swung up and in. They stood looking at the empty garage. There was a door in the far right-hand corner.

'Probably leads into the house,' Collins said, looking at his partner.

'No doubt.'

'What are we waiting for?'

'We go in through that door and anything we find is inadmissible in court. We don't have a warrant.'

'Probable cause?'

'No. Just because the guy gave a false name, it doesn't give us any cause to enter his residence.'

Collins snapped his holster closed and stood with his hands on his hips. It was a warm day and he felt hot in his navy sports jacket and grey trousers. Sweat beaded on his upper lip and he wiped at it.

'So what now?'

Hunter looked along the street in both directions. An old VW Beetle trundled past, its elderly driver peering at the road ahead over the steering wheel. When it passed there was no one else on the street. A typical working day.

Hunter was wearing a black suit, white shirt and navy-blue tie. He felt conspicuous in this neighbourhood. He reached up, pushed the garage door all the way open and stepped inside. Collins followed him.

'I hope this door's locked,' Hunter said, looking back at his partner.

It wasn't. The door swung open into a short hallway that led to the kitchen at the back of the house. Hunter listened for movement but heard nothing. He slid his handgun out of its holster, held it up in front of his face, sighted along the barrel and walked forward.

Collins did the same and followed him.

15

There were unwashed dinner dishes in the sink, dried food encrusted on the plates. Cutlery and a half-filled glass of water were sitting on the table. A copy of the *Denver Post* was beside the dinner setting, the front page reporting on Chase Black's successful appeal. The place reeked of decay.

'Somebody left in a hurry,' Collins said, waving a hand in front of his face.

The door from the kitchen was open, the hallway leading off it stretching to the front door. Hunter looked down the hall and motioned for Collins to follow him. He kept his gun up, pointing straight ahead. It felt hot inside the house, Hunter's shirt sticking to his back. The air in the hall smelled stale, like three-day old sweat.

There were four other doors leading off the hall, two on each side. Hunter motioned for Collins to go into the first room on the left and he went right. Hunter walked into a bedroom. It was a mess, like the kitchen. The bed covers were bunched at the foot of the bed and some clothes lay strewn on the floor. He quickly checked a drawer unit and wardrobe. They were both empty.

'Office-type room in there,' Collins told Hunter when they were back in the hall.

'Computer?'

Collins shook his head.

'Nothing like that. Place has been cleaned out.'

They walked together until they were level with the last two doors. Hunter pushed at the one on his side and it swung into a small bathroom. Same story there – a damp towel lying on the floor with mould on the walls.

Hunter followed Collins through the last door into the living room. He stopped inside the door and stared at the back wall.

'Jesus . . .' Collins said quietly.

The wall was completely covered with photographs, newspaper stories and magazine articles about Black and his trial. Hunter walked past his partner until he was two feet from the wall. He noticed that there were small holes in the wall, like something had been pinned up there and then removed. He rubbed his finger absently over one of the holes.

'What?' Collins asked.

'Something else was up here. There are pin holes.'

Collins came up beside Hunter to look more closely.

'What do you think?'

Hunter turned from the wall and knelt on the floor, rubbing his hand absently over the carpet. He looked down and saw the corner of a clear bag under the couch.

'Look at this,' he said to his partner.

Collins knelt beside him. Hunter took a pen from inside his jacket, pressed the cap end of it on to the bag, and slid it out from under the couch. There was a pin still stuck in one corner of the bag.

'Must have fallen under here when he bolted and he missed it,' Collins said.

Hunter wasn't really listening. He recognised the type of bag. He put the pen under it and flipped it over, revealing the evidence label on the other side. He knew the case number that was printed on the label. Knew it off by heart.

'Is that . . . ?' Collins trailed off as Hunter nodded.

Hunter peered into the bag, saw something inside it. He leaned closer to see what it was.

A child's tooth.

Had to be from the size of it.

'Son of a bitch took a souvenir,' Hunter said.

He looked again at the label on the bag and saw that DeSanto was the only person to have handled that particular piece of evidence. He stood and turned to the wall again, running his hand over it and feeling multiple pin holes.

'Lots of souvenirs.'

'But how? I mean, Steve Ames is such a control freak.'

'I guess it's easy enough if he recovered the evidence himself and no one else touched it. He takes what he likes. Then it's like it never existed.'

'But why take . . .' Collins searched for the right word – 'that, a trophy?'

He knew the answer as soon as the question left his mouth.

'Because this guy might be our killer,' Hunter said.

16

Hunter went to the window looking out on to the front yard. He pulled one of the slats of the blinds down and watched the street. A pick-up truck went by followed by a taxi.

'I think we should have gotten a warrant first,' he said.

'But we didn't. So . . .'

Hunter let the blind go and the slat snapped shut again. He turned and looked at his partner standing in front of that wall of paper; had a sudden vision that it was not Detective Danny Collins but Chase Black. He blinked and it was Danny again.

Collins's head tilted to the side. 'You okay?' he asked.

Hunter looked back at the window.

'Maybe we did get a warrant first,' he said.

'How did we do that? I mean, like you said, there were no grounds for it, really.'

'Use the sleeve of your jacket or something to pick that bag up and bring it here.'

Hunter reached inside his jacket pocket and took out his

cell phone. He scrolled through his contacts until he found the number for the District Attorney's office. He touched the screen to call and put the phone to his ear.

'ADA Angel,' he said when his call was answered.

He waited while he was connected, reaching out and taking hold of one of the cords that controlled the tilt of the blind slats.

'Angel,' a deep voice answered.

'How's it going, Bob? Jake Hunter here.'

'Rock and roll, my friend. As always.'

'I need a warrant.'

'Happy to help. What's the score?'

Hunter looked at Collins and pulled on the blind cord until it was possible to see the street outside through the gaps in the blind.

'It's on the Chase Black case. Or, what used to be the Chase Black case.'

'Today just got a whole lot more interesting. Tell me what you need.'

Hunter told him about the evidence issues and the lab tech's disappearance.

'Me and Danny are out at his house now. Nobody's home, it seems, but we can see through the blinds into the living room. There's some weird stuff. A whole wall plastered with stuff about Black and the trial.'

'You can see this from outside on the street?'

'I'm on his lawn right at the window. Got to get up real close to see it.'

Collins's face was blank. Hunter couldn't tell what his partner was thinking.

'There's something else too.'

'What?'

'A Denver PD Crime Lab evidence bag lying on the floor. Think it's enough for a warrant?'

'Guy was using a false name, screwed with your evidence, has gone AWOL and you can see all this weird shit inside his house. I'd say that would be a yes.'

'How long before you can get a judge to sign it?'

'I'll be there in under an hour.'

17

Hunter and Collins were sitting in their car with the engine running and the air con blowing when Angel pulled up behind them. Hunter pulled his keys from the ignition and stepped out of the car. Angel came towards them, looking even more imposing now that he was growing a beard and his dark hair had been cut short.

They shook hands and Angel passed over the warrant. He looked up at the house.

'This the place?'

'Yeah.'

He walked on to the lawn and went to the window, cupping his hands to the glass and looking in. Collins looked at Hunter.

'You've been quiet, Danny,' Hunter said. 'Everything okay?'

'Sure. I mean, pretty dumb of the guy to leave his blinds open.' He smiled at Hunter.

Angel came back to meet them at the car.

'That is one freaky-looking set-up. How you want to do this?'

'All the doors are locked,' Collins said. 'We tried them already.'

Angel looked back at the front of the house.

'You going to try to kick the door in or call for a breach team?'

Hunter surveyed the house like he was thinking about how to get inside. What he was really thinking was: *how long before I suggest we try the garage door?*

'What about the garage?'

Angel looked at Collins.

'No harm in trying it before we bust a lock, I guess,' Collins said.

Hunter felt a little bad about deceiving Angel. But only a little.

The three men walked up the driveway to the garage door. Hunter twisted the handle and tried to look vaguely surprised when the door swung open. He pushed it up and went through the same routine of sweeping the house with his gun drawn. Angel waited outside.

Hunter opened the front door and came out with Collins, wiping sweat from his face.

'Anything else?' Angel asked.

'Nothing.' Hunter shook his head.

'What do you think this guy was doing?'

'I really don't know. But we'll get the Crime Lab down here and they can go over the place.'

Angel started back towards his car.

'Call me if you need anything else, Jake. Any time.'

Hunter nodded and said thanks.

It was another half-hour before Molly August pulled up with her team in two plain Dodge vans. August came over to Hunter and Collins while the rest of her people took time unloading their gear from the vans.

'Did you know this guy, DeSanto?' Collins asked her.

August shook her head. 'Other than the Black case, I never worked with him.'

'Any friends in the lab that you know of?'

Hunter left them and walked to the house, showing the lab techs the living room and asking them to work in there before checking the rest of the house.

August watched Hunter then turned back to Collins.

'I asked around today. Nobody seems to have known the guy. Maybe they shared a sandwich but that's about it.'

'Did that not raise any suspicions?'

'In the lab?' August raised her eyebrows. 'Place is full of geeks. If he was normal he'd have stood out more.'

Collins laughed.

'What's this about?' August asked. 'You have any idea what he was up to or even who he really was?'

'We don't want to jump to conclusions.'

'I sense a "but" in there.'

'There's a DPD evidence bag in the house.'

Collins told her about the contents. August was quiet for a full half-minute.

'Want to show me inside?' she said eventually.

Collins led her up the path and into the house. Hunter

was in the hall watching the techs get set up in the living room. He nodded at August as she went past him into the room. She stopped inside the door like they had earlier.

'Oh my,' was all she said when she saw the back wall and the bag in the middle of the floor.

'What do you think?' Hunter asked her.

She looked at him and shrugged.

'Looks like obsessive behaviour. But I'm no shrink, you know.'

'Guy had a real close interest in this case, that's for sure.'

'Let us get to work here. You'll be first to know what we find.'

Part Four
Victimology

Memorandum

From: Franck Zimmer
To: Section Chief
Re: Project Eden

Interpol Ref: 735F-27

Sir,

A report has been received from MI5 confirming that the passenger manifest of a British Airways flight from Dublin, Ireland, to London contained the name that we are 99 per cent certain is being used by subject 'Eve'.

Some positive news to report this time in that we have a fairly clear image capture of this passenger's face from cameras within Terminal 5 at London Heathrow Airport. The image is being analysed now and scanned through our facial recognition software. A copy will be e-mailed to you separately.

Our analysts believe that the passenger was wearing a wig and other prosthetic augmentations to disguise her real features. This is a known M.O. of subject 'Eve'.

MI5 operatives were present in Terminal 5 and followed the passenger on the connecting express rail link to Paddington Station in Central London. I regret to advise that the contact with the passenger was lost at that time. MI5 believes that the passenger removed the prosthetics and wig and was, therefore, able to evade their operatives in this manner. It is likely that she travelled to her onward destination via the relative anonymity of the London Underground subway system.

MI5 is on high alert and will utilise the facial recognition software to seek to identify subject 'Eve' from public CCTV systems in London. We will send our image analysis to them. While the prosthetics will mean that an exact match is unlikely, it may be enough to locate her again.

Likewise, Echelon listening stations in the UK are on notice to report any contact that may be linked to subject 'Eve' immediately. She will need to contact subject 'Mamba' again. That's when we should get a lead on her location.

Reports to follow.

1

Thursday: London

Chase Black gripped Logan's hand firmly and shook it once. He held on for a moment and looked directly into Logan's eyes.

'Good to meet you, Logan,' Black said. 'I've seen your work.'

Black's eyes flicked to the television screen in his hotel suite and he smiled laconically. Logan noted the use of his first name. Black was clearly a man who liked to control a situation.

'Mr Black,' Logan said, stepping aside to let Carrie Richardson move forward to introduce herself.

Black, at six-two, was a good couple of inches taller than Logan and he towered over Carrie. She was not a woman to let herself be intimidated and stepped up and gripped Black's hand firmly.

'This is my colleague, Carrie Richardson,' Logan said.

Black nodded at them and looked at his lawyer, Kate Marlow. They were in a spacious and well-appointed suite in an expensive boutique hotel in Mayfair. Logan knew the area well but had marvelled again at the wealth on display on the taxi journey to the hotel. He counted numerous Porsche, Bentley and Mercedes cars either travelling on or parked at the side of the roads. There was also a silver Rolls-Royce glistening in the early morning sunshine. Carrie had nudged him excitedly when they passed by the Tiffany jewellery shop. Even she found time to appreciate a finely crafted piece of gold.

Kate Marlow gave Carrie an all-too-obvious look of distaste as her eyes travelled up and down her slim, five-five frame. She and Logan were dressed in standard CPO gear – combat trousers and black polo shirts with the CPO logo on the sleeves.

'I may not look like much,' Carrie said to Marlow, 'but I wouldn't bet against me if it gets rough.'

Marlow tried to smile, almost managed it, and invited them to sit on a couch by the window. She sat with Black on the opposite couch and poured coffee for all of them from an expensive-looking silver pot resting on the table between the couches. Sun slanted in through the windows, though the room was cooled by the air conditioning that hummed quietly in the background. There was a door behind the couch that Logan figured led to the bedroom of the suite.

'Let's be direct about things,' Logan said to Black. 'I know that Miss Marlow wants us to look after you for the duration of your stay here, but I need to know that you're on board as well. Otherwise it won't work.'

'I appreciate directness, Logan. And I'm entirely comfortable with this arrangement.'

Logan nodded, reached into his nylon dispatch bag, and took out a sheaf of papers that included the contract he had drawn up for the job and Black's travel itinerary for the next few days. He passed the contract to Marlow and asked her to countersign beside his own signature.

She flipped through the ten-page document.

'This is what we agreed via our e-mails?'

'Yes.'

'I still need to read it.'

'Go ahead.'

She put the contract on the table and leaned forward to read it. Logan saw a hint of dark roots where her blond hair was parted. She was wearing an expensive-looking trouser suit with a pink blouse. Everything about her spoke of good grooming and lots of money.

Black leaned back on the couch and spread his arms out. It was a pose that radiated confidence.

'Were you injured in the incident yesterday?' Carrie asked him.

He waved a hand dismissively. 'No, I'm fine. I thought you British types were better than that.'

Carrie laughed. 'You've never been to Glasgow?'

Black shook his head.

'Not so polite,' Carrie said.

Black watched her closely, trying to work out if he was being mocked. Hunter watched him in turn. He was acutely aware of not wanting to jump to any conclusions about the man.

'Maybe you can show me around some time,' Black told Carrie.

'Let's see how we get on before we start dating.'

Something passed across Black's face. Logan wasn't sure what it was, but it looked as if he appreciated the joke.

Marlow continued to read the contract meticulously and seemed oblivious to the conversation. There was a stack of Black's book on the floor next to the table that Logan hadn't noticed before. He reached over and picked the top one up, turning to read the blurb on the inside cover of the heavy hardback.

'Keep it,' Black said. 'Let me know what you think of it.'

'I hear it's been very successful.'

'Sold to sixteen countries around the world.'

Carrie sat forward, resting her elbows on her knees.

'Bet the money doesn't make up for being in jail,' Carrie said to Black.

He shrugged.

Marlow flipped to the last page of the contract, said that it looked fine and signed with a flourish of her fountain pen. She handed the contract back to Logan.

'Let's talk business,' she said.

2

Kate Marlow went over the full programme of events that made up Chase Black's itinerary. It was a mixture of signing sessions at bookstores and speaking engagements at various venues. There was also a party planned for Friday night with the major players at the UK publisher that was paying for everything.

'Our engagement is at your direction,' Logan told her. 'What that means is, if you want us on call twenty-four hours a day, we will be. Or if you want us to cover just the public events, that's also okay.'

'How would that work?' Marlow asked. 'I mean, there're only two of you and you need to sleep, so how can you cover the whole day?'

'We take the night work in shifts.'

Logan looked around the room.

'One of us sleeps for a couple of hours and the other

is on duty in here while Mr Black sleeps through that door.'

He pointed behind Marlow.

'And we keep radio lines open,' Carrie added. 'So which-ever one of us is not on duty is only a shout away.'

'Did you arrange for us to get the room next door?' Logan asked.

'I'm still, uh, negotiating with the hotel.'

'It would be our preferred location.'

'I understand that. I'll make it happen.'

She seemed like the kind of person it was difficult to say no to. Which was a good trait to have in the circumstances.

Marlow looked at Black who had remained silent through the discussion.

'What do you think, Chase?' she asked. 'Do you want them with you all day and night? It's your safety that we're concerned with, after all.'

'What if I need some . . . privacy?'

He looked at Carrie.

'If you get lucky, let us know,' she said, smiling. 'I have no desire to sit here and listen, if you know what I mean.'

'Don't worry, I'll let you know.'

His expression did not change.

'So,' Marlow said. 'It's round the clock unless Chase says otherwise.'

She looked at Black for confirmation and he nodded. Logan figured that the two of them had spent some time together over the last day or two and Marlow appeared entirely comfortable around Black. Seemed she had no concerns about the man.

'Let me speak to the manager again about your room,' Marlow said. 'Then you can get settled in, geared up – or whatever you call it – and we can head out for the first event.'

'Sounds good,' Carrie said, standing and stretching.

Black got up and went into the bedroom, closing the door without saying anything further.

'He's had a tough few years,' Marlow said.

Logan swiped the card that opened the door of the room next to Chase Black's suite and pushed the door inwards. It had taken Kate Marlow only ten minutes to get her way. Logan wasn't sure that he liked Marlow, but he admired her ability to get things done.

The room was small but decorated and furnished to a high standard. He put his cabin bag and dispatch case next to the single bed nearest the door.

'What, we got separate beds?' Carrie said, following him into the room and seeing the twin beds.

Logan had known as soon as he walked in the door that she'd make some sort of crack about it. Wouldn't be Carrie otherwise. He smiled anyway.

'Yeah,' she said when she saw his face. 'I knew it. You're disappointed too. Want to get Miss Marvellous on to it? I'm sure she could swing us a double room no problem.'

'It's Marlow.'

'That's what I said.'

She sat on the other bed, looked at her watch, then rubbed her eyes.

'Man, I hate the early rises.'

Logan wasn't such a fan either. He had got up with his

alarm at four-thirty that morning to get to the airport for the first flight to London at six. His bag was packed already, so all he had to do was shower quickly, dress and get to his car. It took him around half an hour in total.

His mood wasn't helped by the less-than-enthusiastic conversation with Becky the previous night after dinner with Ellie. She knew enough about the Chase Black case to think that it was not a job CPO should be taking on.

'He's a killer,' she'd said.

'That's the policewoman in you talking.'

'That's what I am.'

She'd fixed him with a hard stare at that. The evening did not end as intimately as Logan had hoped.

'What's the first gig?' Carrie asked, pulling Logan from his thoughts.

'Waterstone's bookshop on Trafalgar Square at eleven.'

'Any particular concern about it?'

'Nope. Should be standard crowd control-type thing. The shop will have its own security guy at the front door, so we don't have to worry about that.'

'Just your basic signing. One customer at a time?'

'Right.'

'Easy money.'

Logan hoped she was right.

3

Logan and Carrie changed into inconspicuous clothes – trousers and light jackets – and rode down in the lift with Black and Marlow. Both of them were dressed more formally in dark suits.

Marlow had explained that the publisher had arranged for them to have a dedicated car and driver for the duration of the tour. Logan told Black and the lawyer to wait in the lobby with Carrie. He went out through the revolving door and stood on the pavement, taking his time to look in every direction. There was nothing that caused him any concern so he turned and waved at Carrie through the glass of the doors.

Earlier, he had made a point of coming down to introduce himself to the driver, a thin man of Middle Eastern descent, and to check out the car. It was a black MPV with darkly tinted rear windows and three rows of seats. The big rear doors were electronically operated and slid back silently on the press of a button.

Black got in the rear seat beside Marlow with Logan and Carrie in the middle row directly behind the driver.

'Keep the doors locked at all times unless I say otherwise,' Logan told the driver when he was in his seat.

'Yes, sir,' he said, activating the central locking.

'You ready for your public?' Marlow asked Black.

'Looking forward to it.'

Logan thought that he heard a slight waver in Black's voice, as if he was nervous. He turned to face Black.

'Don't worry, we'll look after you,' he said.

They drove along Green Park before turning towards Buckingham Palace and the wide, red expanse of the Mall. Logan always liked driving on the Mall. He wasn't a huge supporter of the Royal family, but there was no doubt that their presence gave London something no other city had.

They passed through Admiralty Arch and on to Trafalgar Square with Nelson's column stretching high above them. Tourists milled around the square, some of them climbing up on to the lions carved in stone at the foot of the column to have their photographs taken. Logan saw that a queue had formed outside the Waterstone's shop on the west side of the square. The entrance was roped off and a large man with a flat nose stood at the front of the queue with his arms crossed. There was no mistaking store security.

'We're going round back,' Marlow said, leaning forward in her seat.

The driver nodded and went past the shop entrance before

turning right and then right again to get to the alley that serviced the rear of the shop.

There was a woman publicist at the back door with the shop manager. Logan asked Carrie to go inside to check the shop and speak to the front-of-house security before he allowed Black to get out of the car. She went past the two women at the back door and Logan closed the door after she had left.

'You're being very cautious,' Marlow said. 'I mean, that's a good thing.'

Logan turned in his seat to speak to her.

'I learned from the best,' he told her. 'My partners in the company were US special forces soldiers and then Secret Service agents. They worked all over the world with American politicians in their care.'

She looked impressed.

'Their primary rule is to treat everyone the same,' Logan went on. 'So a book signing is the same as the President going to a base in Afghanistan.'

'The threat level isn't quite the same, though, is it?' Black asked, leaning forward. 'I mean, come on.'

'We assume that it is.'

'But no guns for you.'

'No.'

Carrie appeared at the door again and waved them in.

Logan was a little surprised at the size of the media presence inside the store. There were TV crews from the major UK news channels and a couple of US networks as well. He walked behind Black with Carrie and Kate Marlow ahead of them. The shop manager had opened the door from the rear store area on to the shop floor and they had been blinded by the powerful TV lights and multiple flashes from photographers.

Black was taken aback and stopped for a moment. Then he smiled, waved and walked forward to join the woman publicist at the desk set up for signing. It was piled high with books and faced the front of the store where the queue had grown longer.

Logan asked the store manager to lock the door behind them. When he had checked that it was secure, he and Carrie took up positions at the front of the table – standing off to the side so as not to look too obviously like security.

'Are we ready?' the store manager asked.

Marlow looked at Logan. He nodded at her.

'Open the doors,' Marlow said.

4

Logan had agreed with Carrie how to monitor the crowd once the event got going. She would watch the line of people coming in through the door and waiting at the temporary barrier eight feet from the table. Logan's job was to watch each person approaching the table and be ready to move fast if anything looked off-kilter.

The first half-hour passed without incident with a steady stream of customers, mainly women, presenting their book for signing and saying a few words of encouragement to Black. Some of them had friends take photographs. Outside, the queue seemed to grow longer with each passing minute. Logan was surprised by how popular Black was turning out to be.

Carrie saw the trouble coming.

Saw him as soon as he came in the door.

He was avoiding eye contact with anyone, mainly looking down at the floor. His right hand kept going inside the pocket of his windcheater jacket and Carrie could see something bulging at the bottom of that pocket.

She turned her head and looked at Logan. He saw her. Knew what the look meant.

Logan followed Carrie's gaze as she turned back to the guy in the queue. He saw immediately why she had singled him out. He looked back at Carrie and nodded. She went behind the desk where Black was sitting and spoke to the manager of the store. The woman looked a little startled at first, then set her lips in a thin line. She went to the storeroom door and unlocked it, then walked to the two staff members who were stopping the customers at the temporary barrier. Carrie stayed by the storeroom door.

Logan waited until the customer at the desk was done talking to Black, then moved to his side and told him they were taking a break. He put his hand under Black's elbow and lifted it, telling Black that he should move.

It all went smoothly.

Logan walked with Black and Kate Marlow until they were in the store area. Carrie followed them inside as the manager told the remaining customers that Mr Black was taking a short break and would be back soon.

'What is it?' Black asked as Logan closed the door behind them.

'Someone in the line of people we want to check out,' Logan said.

'Anything I should be concerned about?'

'Being concerned is *my* job. Stay here and I'll check it out.'

Marlow looked pale.

Logan went back out into the shop alone. Carrie stayed with Black. Never leave your client unprotected.

Logan locked the door after he was through it. The store manager approached him and he gave her the key before walking through the crowded shop to the security guard at the front door. Logan motioned for the guy to step inside the front door.

'I'm Mr Black's personal security,' he said.

The man was impassive.

'What's your name?'

'Rick.'

Just Rick.

'We may have a problem.'

Just Rick's eyes flicked behind Logan to the line of people snaking through the shop.

'Guy with his hand in his pocket looking shifty,' Logan said.

Rick's eyes continued to scan the crowd. Logan guessed that he was a man to have in your corner when things got bad, but probably had little by way of training. Which was probably why he had not noticed the man when he entered the shop.

'Got him now,' Rick said.

'Shall we go talk to him?' Logan asked.

'I think we should.'

'I'll speak to him. I'm less intimidating than you are up close.' Logan smiled. Rick did not. 'You circle behind and get close enough to take him if need be,' Logan said. 'Watch his hands.'

Rick nodded. It appeared that he liked to communicate as economically as was humanly possible.

Logan kept his eyes on the man in the line as he moved towards him. He waited until Rick was in position before he made the final approach. The man was still looking at his shoes with his right hand on whatever was in his pocket when Logan stepped in front of him.

'Excuse me, sir,' he said, smiling. 'Can I get you a book?'

The man looked up at him, startled.

'What?' A frown creased his forehead.

'A book, sir. You know, for Mr Black to sign for you.'

'I, uh . . .'

'It's really no problem at all. There are plenty available.'

The man was thin, with lank hair that he patted flat on his head while his eyes darted around.

Logan put his hand on the man's left arm.

'If you don't want to get a book signed, can I ask you to step out of the line, please. There are plenty of people here who have copies to get signed.'

He stepped forward and pushed firmly at the man's arm. The man was surprised and stumbled as he went back.

People in the queue were turning to look. Curious, if not quite concerned yet, by the commotion.

Rick moved forward, ready to grab the man's other arm and neutralise the threat of whatever it was he was holding. But the man was quicker and stronger than he had expected and pulled the hand from his pocket, trying to wrench his other arm free of Logan's grip.

Logan knew then that he should have brought Carrie out with him. Never trust your safety to anyone outside the team. But it was too late.

The man started to lose his balance and fall back, now with both hands on the item he had pulled from his pocket.

Logan tried to get both hands on him as he fell into Rick, knocking him backwards.

'Murderer!' the man screamed as he went down.

He threw both his hands out and Logan saw a splash of red; felt something cold and wet hit him in the face.

The people around them scrambled to get out of the way as both Logan and Rick fell on the man and secured his hands, pinning him to the floor.

'Murderer!' he shouted again, his voice hoarse.

Logan was aware of the TV lights being trained on them and flash photography popping.

He looked at Rick and saw rivulets of blood running down his face from out of his hair. For a terrible moment he thought that Rick had been shot or slashed with a knife, though he had no recollection of hearing a gun go off.

Women started to scream around them.

Logan wiped his hand across his face where he had felt the cold liquid hit him and it came away covered in blood.

A glass jar rolled out of the man's hand, the remaining blood in it slopping out on to the floor.

'Their blood is on his hands,' the man shouted.

Logan felt relief wash over him. He looked around for the shop manager, raising a hand to shield his eyes from the lights. He saw her open-mouthed several feet away.

'Call the police,' he told her.

Then he realised that he would be all over the TV and Internet in a matter of hours, if not minutes. Again.

So much for keeping a low profile.

5

Thursday: Denver

Detectives Arturo Sanchez and Sally Kaminski were the homicide unit 'hot' team which meant that they would be first on-call for any new cases that came into the unit. Kaminski looked up at Hunter when he came into the open-plan area. She was on the phone, cupped her hand over the mouthpiece, and mouthed 'What?' at Hunter. He waved a hand at her, conscious of how he looked at 5 a.m. He'd seen himself in the mirror that morning – dark smudges under his eyes.

He had found it difficult to sleep. Had lain in bed staring at the ceiling for more than an hour before finally drifting into a fitful sleep. He had given up at four in the morning and had decided to come into the office.

Had they made such a massive mistake with Chase Black? The question gnawed at him, a constant strum of tension in his stomach. Like his guts were stretched a fraction too tight.

The last time he had spoken to Molly August was at ten last night when she and her team were still hard at work sifting the evidence recovered from the house on South Grape Street. The house formerly occupied by Crime Lab technician Joel DeSanto. Or whatever his real name was.

'You getting overtime for this shift?' Hunter had asked August when he found her in her office.

'Nope. How 'bout you?'

'Same. Never crossed my mind.'

She made a noise somewhere between a laugh and a grunt, looking down at a number of printed sheets of paper spread across her desk. It was a lot less tidy than under normal circumstances.

Hunter pulled a chair out from her desk and sat heavily. 'Did we screw up?' he asked.

She made that noise again and leaned back in her chair. 'You mean any more than already identified?'

'I mean, is Chase Black innocent?'

'That's a big question.'

'It's the only one I'm interested in right now.'

'I don't know. That's the honest answer.'

'It's not exactly the one I was hoping for.'

She leaned forward with her hands clasped in front of her on the desk. 'Look, Jake, we're all in this together. As much pressure as you feel from your boss, we're under the same scrutiny. Me and Steve. This is a jobs-on-the-line kind of fuck-up. A real career killer, you know.'

He'd never heard her use profanity before. Not once.

Which was unusual in the highly pressured environment in which they worked. It was part of the vernacular for cops. He looked closely and saw in her face the same tension he felt, her skin stretched tight across her cheekbones. 'Did you recover hair samples from the house?'

'Yes. Lots of different ones.'

'You know what I'm asking.'

'Does his hair match the samples from the two previous scenes?'

Hunter nodded.

'I'm not sure we'll ever be able to make a definitive call on that.'

'Why not?'

'Think about it. I mean, even if we do match a hair from that house to the ones we have already, we can't say for sure that it's his. We don't have a control sample direct from him to match any of them.'

Hunter closed his eyes, felt light-headed from lack of sleep. 'The odds of a match to anyone else are pretty slim,' he said finally. 'You would agree with that?'

'Not conclusive, but you're right.' She nodded. 'The chances are it would be his.'

'I don't think that this case can rest on a "chances are" assessment, do you?'

'No.'

'Let me know when you have anything we can use.'

Hunter scrolled through his e-mail messages. There was one from August at 11.02 p.m. saying that she was calling it quits for the night.

There was one more e-mail at around midnight. This one from his friend at the FBI, Dean Graves. It had 'ViCAP' in the subject line and the message itself consisted of three words:

I'm on it.

Hunter smiled and closed the message. He wanted to order his thoughts, to make sense of where the investigation was. Fatigue clouded his mind so he went to get a coffee. Arturo 'Choons' Sanchez was at the machine waiting for his last fix of the night shift. Hunter nodded a greeting.

'You look like shit, Jake.'

'Thanks.'

That was the end of the conversation. Sanchez, unlike Molly August, tried hard to punctuate every sentence with at least one profanity.

Hunter drank half of the coffee quickly, feeling it scald his tongue and burn down through his body. It felt good.

He opened a blank document on his computer, typed the date as a heading and went to work.

6

Thursday: FBI Academy, Quantico, Virginia

The first thing Dean Graves did that morning when he got to his office at the FBI Academy was grab his Browning Hi-Power and head for the gun range. It was therapeutic.

He checked in with the range supervisor and took enough rounds to fill three magazines for his weapon. Graves squeezed the trigger and let loose his first live round, thinking about his friend in Denver, Jake Hunter. He was worried about the younger man. Didn't like seeing his case going so badly wrong, and so publicly.

Graves emptied the first magazine and watched smoke particles swirl in the air. He set the gun down on the ledge in front of him and pushed the button to bring the target up so that he could check his score. He eyed the shredded card target and thought he hadn't done too bad, not for an old man anyway.

He ripped through another couple of targets and decided to get back to his office and speak to Nick Levine again. Make sure he was giving Hunter all the help he needed. Then he would go and see the Hostage Rescue Teams under his command as part of the FBI's elite Critical Incident Response Group. It had been a few months since CIRG had been fully deployed and he wanted to make sure everyone was still alert and in shape.

Graves was sitting in his office sipping a coffee when Levine walked in.

'You looking for me, sir?'

Graves nodded and told Levine to take a seat.

'You know I have history with Detective Hunter.'

Levine nodded. 'Yes, sir. I read up on it.'

'He needs to get all the help he can on this. Now that it's official with his lieutenant, make sure he gets a five-star service.'

'Yes, sir. Of course.'

Graves liked Levine. He was relatively new to the team, no more than eighteen months in, but he was smart and hard working. Those two traits went a long way with Graves who was no stranger to thirty-six-hour shifts if the job required it.

The thing in Denver was starting to spark Graves's instincts. Too many dead and a killer loose – whether it was Chase Black or someone else. Now that the Bureau had been asked to assist, technically he would be within his authority to go to Denver and assume control of the investigation. But that would be a death sentence for Hunter's career. Like it or not, all he could do was help from a distance.

He didn't like it.

'I think I've made clear the level of importance that I want this assignment to be given. Keep me posted, okay?'

Levine nodded and stood. He hesitated before leaving, looking back at Graves.

'Something on your mind?' Graves asked.

'Well, it's just . . .'

'Spit it out, Nick.'

'We could do more on the ground. In Denver, I mean.'

'I know that.' Graves stared at Levine. 'This one is going to have to play out on its own. For now.'

'Understood, sir.'

The Hostage Rescue Team was divided into two sections, Red and Black, with two seven-man assault teams and two seven-man sniper teams in each section. They had their own separate compound on the Quantico base where they practised for engagements. Graves walked along the hallway of the HRT building and looked at the photographs on the walls from past missions all over the States. He found the Red section supervisor, John Sullivan, in one of the classrooms at the back of the building.

'Hey, Big Dog. Come to check up on us boys at last,' Sullivan said.

Graves smiled and shook his hand. Sullivan had been the one to give Graves his team call sign, Big Dog, and he knew Graves enjoyed it. Graves liked the fact that Sullivan did not have a military background, unlike a lot of the HRT squad. He was one of the former FBI field agents to have made it through the tough HRT qualification programme.

'How was Arizona?' Graves asked. 'The boys stand up to the heat?'

'Sure did. A couple of the new guys took some time to get used to the workload but we brought them up to speed.'

'I know that they need a proper operation to stay sharp and these training exercises only take us so far.'

'Sure, but if we're quiet, then the world must be a safer place, right?'

'Maybe our part of it.'

Graves sat on one of the desks and Sullivan did the same.

'What brings you over here, sir?'

Sullivan knew his chief well enough to recognise when he wanted to talk about something. Graves was not one for idle chat in the workplace.

'I got a call for some assistance from Denver PD. Jake Hunter of their Homicide Unit called in a favour.'

Sullivan nodded. Everyone in HRT had heard about Graves's history with Hunter in Denver.

'Nick Levine's giving them some profile stuff.'

'Nick's a good man. It'll work itself out, right?'

'I guess. But Jake's never called in the favour before and, I don't know, it doesn't sit right with me.'

'This the serial killer investigation? The one that got released a few months back?'

'Yes.'

'Cops can handle that. No need for us to go rolling in loaded for bear, is there?'

'No. It's not one for a full deployment. But you and some of the other guys have investigative backgrounds, right?'

Sullivan nodded.

'You think maybe he might need some help? We could send a couple of boys just in case.'

'Only if Jake calls for it. But do an old man a favour and stay sharp.'

Sullivan said sure. Graves left without saying anything else.

Graves paused in the hallway on his way out and stared at a photograph taken at Ruby Ridge. The gallery reminded all HRT operators of the good times and the bad. He thought of the dark interior of the bank where he and Hunter had run through the fire together and lived.

He turned to head for the door as Nick Levine pulled it open and came inside, breathing heavily as if he had been running.

'What is it?' Graves asked.

'We have something on the killings in Denver.'

7

Thursday: Denver

It was amazing what could be achieved on a cup of coffee and four hours' sleep. Hunter felt more focused than he had since Chase Black had walked out of jail on that cold morning six months ago. He sat back and looked at the notes he had typed. Clarity was what he needed, and he felt that he had achieved some measure of it:

1. Matching hair fibres at 2 separate scenes – not Black & not any family members
2. Black's blood found at scene handled by DeSanto
3. Blood evidence tainted by DeSanto not signing in at the scene
4. Original blood sample from Black taken by DeSanto
5. DeSanto using false name

6. Trophies from the crime scenes at his house
7. DeSanto is in the wind
8. DeSanto misfiled the hair samples found on scene (because they were his?)
9. Matching hair fibres at DeSanto's house (?)

It was clear that DeSanto had to be treated as a serious suspect. But the third item on the list troubled Hunter when he tried to analyse it rationally. Maybe that was the problem – that it could not be done rationally.

He tried to get it clear in his head again. They had obtained Black's blood sample legitimately. Black had volunteered it, in fact, so there was no question of it being tainted evidence. DeSanto was the technician who actually took the sample from Black. He would have recognised Black as someone that they were looking at as a potential suspect in the beginning.

But, at the same time, if DeSanto was the killer and he was trying to frame Black by planting his blood sample at the crime scene, why did he do something so basic as not signing in? There was no doubt that he was using a false name but the other Crime Lab employees Danny Collins had interviewed recognised him as having genuine experience and ability at the job. And he had signed in at every other scene he had ever worked while employed by the Lab.

It made no sense. He would have known that the failure to sign in would taint the evidence. Hunter tried to put himself in the man's position. If *he* was going to frame someone to cover his own tracks, he would make damn sure that everything about it was done entirely according to the rules.

Which brought him back to the same question – why?

He didn't have an answer. He highlighted the sentence onscreen and changed the font colour to red. One for Nick Levine, the profiler. The psychological stuff was his field of expertise, not Hunter's.

He wondered if they might be able to trace DeSanto in the past to another lab somewhere. Or maybe a teaching facility – as either a student or a tutor. He scribbled a note to check that out on a piece of paper on his desk and under-lined it. Maybe that was the way to find his real identity.

Hunter went to see Art Morris when he saw him arrive and filled him in on all developments. Morris told him to stick with it. Which, for Morris, was about as close to enthu-siasm as he got on a case.

He went from Morris's office to the elevator bank and shared a ride down to the ground floor with Kaminski and Sanchez as they were leaving to go home. It was around eight.

'Your day getting any better, Jake?' Kaminski asked as the doors slid shut behind them on the third floor.

'Honestly? I don't really know.'

'Chase Black giving you nightmares?'

Hunter puffed out his cheeks and released a long sigh. 'Not in the way that you would think,' he said.

The elevator shuddered to a halt and the doors opened. Danny Collins was waiting in the corridor outside the bank of elevators.

'You leaving?' he asked Hunter.

Kaminski and Sanchez stepped out of the elevator. Hunter considered his partner for a moment and then inclined his head, telling Collins to join him.

'I was going for a walk. Get some fresh air.'

Collins pressed the button for the third floor and the doors closed again.

'And now?'

'I changed my mind.'

Hunter explained what he had done so far and his concern about DeSanto's failure to sign in at the crime scene. A short stubble had formed on Collins's chin and he rubbed at it.

'No word from Molly on any hair fibres?' he asked.

Hunter shook his head. 'I'm hoping we'll hear something today.'

When they were at their shared desk Hunter asked Collins to trace DeSanto's past employment and studies.

'Where do I start?' Collins asked.

'We've got a date of birth, right?'

'Yeah, but what if it's fake too?'

'Most lies, good ones, anyway, are centred around some truths. I mean, think about it. Someone asks for your date of birth, you answer automatically.'

'I suppose . . .'

'If you've got to stop and think each time, or if you get the false one mixed up with the real one, that could be trouble. Shatter the veneer of the life you've created.'

'So even if most of the stuff is false, the date of birth could be real?'

Hunter nodded.

'Start with public records here in Denver and check those

people born on that date. Run down all the male children you find. And at the same time check nationwide for forensic teaching facilities. There can't be that many of them. Identify students with the same DOB and speak to the schools.'

Collins scribbled on the pad sitting on his desk.

'And speak to the lieutenant if you need any more resource on it. I brought him up to speed already.'

Hunter looked at his computer screen as a new e-mail opened in his inbox. The FBI crest was prominently displayed.

'What are you going to do?' Collins asked.

Hunter scrolled down the e-mail and frowned. Collins watched from across the desk as Hunter's eyes narrowed and anger filled his face.

'What is it, Jake?'

Hunter looked at his partner. 'We got a ViCAP hit. Dean Graves sent it to me.'

Collins walked around the desk to look at the e-mail. Hunter pointed at the screen.

'Girl got killed over in Dillon last week. Just married. Husband found her gutted, bound to their bed. Hit on enough of our entries on the system to throw it up as a possible match.'

'The Draytons stayed in Dillon.'

Hunter nodded.

'And Chase Black was still in prison last week,' Collins added.

'I know.'

8

'Sergeant Fields,' a woman answered on the second ring.

'This is Detective Hunter with Denver PD Homicide. How are you doing today, sergeant?'

'Not too good, detective. But you probably don't want to hear my woes.'

Hunter thought he heard a trace of New York in her accent.

'What can I do for you?'

'Well, I'm looking at an e-mail on my screen that has your name on it.'

'Those damn Internet dating sites.'

Hunter wasn't sure if she was joking, decided to ignore that comment until he got to know her a little better.

'It's from the FBI. We got a hit on a case of ours that matched up some with a murder you had over there last week. Girl by the name of . . .' Hunter scanned the e-mail looking for the victim's name.

'Kimmy Dawson,' Sergeant Fields said before he could find the name.

'You knew her?'

'Only a little. But then I know most folks here a little. We're not a big town, sir. Not like Denver.'

'How many homicides do you get in a year?'

'Uh, if we get one it's considered a major event. And nothing like this before. Ever. Last one I remember was when Everett Trill hit his wife over the head with a bottle and severed her carotid artery in the process. That was nearly three years ago.'

'You don't sound like a Colorado native. New York?'

'Good catch, detective. I moved away from there to find the quiet life. A lesser class of criminal.'

'You were a cop back east?'

'Only for a little while.'

He sensed melancholy in her voice – not sure if it was at what she had seen in New York, or what she had left behind.

'Listen to us shooting the breeze while the bodies are getting colder,' she said. 'What do you have, detective?'

'You heard of Chase Black?'

'Hasn't everyone? What's he got to do with—' She stopped abruptly. 'Are you saying that your ViCAP hit relates to those murders?'

'I am.'

'If I wasn't a lady I would have said holy shit.'

'I wouldn't have held that against you.'

'Can you hold on a second? I think I'd better get my boss in on this call.'

There was a noise as she put the phone down on her

desk and then footsteps followed by a muffled conversation. Hunter waited then heard two sets of footsteps approach.

'I have you on speaker now, Detective Hunter. My boss is here – Chief of Police Franklin Patton.'

'Morning, chief.'

'*Was* a good morning till Sergeant Fields here told me what you got from the FBI. I assume you're not pulling our chains on this.'

'That's correct, sir. This is genuine, direct from the Bureau.'

'Tell you the truth,' Patton said, 'this is kind of out of our league, you know. We already sent the forensics to the FBI lab.'

'I understand. How many officers do you have?'

'Eleven total.'

'Thirteen, if you count the dog and the horse,' Fields added.

Hunter smiled. He decided that he liked this woman.

'Got the lowest crime rate in the whole of the State,' Patton said. 'Or we did until Kim Dawson got cut up.'

'Tell you what,' Hunter said. 'How would you like some help from us city boys?'

There was a moment of silence and Hunter could picture the two officers on the other end of the line looking at each other.

'We'd like that plenty,' Patton said.

'I'll need to clear it with my boss. But I don't think it'll be a problem.'

'Let us know if you need anything to help with that conversation. We'd be glad to have all the help that we can get.'

'Leave it with me. I'll see what I can do.'

9

'Chief Patton, my name is Arthur Morris. I'm the division head here at Denver PD Homicide.'

Hunter and Collins were huddled together on the far side of Morris's desk with the phone on speaker mode. Morris leaned forward with his elbows on the desk.

'Good to talk to you, sir. I'm here with my sergeant, Sutton Fields. Sergeant Fields is leading our inquiry. She used to be a detective over in New York.'

'Homicide?' Morris asked.

'No, robbery,' Fields said.

'She's the closest thing we have to bona fide murder police,' Patton added.

'Where are you with your investigation right now? I mean, do you have anyone in custody?'

'No,' Fields said. 'We've gone at the husband as you would expect. He's a mess and I don't believe he killed her.'

'Any other leads?'

'Not so far.'

'What are you doing about the forensics work?' Hunter asked. 'We've got a good lab here. We could join the dots with your case.'

'We sent it to the FBI. Maybe your people can hook up with them?'

'I'll speak to them about that. Can you e-mail me the case reference?'

'I'll do that now,' Fields said.

'What do you need from us?' Morris asked.

'Whatever you got is what we need, you know.'

'Leave it with me for now,' Morris said. 'We'll discuss resources here. There's a major ongoing murder investigation and I can't dilute our focus from that.'

'I understand,' Patton said. 'I expect you have clearance rates to think about.'

'Right. We'll be in touch later today.'

Morris sat back in his chair and looked at Hunter.

'We're going over there,' Hunter said. 'This is not a dilution of our case. This *is* our case.'

Collins glanced sideways at his partner.

'You don't know that, Jake. I mean, from what you told me about their case it doesn't fit precisely with ours. ViCAP is not an exact scientific tool.'

'I know that. But it's not like Dillon is on the other side of the world. Our chief suspect is probably not in Denver any longer.'

'You're not talking about Chase Black this time?'

'Correct. I'm talking about DeSanto. And Danny reminded

me that the Draytons were staying in Dillon. That can't be a coincidence.'

'If you're right about all this, and you go to Dillon, how do we run the case here? There's little or no capacity for anyone else.'

'It's mainly lab work here. We can co-ordinate from Dillon. Kaminski and Choons can keep it going here.'

Morris frowned and steepled his fingers under his chin. It was not a gesture Hunter associated with a homicide detective — more like a college professor.

'Fine,' Morris said. 'Drive over there tomorrow. Get the lie of the land. But stay in touch. I don't want this to be part two of your personal crusade on this case.'

Hunter ground his teeth together, his jaw muscles bulging outward. Morris either didn't notice his anger or chose to ignore it.

10

Thursday: London

'I need a drink,' Chase Black said from the rear of their car as they pulled up in front of the hotel.

It had been a long day for Logan and Carrie after the early flight from Glasgow. The last of the signing sessions had finished after six and it was close to seven now. Logan hoped that Black meant a quiet drink in the hotel bar rather than a night on the town.

'Somewhere lively,' Black said, sounding enthusiastic.

So much for a quiet night in, Logan thought.

'Know anywhere good?' Black asked, tapping Logan on the shoulder.

Logan turned to look at him and shook his head.

'How 'bout you, Carrie?' Black asked.

'Not my town,' she answered.

'You guys feeling the pace?'

'No,' Logan lied. 'Whatever you want to do is fine with us.'

'Great. Kate, do you know anywhere we can go? Been stuck in this car or in a book store all day long.'

Kate Marlow looked even less enthusiastic about the prospect of a night out than Logan, but said she would speak to the concierge to get a recommendation.

'And get your dancing shoes on, everyone.'

Carrie turned in her seat and looked at Black as the car slowed to a stop.

'We'll be on duty, Mr Black. No booze and no dancing.'

'I'll have enough fun for everyone.'

Logan went into the hotel foyer first to check it out before everyone else. He felt scuzzy and self-conscious. After the incident at the store on Trafalgar Square he'd only had time to quickly wash the blood off in the store toilet and dress in clothes that Carrie had bought for him. He motioned for the others to join him when he was satisfied that it was all clear. They got into the first lift to arrive. A young couple holding hands moved to join them. Logan stepped forward and held his hand up.

'Take the next one,' he told them.

The doors slid shut, cutting off their complaints.

'We have to agree a curfew,' Logan said to Black as the lift moved up.

'Why?'

'There're only two of us and we can't both be awake twenty-four hours a day and be at the top of our game.'

Black frowned.

'Probably for the best,' Marlow said, putting a hand on Black's forearm.

'You want discreet security from a small team, you have to make compromises,' Logan said.

'So what? Like, curfew at five a.m?'

'Midnight,' Logan said.

'I'm the client,' Black said. 'What if I say no?'

'Then you're on your own,' Carrie said. 'I need my beauty sleep.'

'What do you think of this guy?' Carrie asked Logan back in their room. 'I mean, I can't really get a handle on him. Is he a sleaze or charming?'

'Might be both. I haven't made my mind up yet.'

Carrie took her jacket off and unbuttoned her blouse. Logan looked at her and raised his eyebrows. She pulled the blouse off and threw it on the bed. She saw Logan watching.

'What?' she asked, her hands on her hips.

'I know that you're used to having less than total luxury on detail and changing together as a team, but there is a bathroom attached to this room, you know.'

She stepped forward until they were less than three feet apart. Logan's eyes moved down past her bra to her well-toned abdomen then back to her face where a smile flickered on her lips.

'You getting shy?' she asked, her hands moving to the waistband of her trousers.

She undid the button on her trousers and pulled the zip down, sliding the trousers over her hips and stepping out of them.

Logan went past her and opened the bathroom door.

'I'm going for a quick shower,' he said.

He looked back and saw her unhooking the clasp on her bra. He closed the door and clicked the lock into place.

'You're no fun,' Carrie called from the other side of the door.

11

'Saw you on the TV,' Alex Cahill told Logan over the phone.

Logan was sitting at the table by the window of his room. Carrie was in the bathroom getting ready.

'Yeah, that was a weird one. You picking up my dry-cleaning bill?'

'How did the rest of the day go?'

'Uneventful. But he wants to hit the town tonight.'

'You give him a curfew?'

'Of course. But I'm not sure that he'll stick to it, you know. He's not an easy guy to read.'

'I've heard that said before about serial killers.'

Logan laughed. Carrie came out of the bathroom in a pair of tight jeans with a short, fitted jacket over a white vest. She looked good.

'How's Ellie doing?' he asked Cahill, going back to looking out the window.

'She doesn't miss you even a little. All the girls went out to the cinema. I'm home alone.'

'I suppose that's the way it should be for a fourteen-year-old.'

'Carrie looking after you all right?'

Logan stiffened at the question. 'What do you mean?' he asked.

Cahill was quiet for a moment. 'You okay, buddy?' he asked after the pause.

Logan blew out a breath. 'I honestly don't know, Alex.'

'Keep focused on the job.'

'Always.'

Kate Marlow was very glamorous in a little black dress and towering heels. Black looked tanned and affluent in black trousers and a pink check shirt. Logan felt inadequate in his jeans and now wished he'd brought something else to wear.

They went through what was becoming standard procedure before they got into the car and headed for a club in the West End that Marlow had chosen. She was suddenly more relaxed and talkative, chatting away to Black behind Logan and Carrie. Logan wondered if Marlow was attracted to Black. And maybe the element of danger surrounding his past made it more of a thrill. He noticed that she didn't wear a ring on her left hand.

There was a queue outside the club on Haymarket, west of the bustling hub that was Leicester Square. Two large gentlemen in matching black suits and shirts, one with a clipboard, were the guardians of the entrance. There were some photographers leaning on cars parked by the kerb.

'Pull up right at the door,' Marlow said to their driver. 'We should be on the list.'

Logan hated this part of the job. He knew that Marlow and the publishers wanted everything about this trip to be high-profile. Wouldn't be surprised if they had tipped the photographers off about Black's intention to be at this particular club tonight. He and Carrie would be reduced to bit-part players – no more than holding the doors for their clients.

The photographers went to work when Marlow and Black stepped out of the car. Marlow gave it her best, full-wattage smile. Black moved into the club past the bouncers without reacting. Logan told the driver to wait on the street and he and Carrie followed their client into the dark interior.

12

Marlow had arranged a semi-private table on a mezzanine terrace that overlooked the bar and dance floor below. The house DJ was thumping out endless American R&B that did nothing for Logan. Black seemed to be enjoying it as he sipped at a Jack Daniel's and chased it with a bottle of beer.

'Great choice,' Black shouted at Marlow.

Every conversation would have to be conducted at that level to be heard over the sound system.

Marlow gave Black the killer smile again. He watched her for a moment, downed the last half of his beer in one swallow and got up.

'Let's go,' he said, taking Marlow by the hand and pulling her from her seat.

Logan looked at Carrie and nodded. She followed Black and Marlow downstairs to the dance floor. Logan went to the mezzanine balcony and leaned on it, watching the three of them descend the stairs. Carrie stayed by the side of the dance floor watching Black and Marlow do their thing. Which, he had to admit, wasn't too bad. Logan was not a dancer and he envied anyone who could do it well. Which Black could.

Logan scanned the crowd. Black was attracting attention from a number of women. He stood out. Logan looked at Carrie and they shared a shake of their heads. Carrie went back to watching their client. Logan's eyes stayed on her.

He wondered what she had been trying to achieve back at the hotel. She knew that he was involved with Becky and all of the good-natured banter he had assumed was just that. Now he was beginning to wonder if she might actually feel something for him. That would complicate things. He wasn't a fan of complicated. Had more than enough of that in his life already.

Logan's phone buzzed in his pocket. He pulled it out and did not recognise the number displayed on the screen. He looked around and saw the door for the toilets. He pushed through the door and went into one of the stalls. The sound was muted in there.

'Logan, it's Jake Hunter.'

Logan put a finger in his other ear.

'Jake, how are things?'

'Good. Sounds like you're in a club or something.'

'Yeah, turns out your man Chase Black likes the nightlife.'

'How's it going?'

'Good so far. Minor incident this morning but we handled it. He seems like a decent enough guy on the surface.'

'It's possible that he is a decent guy underneath as well.'

'What do you mean?'

'We've got some new evidence. A new suspect.'

'Black might really be innocent?'

'It's possible. Look, the guy has always felt wrong to me. You know what I mean?'

Logan wasn't sure he did know. He said nothing.

'Anyway, I thought you'd appreciate the heads-up. That he might not be the guy.'

'I do, Jake. Thanks.'

'I gotta go. Take care of yourself, Logan.'

Black and Marlow called it quits and were back at their table ten minutes later. A light sheen of sweat showed on both their faces.

'That was fun,' Black said.

Marlow laughed.

Logan pulled Carrie aside and told her about the call from Hunter. She shrugged: still got a job to do. Logan nodded.

'Drinks are on me,' Black shouted as another tune pumped out of the speakers. 'C'mon, Logan, you're helping me carry them.'

Logan followed Black to the bar on the lower level of the club. Not because he was agreeing to Black's request, but because someone had to stay close to him at all times.

It took them the best part of five minutes to get through the crowd at the bar and place the drinks order. Lights flashed and strobed in the dark. Logan could feel tiredness starting to slow him down. That was not good.

'So, you and Carrie,' Black said as they waited for the drinks order, his eyebrows going up.

Logan shook his head.

'Business partners only.'

'Pity. She's got something. Good things and small packages, you know?'

Logan looked up at the balcony and saw Carrie watching them. She waved at him and smiled. He rubbed at his temple, feeling a headache start. The music seemed to get louder and the lights faster and brighter.

A woman pushed past Logan to get to the bar. She bumped against Black's elbow and dropped her bag. Logan bent to pick it up and saw that a photograph had fallen from it. He picked both up and looked at the photo for a second. It was of a little girl and looked like it had been taken some time ago. The corners had punch holes in them and it was faded from exposure to the sun.

The woman put her hand on Black's arm and leaned in to speak close to his ear. He laughed at what she said and put his hand on her back, his fingertips touching the bare skin of her shoulders which were exposed. Logan thought he saw her recoil from the touch for an instant, but the smile stayed on her face.

'Excuse me,' he shouted at her, holding out the bag and the photo.

She looked at him and saw the photo. Her face froze momentarily.

'This is my bodyguard,' Black said, still laughing.

She looked from Logan to Black and back again, the smile faltering. Logan shook his head and handed her the bag and the photograph.

'He's kidding,' Logan shouted.

She took the bag and put the photo inside it.

'Let me buy you a drink,' Black told her.

She said okay, glanced over her shoulder at Logan and leaned into Black.

13

Black went with the woman to a table at the back of the lower level of the club. Logan looked up at Carrie as he followed and pointed at his eyes. She understood the message – keep watching.

Logan took the measure of the woman. She was tall at around five feet nine with her dark hair cut in a bob. She wore heels that took her up to close to six feet. Her dress looked expensive and finished above her knees. From behind, he could see that her legs were well toned and firm, as though she was used to a lot of physical activity. The dress was sleeveless, exposing her arms. They were also well toned, to the point where the muscles were well defined. Not that she was the size of a body builder – more like an Olympic sprinter.

He wondered what line of work meant that she had to stay in such good shape.

But the thing he noticed most was that her nails were cut short and not painted. That seemed out of place. He would have expected her to take the same level of care about the appearance of her hands as the rest of her. That meant she worked with her hands, that she viewed them as her tools.

It was something that Cahill had drilled into him about people – watch their hands. That's where the gun or knife comes from. Learn about people's hands.

She took Black to a table in the far corner where they sat closely and talked. She glanced at Logan as he took up a position ten feet away, leaning on a pillar at the edge of the dance floor. She said something to Black while her eyes maintained contact with Logan. Black laughed. Logan thought that he had seen her mouth form the word 'boyfriend'.

They talked for a few minutes and she reached into her bag and pulled out a pen and what looked like a business card. She wrote on the card and slipped it into the pocket of Black's shirt.

Logan felt his phone vibrate in his pocket but he ignored it. Black got up and came over to Logan.

'Give me a break, man,' he said, still shouting to be heard over the din. 'I'm not going to get anywhere with you watching.'

Logan looked at his watch.

'It's not midnight yet. I'm on call till then.'

Black looked at the woman and up at Carrie on the balcony.

'I'm the client, right?'

Logan said nothing.

'So I can call this off at any time. That's up to me.'

'Technically, the publisher is paying the bills so you're not actually the client.'

Black opened his palms out.

'One guy to another,' he said.

'You want my opinion?' Logan said. 'Walk away. I think she's bad news.'

'What? You're crazy. Have you looked at her?'

Logan kept his eyes on Black.

'Look at her nails. Then look at the rest of her. Tell me what you think then.'

'Now I *know* you're crazy. Who cares about her nails, man?'

Logan shrugged.

'Take my advice or don't. But I'm telling you that something is off here.'

The woman got up and walked to them, resting her hand on Black's shoulder and staring at Logan.

'You want him?' she asked, smiling.

This close, Logan could smell her perfume and see the startling blue of her eyes. Her voice was strong and carried over the music. It didn't seem like she had to shout. Logan felt woozy – put it down to being tired.

'Do you?' he replied.

She looked at Black. His face was blank, his mouth open.

'Yes,' she said, turning to Logan. 'Are we going to have to fight over him?'

The smile stayed on her face but Logan did not see any trace of humour in her eyes.

'That depends,' he told her.

'On what?'

'Exactly what it is that you want from him.'

The smile faded and her eyes narrowed a fraction.

'You're actually his bodyguard, aren't you?'

Logan shook his head and said no. His voice felt weak compared with hers.

'Are you afraid of me?' she asked. 'Mr Bodyguard.'

'Should I be?'

Logan wanted to sound nonchalant, but he heard the uncertainty in his own voice even as he spoke. This woman made him feel more uncomfortable than anyone he had met. He couldn't pinpoint why.

'I'm going to call it a night,' she said, turning her face to Black.

'No,' Black said.

Logan watched without saying anything.

'You're got my number,' she told Black, patting the pocket of his shirt where she had put the card.

She looked at Logan again. Her eyes sparkled. But it was only the pulsing lights. They were otherwise devoid of any emotion: black holes with a gravitational pull that was hard to resist.

'I'll be in touch,' she said.

Logan got the impression that she was talking to him.

She walked away without speaking again. Black stared after her.

Logan moved towards Black, taking hold of his elbow. He had an urge to turn quickly, as if someone was racing towards his back to do him violence. He looked over his shoulder. The woman was watching him from the door leading out of the club. Black placed his palm flat on Logan's chest.

'We're leaving,' he said, walking away from Logan. 'I'm done for the night.'

Logan turned to follow him, saw that the woman was no longer by the door. He looked around the club, his eyes straining against the intermittent dark then light. He thought he saw her walking between the tables but when he looked again it was a different woman.

14

Black did not want overnight cover. Logan was glad. He was dead tired and had not relished the possibility of alternating shifts with Carrie.

'What's the story with that woman in the club?' Carrie asked when they were in their room at the hotel. 'You've been wired to the moon since you spoke to her.'

'I don't know. Something was off about her. I can't explain it any better than that.'

'Something dangerous?'

'I honestly don't know.'

Carrie took her jacket off and stretched her hands above her head.

'You speak to Becky today?' she asked, rising up and down on the balls of her feet to stretch her calf muscles.

'No.'

She stopped moving, hooked her thumbs in the waistband

of her jeans. The jeans moved down on her hips a little. Enough to expose her skin. Logan stared.

'Everything all right in Wonderland?' she asked.

He turned away from her and said it was fine.

'Call her now if you like.'

Logan looked back at Carrie, unsure what she was trying to achieve with this conversation.

'We're fine,' he told her.

'So you said. Look, I'm going to get undressed so you can stay here and watch like last time or go to the bathroom until I'm done. What's it to be?'

Logan went to the bathroom and closed the door. He sat on the edge of the bath and turned his phone over on his hands. It was almost midnight now. He felt like he should call Becky. Wasn't sure if he *wanted* to.

He called anyway.

'Hey, Logan,' she answered.

Her voice was warm. She sounded like she was right there in the bathroom with him. He wished she was, pushing the phone hard against his ear as if that would bring them closer together.

'I miss you,' he said.

'Do you? Even after I was a little bit of a bitch last night?'

He did. Told her so. He was surprised at the emotion bunching in his throat.

'You sound weird,' she said.

'It's been a strange day, you know.'

'I guess. Saw you on the TV.'

'Yeah?'

'You looked good. All that blood notwithstanding.'

He laughed and ran a hand up over his head.

'This guy,' he started to say. 'Chase Black . . .'

'You don't need to justify yourself to me, Logan. I under-stand. I mean, I know it's what you do now and I have to get used to it.'

'If I don't have to justify myself to you, then who?'

'Your daughter.'

'I *want* to tell you.'

'Go ahead.'

'It looks like he might not be the killer. The police in Denver are looking at a new suspect.'

She let out a breath. 'That's good. Keep you out of harm's way.'

'That would be nice.'

She laughed. 'You must be tired. Been a long day. Get some sleep and be ready for tomorrow. I love you.'

He said he did too.

'Yeah, well, don't be making any moves on Carrie.'

He tried to smile at her joke and failed. He ended the call and stared at the bathroom door.

Carrie was asleep in bed when he came out of the bath-room. He changed into a T-shirt and shorts and quietly slipped under the covers. He was asleep within a minute, dreaming of a woman with an athlete's body and eyes as deep and cold as the universe.

15

That was exciting. And I thought it was going to be so easy. More fool me. That was a real, live bodyguard he had in the club. So much testosterone in the air.

Still, I got the measure of him. I can sense it, you know. Sort the good from the bad. And Chase Black vibes are bad.

Like I said before, I'm always right about these things.

The bodyguard seemed like such a boy scout. It would be a shame if he got in the way. And his partner too — the woman. He probably thinks that I didn't see her: that tough little package standing on the balcony.

So, a little more planning is going to be required. A little more skill and care. And perhaps something so bold that it will take them all by surprise. But that's okay. I don't mind having to work at it — makes the outcome all the sweeter.

One more bad man wiped from the face of the planet. The way I look at it, I'm doing the world a favour.

Part Five
Confluence

Memorandum

From: Franck Zimmer
To: Section Chief
Re: Project Eden

Interpol Ref: 735F-27

Sir,

MI5 has been unable, so far, to trace subject 'Eve's' location within London. They continue to focus their resources on facial recognition analysis from public CCTV recordings. It is, you will appreciate, a difficult and time-consuming process.

Meantime, we have received further information that may shine some light on subject 'Eve's' target. As you know, we have an asset within the European network. He is in deep cover and cannot report with any frequency. Contact was received today for the first time in some weeks.

Enquiries have been made through the network about an engagement to neutralise the American designated subject 'Night' (dossier attached). We know that subject 'Night' is in London. He is a high-profile target. News reports from the UK have been e-mailed to you. Subject 'Night' was the intended victim of a protest attack today. Nothing significant occurred. He has private security – CPO. They are known to us and are an excellent outfit.

GJ Moffat

I have taken the liberty of alerting MI5 to the threat to subject 'Night'. He was, for obvious reasons, monitored on entering the UK. His status is such that he is on the low-level watch list.

We are proceeding on the working assumption that the target of subject 'Eve's' recent activity is subject 'Night'. MI5 will undertake surveillance of subject 'Night' from tomorrow with a view to apprehending subject 'Eve' if she makes her move.

Reports to follow.

1

Friday: Denver

Jake Hunter sat in his car with the engine idling and called Danny Collins.

'I'm outside,' he told Collins when the phone was answered. 'Waiting.'

'Hold on, chief. I'll be there.'

Hunter reached forward and pressed a button on the portable GPS device fixed to his dashboard. He looked at the address for the Dillon police department building on a page printed from the department website and patiently typed it into the GPS device. He knew where Dillon was, roughly. but it would be easier with the GPS. Collins's sense of direction and map-reading skills were not his strong suit.

Collins walked out of his apartment building towards the car, raising a hand in greeting. Hunter nodded in return.

Collins was such a free spirit that Hunter frequently wondered how it was that they had clicked so well almost immediately upon being partnered in Bowman's squad. Hunter thought of himself as many things, but a free spirit was not one of them.

But he'd been the one to move the evidence around in DeSanto's rented house and open the blinds. He'd been the one to lie to his friend, ADA Angel, about the probable cause for the warrant.

Maybe they weren't so different deep down.

Collins opened the rear door of the sedan and threw an overnight bag on to the seat. He slammed the door shut then opened the front passenger door to sit next to Hunter, rubbing his hands together, though it was far from cold even at seven in the morning.

'Road trip,' Collins said. 'You bring the beer?'

Hunter smiled. 'You could've put your bag in the trunk, you know.'

Collins looked over his shoulder and back at Hunter.

'My go bag? In the trunk? No way.'

'*Go bag?*' Hunter asked, slowly. 'You hear that on *CSI* or something?'

'Dunno.' Collins grinned. 'But I like it. Sounds important.'

Hunter leaned forward and touched the screen of the GPS device where the word 'GO' was displayed. The screen flicked to a street map view of their location and a woman's voice told him to drive straight ahead for point five miles then turn right. So that's what he did.

Once out of the city, they headed west on I-70. Most of the popular ski resorts in Colorado were in the west along

I-70 and through the Eisenhower Tunnel that cut a ragged hole through the Rocky Mountains.

As the car passed from the bright sunshine into the artificial light of the tunnel, Collins rested his head back on the seat, folded his arms and closed his eyes.

'Wake me up when we get there, Dad,' he said.

Hunter punched Collins lightly on his arm.

'What?' Collins asked, squinting at him with one eye still closed.

'We forgot about something.'

Collins sat up and opened both eyes. 'What now?'

'Nothing bad. I mean, just an idea that we had. That I had. Actually, a couple of ideas.'

Collins looked none the wiser.

'You remember what the profile said about the killer? That he had probably killed before?'

'Sure, yeah.'

'We were going to look harder at Black's past. I mean, spread the net beyond Denver and see if we could find anything that might be worth looking at.'

'Okay. But now we're past that. Aren't we?'

Hunter looked at Collins quickly and back at the road ahead.

'Why should we be? I was thinking about it last night and maybe we should still be looking at that as an alternative to DeSanto.'

'Or whatever the hell his name really is.'

'That's the other thing. Checking schools that run forensic courses against the date of birth we have for DeSanto.'

'I kinda lost track of that one.'

'Someone else in the squad can take it on.'

Collins nodded.

'So, what do you think?' Hunter asked. 'Should we check into Black's past?'

Collins dropped his hands to his lap and drummed his fingers on his thighs. 'What do we know about Black already?' he asked. 'I mean, from the previous investigation.'

Hunter's brow creased into a frown. 'Not much, I don't think.'

He tried to recall what detail they had.

'After his arrest, I don't think it mattered beyond checking his date of birth for our records. We had his blood, you know. We didn't need to know much more.'

'If that is his date of birth.'

'Don't even go there, Danny. I'm serious.'

'He's from a broken home, though, right? He told us that.'

'Yes. His father died when he was young.'

'Maybe we can track his mother. He must have lived with her. Find out where she went, that's where he'll be. Check any unsolved murders.'

Hunter glanced at him again. 'Sometimes, Danny, I think you might make it as a detective.'

'Fuck you very much.'

Hunter laughed. 'We'll call the squad when we get to Dillon. See if they can make a start on it.'

2

Hunter edged the car left and took the Dillon exit off I-70, seeing the blue water of the lake sparkle in the morning sun beyond the low-rise buildings that made up the town. Jetties jutted out from the marina into the lake and modest homes whipped by at the side of the road.

Dillon is a town irrevocably linked to Denver and the old West. While prospectors initially flocked to Denver, it wasn't the gold strike that enabled the town to prosper and grow but silver. And then, in the latter half of the twentieth century, its reputation was as a cow town whose fortunes were changed for the better on oil and energy income. Now it was a modern metropolis. Not large, by American standards, but welcoming and on the edge of so much natural beauty, and with a relatively mild climate, that it was an attractive place to settle. To raise a family.

Dillon's origins were no more auspicious: probably

243

nothing more than a mountain trading post and a few log cabins at the confluence of three rivers. But then, as Denver expanded and prospered and the need for water reserves grew, an artificial reservoir was created. So the meagre foundations of the town had to be relocated to its current location on the northeast of Lake Dillon.

Hunter nudged Collins awake as two yachts raised sail on the lake and drifted out from the marina. Mountains loomed in the near distance. It was close to nine in the morning.

People die in stinking, garbage-strewn alleys or in crack houses in a pool of their own filth, Hunter thought. And they die in places like this, with their insides torn out by some psycho.

What a world.

The town itself looked like any other Smalltown, USA. Some of the storefronts were a little tired and in need of a lick of paint, but otherwise it looked like a nice place to live.

Hunter followed the GPS directions on to Lake Dillon Drive until the voice said 'arrive at destination on right' at the intersection with Buffalo Street. He saw the three-storey, brown-brick police department building and pulled into a small parking lot in front. They rolled to a stop next to a white SUV with blue/green police livery.

They got out of the car and stretched. Hunter took his suit jacket from the car and draped it over his arm. Collins did the same. The entrance door to the building was at the bottom left corner as they faced it and they walked out of the sun into a reasonably modern, air-conditioned office building.

A civilian receptionist sat behind a long counter and

smiled at them as they came in. Hunter saw something on the notice board to the left of the counter announcing that the town had the lowest crime rate in the state. He remembered Chief Patton saying something about that when they first spoke.

'Morning, gentlemen,' the woman said as they reached the counter. 'What can I do for you?'

She was in her early forties, plump and with a bouffant hairdo that would not have looked out of place in the eighties.

'Detectives Hunter and Collins from Denver PD here to see Chief Patton and Sergeant Fields.'

She wrote their names on a notepad in front of her and asked to see their identification. When she was satisfied with that, she picked up the phone and called someone to announce their arrival.

'Sergeant Fields will be down shortly, detectives.'

Sutton Fields was not at all how Hunter had pictured her from their interaction on the telephone. He had a vision of a short, hard-faced NYPD veteran. Instead, the woman who came through the door to the side of the reception counter was tall at five-eight and slender in a neatly pressed uniform – trousers, shirt and tie – all in navy blue. Her fair hair was tied back in a ponytail and she swept loose strands off her cheek and behind her ear as she walked forward and held out her hand to greet them. The only physical sign of the toll that a hard tour in a major city could take were crow's feet at the corners of her eyes and the faint, permanent frown lines creasing her forehead. He made her for late thirties.

'Good to see you guys,' she said as she shook their hands and smiled. 'You've no idea how good.'

'We've got the common goal of wanting to get this guy behind bars,' Hunter said. 'Before he kills anyone else.'

'My guy or your guy?'

'I figure there's a good chance they're the same.'

Fields rested her right hand on the gun fitted tightly in the leather holster on her belt. Hunter noticed that there was a sheen on the holster, like it had recently been polished.

Look after your tools and they will look after you.

'You had breakfast?' she asked. 'Cause, I mean, we've got coffee and pastries upstairs with the chief.'

'There's always room for more,' Collins said. 'Lead on.'

Franklin Patton, the Chief of Police in Dillon looked every inch the career small-town cop. He was lean like a middle-distance runner with receding hair cut short and neat. Frameless glasses covered his eyes and the two gold stars on each tip of his shirt collar marked him out as the top man. His uniform was the same as Fields and it seemed like he ran a tight ship: Hunter had seen two other cops out in the corridor on the way to the Chief's office and they were similarly neat.

Patton stood and shook their hands firmly as Fields made the introductions.

Patton sat behind a solid teak desk that looked like an antique. A laptop computer was on the desk to his left and a neat stack of papers was on the right in a wire basket. Otherwise the desk was clear except for a pot of coffee, four cups and a plate of pastries. All as advertised. Framed commendations hung on the wall behind him.

Hunter and Collins sat in two chairs on the opposite side

of the desk while Fields poured the coffee then leaned against the window sill with her arms folded across her chest. Hunter figured she preferred to stand. Maybe a legacy from New York – always ready to move.

'Bad business,' Patton said, shaking his head.

Hunter nodded, sipping at his coffee. 'Yes, sir. And we're here to help in any way that we can.'

'Where do you want to start?'

'I can show you the crime scene. The house,' Fields said.

'You still have it secured?' Collins asked.

'Not really. I mean not officially. But the husband hasn't been back since we let him go. He's staying at a motel. Far as I know the place is as we left it.'

'Okay, sounds good.'

'What about the forensics?' Hunter asked.

'Not heard from the FBI with any results yet.'

'Okay, I can chase that. I know some people there and our Crime Lab team already touched base with them when you sent over your case reference. I don't think we'd heard from them before we left.'

Patton leaned forward and placed his hands palms down on the desk. 'Sounds like you might want to be here longer than today,' he said.

'We brought some things. Booked into the local Best Western for two nights.'

Patton looked at Fields who grinned.

'You wanna finish your coffee or get going?' she asked. 'Cause I'm ready now.'

Collins looked at Hunter, the corners of his mouth turning down.

'We'll finish our coffee,' Hunter said.

Collins grabbed a pastry and took a large bite out of it, flakes of pastry sticking to his face and falling to the floor. The other three stared at him.

'Gotta keep our strength up,' he said through a mouthful of food.

3

Hunter told them briefly where they were with the investigation in Denver while Collins ate: about DeSanto, the bad evidence and what they found at his house. Patton and Fields listened in silence. When they were done, Fields led them to the police SUV that they had parked next to in the lot in front of the department building. Hunter got in the front seat beside her with Collins in back. The big engine growled to life and Fields swung the vehicle out into the street.

'We never talked about Chase Black,' Fields said as she straightened the wheel and pressed down on the gas pedal. 'You're the one who arrested him last time?'

'That's right,' Hunter answered.

Hunter looked at her but she kept her eyes on the road ahead.

'I read up on it after we spoke,' she added.

'Yeah, I led the investigation. And we had Black dead bang on a blood sample found at a scene. No question.'

'Until this thing with DeSanto?'

Hunter said yes.

'So you think this guy, this DeSanto, is the one? And that he messed up your case from the inside?'

'That's the theory we're working on for now.'

'Except DeSanto isn't his real name,' Collins added.

'You find out who he really is yet?'

'We're working on that.'

They were quiet for a few minutes until Fields slowed the car and turned into a long street not far back from the lakeside. On the right of the street, the ground fell away gently to the still water and on the left houses were widely spaced on a steeper incline. Fields pointed to the sixth house and pulled up on to the driveway that ended at a door on the side wall. Police crime scene tape flapped loosely from the door in a light breeze.

They got out of the car and walked together to the door. Hunter looked closely at the frame and saw no signs of a forced entry.

Fields pushed a strand of the tape aside, reached into her trouser pocket for the door key and pressed it into the lock. The door creaked open on rusted hinges.

'How did he gain access?' Hunter asked.

'We don't know. There's no sign that any of the entry points, doors or windows, were forced.'

'Different from our scenes,' Collins said.

Fields looked at Hunter as he stepped past her into the hallway.

'What do you make of that?' she asked. 'I mean, that he got in without using force.'

'Could be any number of things,' Collins answered as Hunter walked along the hall and they followed behind him.

The hall opened up into a large living space with a kitchen and eating area at the back and a living room at the front with big windows looking out over the lake. Sun streamed in through the open curtains and the place felt stuffy and hot. The smell of death lingered faintly: blood, piss and evacuated bowels.

Collins rubbed at his nose.

'This how it was found?' Hunter asked, looking around. 'Neat, I mean.'

'Yes.'

He nodded and walked to the kitchen, looking out into the backyard.

'Ground's hard this time of year, dried out by the sun,' he said. 'No chance of getting casts of footprints outside.'

He didn't say it like it was a question but Fields said 'no' all the same.

'Want to go upstairs?' she asked.

Hunter nodded and followed her back to the hall and up the stairway that was illuminated by light from a window in the roof on the half-landing. The familiar smell grew stronger as they climbed. Hunter knew that a human being's sense of smell was closely linked to taste; that what you smelled was actually particles of matter being inhaled. Right now, he was mainlining the dead woman's blood.

The stairs ended in another hallway, with four doors off it.

'Bathroom there,' Fields said, pointing at the first door on the left. 'We got some trace evidence from the sink. Her blood mainly. But some hairs too. Not hers and not the husband's.'

'He washed his hands before he left,' Hunter said.

Fields walked to the last door at the end of the hall and pushed it open. Hunter walked forward, the smell now all pervasive. He flashed back to the Dale house: saw the kids' bodies ruined and devoid of life. Saw his wife's expanding belly and felt the heartbeat of his own child pumping inside her womb as he rested his hand on his wife's taut skin.

'Jake . . .'

Hunter turned at the sound of his partner's voice.

Fields stood inside the room watching them and holding the door open.

The bed frame was bare except for the mattress. The blood had soaked through it and had dried and crusted on it. He didn't see any evidence of the bindings used on the woman.

'You take the bed linen and the bindings?' he asked.

'Yes. FBI Lab has them now.'

Collins walked to the window that looked down on to the lake. He unlatched it and pushed it open, breathing deeply as fresh air flowed in.

Hunter and Fields watched him for a moment and then went back to looking at the bed.

'We can compare the hair samples you recovered with some new evidence we have,' Hunter said. 'We think they belong to the killer.'

'Help us identify him,' she said.

'Only if we catch him.'

Fields nodded.

'Any blood unaccounted for?' Hunter asked. 'I mean, not from the husband or wife.'

'No, nothing like that. No stray blood, saliva or seminal fluid.'

Hunter hunkered down beside the bed and put a hand on the wooden floorboards to steady himself. He looked under the bed and saw two pairs of slippers: his 'n' hers. He thought that it was perhaps the saddest thing he had ever seen. He put his other hand on the woman's slippers and knew that they would never again feel the warmth of her skin.

Perpetual cold was all she had to look forward to now.

Collins turned from the window.

'Place looks totally undisturbed,' he said. 'Like she led him up the stairs, lay down on the bed and let him kill her.'

'Is that different this time?' Fields asked.

Hunter shrugged.

'He never killed just one person before. Not in Denver anyway.'

'What if he confronts them at the door with a gun? You know, controls them that way until he gets to the kill zone in the bedroom.'

'Could be that. Could be something else.'

Hunter stood and looked at Fields.

'I think we've seen enough,' he said.

4

'You want to speak to the husband?' Fields asked when they were back in the car. 'I can arrange it.'

'You went hard at it with him?' Hunter said.

'I did.'

Hunter shrugged.

'We can watch the recording of your interview but I don't think we need to see him in person.'

'We haven't known one another long enough for you to trust whether I did it right. Maybe the husband did it and made it look like yours.'

'You don't believe that.'

'No.'

'It's your case, your call.'

'You trying to make friends, Jake?'

Hunter smiled.

'Cause, I mean, you don't know me at all. I coulda

gotten hounded out of the NYPD for being no good. Or worse.'

'You didn't.'

She looked sideways at him.

'You check up on me?'

'Maybe.'

She was quiet for a moment.

'So what do you want to do now?' she asked.

'I'd like to go back to your office, check on how our lab guys are doing with the FBI. Listen to the husband's interview. Let it all sink in.'

'I can arrange that.'

Collins leaned forward from the back and rested his elbows on the top of the front seats.

'You know,' he said, 'if this is the same guy, he came here sometime in the last five, six months. We know that's when DeSanto left Denver. Is there any way of checking local businesses and realtors for new employees or leases?'

'Other than talking to them all?' Fields asked.

'Yeah.'

'The IRS might have tax records,' Hunter said. 'For employees.'

'Not if he's getting paid cash off the books,' Fields said.

'But it's a good idea. How many businesses, vacant properties and hotels are there in town?'

Fields puffed out her cheeks.

'I don't know. Couple hundred at least, I would have thought.'

'Not too bad if we have some more of your officers canvassing. We could do a first sweep by phone.'

'I can speak to the Chief. I'm sure he'd be okay with it.'

'What if we need overtime?'

'Budgets are tight.'

'Same all over. Welcome to the new world order.'

'Any new police?' Collins asked.

'No,' Fields told him. 'That would have been too easy, huh?'

'Everybody opens the door to the cops.'

'Everybody decent.'

5

While they had been out at the house, Patton had arranged for the department muster room – no bigger than a large office – to be set up as a makeshift incident room. There were three desks, one with a computer, a whiteboard and a separate table with all of the paperwork on the Dawson case spread out.

'This where you have your roll call?' Hunter asked as they walked in.

'You could call it that,' Fields said. 'Usually no more than six of us here for it at any one time, what with the different shift patterns.'

'It's good of you to accommodate us.'

Fields went to the desk with the computer and switched it on, drumming her feet on the floor while it booted up. Hunter and Collins went to the table with the paperwork, Hunter picking up the pile of photographs from the house and leafing through them.

When he got to the first shot of Kim Dawson's body he stopped. It looked very much like the scenes he had encountered in Denver. He nudged Collins and tapped on the photo with his finger.

'Look familiar?'

Collins looked at it and nodded.

'Yeah. A lot.'

Hunter continued to look through the rest of the photos. He found a close-up of the victim's feet, bound to the bed. He brought the photo closer to his face to see more clearly.

'Your ViCAP entry indicated that he tied her with fishing gut,' he said, turning to face Fields.

She looked over at him as he turned the photograph towards her.

'Yes.'

Hunter looked at the image again. He had never fished in his life so didn't know how many different types there were. It looked different from the type that had been used on the Denver victims.

'Did you find anything like it in the house?'

'Yes, as a matter of fact, we did. The husband fishes. Whoever killed her used stuff from a tackle box in the house.'

'So the killer took the time to access his gear.'

'Uh-huh.'

'Risky move,' Collins said. 'He always brought his own to our scenes.'

'Why change now?' Fields asked.

'I don't know,' Hunter said. 'We should think about what it means.'

'If it means anything.'

'Right.'

Fields leaned forward as a short piece of music played from the computer.

'Now we're in business,' she said, grasping the mouse and tapping on the keyboard with her other hand.

'You got the interview recording on there?' Hunter asked.

Her eyes flicked across the screen as she moved the mouse around and clicked on the buttons under her fingers. She frowned after a moment.

'No, it's not on here. Someone forgot to transfer it over and I can't access it on the main system from this machine.'

In addition to being the only officer with any experience in a city detective bureau, Sutton Fields was also the department tech guru. Which didn't mean much except that she was more comfortable with computers, monitors, leads and plugs than anyone else.

She stood and asked Collins to help her carry a projector in from another room.

'Make it easier for us all to watch it together than trying to huddle round the computer. I'll get the film on a memory stick and we'll be good to go.'

'Is there a phone I can use to call our crime lab?' Hunter asked.

She pointed at one of the other desks where a small phone sat charging on its base station. Hunter sat at the desk as Fields and Collins left the room and picked up the phone to call Steve Ames.

'Steve's not here, Jake,' Molly August said when she answered the call. 'He's out on scene. This about the Dillon case?'

'Yeah, me and Danny are here now. Has anyone there been in touch with the FBI lab?'

'I don't think so, why?'

'We were out at the crime scene here this morning and there are at least two things we should check specifically.'

'Hang on, let me grab a pen.'

He waited for her to say she was ready.

'Okay, most important thing is that they recovered hair fibres that do not match either the victim or her husband. You should check if they match what we have.'

'What's the second thing?'

'The bindings.'

'Same stuff?'

'No, that's the weird thing. He used fishing gut, but it was the husband's. Seems like he used what he could find in the house.'

'Doesn't that seem strange? I mean, taking the risk that there would be something there. Why change when, for all the previous murders, he brought his own stuff?'

'I don't know. I'm going to speak to the profiler about it. See if he has any ideas.'

'You think it might be significant?'

'It feels like it is.'

'Anything else?'

'Can you call me after you've spoken to the Feds? I want to keep up the momentum.'

She said she would and ended the call.

Collins and Fields came back into the room carrying a projector and a stand for it. They went to work setting it up in front of the whiteboard to use that as a screen.

Hunter checked his cell phone to find the number for Nick Levine, the FBI profiler, and called him using the landline. His phone was only showing one signal bar and he wasn't sure how good the sound quality would be.

When he was connected to Levine, Hunter explained about the bindings they had found in Dillon and asked what Levine thought about it.

'That's unusual. I mean, for a killer who was previously so methodical and organised to make such a simple mistake.'

'What does it mean?'

'I'll have to think about it, Jake. Review our database and see if I can find anything similar from other cases.'

'What does your instinct tell you? I'm not going to hold you to it, Nick.'

Levine was quiet – thinking about this new information. Hunter watched Collins struggle to get the projector stand upright while Fields stood holding the projector.

'A serial killer learns on the job,' Levine said. 'By that I mean that he gets better at the organisational aspects of the killing.'

'Like any job,' Hunter interjected. 'The longer you do it, the better you get.'

'Exactly. And you have to remember that it is kind of how the killer sees it. He takes pride in what he does. He wants to get it right. To be admired for his art.'

'We're not dealing with a rational mind.'

'Not in many ways, that's correct. But if you have a killer who has evolved his technique to the point where the pattern is set – which is what you had in Denver – it is very rare to see the killer fall back. To get worse at it, so to speak.'

'I understand all that. So where does it take us so far as *our* killer is concerned?'

'I'll be honest, Jake, my first thought is that it might not be the same guy.'

Hunter did not respond.

'I know that's not what you want to hear. But we have to consider it as a possibility.'

'There's no other explanation?'

'This is my instinctive response, Jake. Look, I don't want you to take what I just said as a working assumption for your investigation. Like I said, I need to do some more research on it.'

'Fair enough.'

'Anything else?'

Collins finally managed to get the stand upright. Fields put the projector on it and took a lead from the rear of the machine to the computer on the other desk where she plugged it in.

'Yeah. Have you compared the ViCAP entries in detail? You know, for Denver and for Dillon.'

'No. But I'll do that also.'

'It's urgent, Nick. This guy is still out there.'

'I know.'

6

'We're set up,' Fields said as Hunter hung up on the call with Levine. 'Want to watch it now?'

Hunter looked at his watch, saw that it was not yet noon. It seemed later.

'Let's do it.'

Hunter pulled his chair from the desk and put it beside the projector stand, eight feet back from the front of the whiteboard. Collins did the same while Fields set up the film on the computer. When she was done, she closed the blinds and turned off the light.

On the board, the images played out.

Fields walked into an interview room with the husband and another officer. Hunter studied the husband's face. He looked tired and his long hair hung unwashed around his face. He was like one of those California surfer dudes, tanned and healthy and always flicking their long hair back when wet. Like in a Calvin Klein ad. Or, at least, that's what he would have looked like before someone gutted his wife.

Hunter had seen plenty of grieving family members who turned out to be killers. He had a legendary sixth sense in the department for calling out the liars before anyone else.

Except Chase Black, it seemed.

The husband's grief looked real. Hunter said so to Collins and Fields.

'Was what I thought too,' Fields said.

Onscreen, the man slumped into a chair beside a small desk. He made no move to push the hair away from his face. Instead, he looked down at his lap where his hands lay unmoving.

Hunter watched closely for the next hour as Fields went through her interview with him. She started off sympathetic, getting him to trust her and to start opening up. It worked. He became more animated after ten minutes or so.

Fields moved on from getting to know you and sympathy to more detailed questions about the husband's movements on the day of the murder. After that she moved on to his relationship with his wife.

Hunter knew what she was doing: slowly building up to the point where he would realise she was probing at the veracity of his story.

It took him until about forty-five minutes into the interview before he cottoned on. Fields was good by any standards. She was patient and didn't rush it. Didn't jump in and start shouting in his face, accusing him straight away.

The husband essayed a genuine 'My God, you can't

believe that I . . .' line. He didn't quite use those words, but Hunter had heard all the variations. He didn't get angry about it; just looked hurt. Started to tear up.

Then he got a little bit angry. He swore, which he had not done up to that point. It all came across as genuine.

The film finished with some placatory words from Fields and a reassurance that they were doing all they could to find out who killed his wife.

Fields turned in her seat to face Hunter when it was done. 'What do you think?'

'I agree with your assessment.'

Collins nodded.

'Not a false note in the whole thing that I could detect,' he said.

Fields got up and opened the blinds as Chief Patton came into the room. He nodded at Hunter and Collins and sat awkwardly on the edge of one of the desks. He wasn't a man that did 'casual' very naturally.

'You watch the interview with the husband?' he asked.

'Yes,' Hunter answered. 'I don't think he did it.'

Patton took his glasses off, breathed on one lens and wiped it with his tie.

'What about the house?'

Hunter shrugged.

'Not much to see,' Collins said.

'We've chased up the FBI and our own Crime Lab. They'll put a rush on further forensic examination and comparison of the evidence.'

'Danny had another idea,' Fields said as she turned back from the window.

'What was that?'

'Well, if the Denver killer is here now he only arrived in the last few months. So he's new to town.'

'If he's *in* town.'

'Right, but we have to start somewhere.'

Patton nodded once.

'We should start a canvas. Get around all the local businesses, hotels and other lodgings. Check to see who's new in town. Run background checks and interview all of them.'

'What if we end up talking to the guy? It'll alert him to the investigation. Scare him off.'

Collins shook his head. 'We have a photo of him from our records back in Denver. We can get a copy issued to all of your people.'

Patton regarded both of them silently for a moment before he spoke again. 'How many of my people do you need for this?'

'I was thinking me plus another three or four,' Fields said. 'I'll pick them.'

Patton pinched his lower lip. Hunter hoped that he respected his own sergeant enough to go with her recommendation. Even if he thought the two city boys were incompetent for letting a killer operate in their own lab, right in front of them.

'Let me go speak to the people I have in mind,' Fields said. 'See if they are up for the detail.'

Patton stood and said all right.

Fields walked past Hunter to follow Patton out of the room. She put her hand on Hunter's shoulder as she passed.

'I'll get it done, Jake,' she said.

7

Fields came back after a half-hour and asked Hunter and Collins if they wanted to grab some lunch before starting on anything else. They said yes and followed her out of the building and along Lake Dillon Drive to a small diner. It was busy with locals and all of the tables were taken. They found three stools together at the far end of the counter that ran along the left-hand wall. The servers wore black T-shirts with the diner's logo. The table and countertops were in a bright red Formica. It looked clean and the food smelled good, hamburgers and onions sizzling on a hot plate behind the counter.

'What's good here?' Collins asked.

'Everything,' Fields said. 'They run an all-day menu so you can have breakfast if you like. I recommend the pancakes.'

Hunter ordered a short stack of blueberry pancakes. Collins and Fields went with burgers.

'What's the Chief like to work for?' Hunter asked.

'What you see is what you get. He likes things neat and tight. Do as he says and you get along fine.'

'A boss is a boss?'

'Right.'

A male server brought them their drinks, setting the cold glasses down on napkins.

'Why did you leave New York?' Hunter asked. 'I did check and your record was flawless. In fact, you were one of their best, from what I could see.'

She took a sip of her drink and put it down, moving the ice cubes around with a straw.

'The work was good,' she said. 'No, it was great. I loved it.'

'But . . .'

'No buts. Not about the work anyway.'

She prodded at an ice cube with her straw. Hunter realised that they could be straying into territory that cops usually left alone – personal relationships. Leave two cops in a car alone on a surveillance gig for a number of hours and they will talk about work for most of the time: the murder with no real suspects that is holding the clearance rate up; the boss that makes their lives hell or the new guy that sucks. The rest of the time it's sports and food.

Never relationships.

Hunter decided to leave it alone. Turned out Fields was happy to talk about it anyway.

'I ran away from a bad relationship.'

Hunter turned in his seat and looked at her.

'Someone in the department,' she said. 'I tried to end it

and he didn't take it well. It started to affect his work. And it was bleeding into mine. So I left.'

'You had a career there.'

'And I've got one here. I'll be next in line after Patton and that suits me. I like it here.'

'Better than the city bureau?'

'Different.'

'What about you guys?' she asked.

The same male server came over with their food. A square of butter was melting on top of Hunter's pancakes and he poured a healthy measure of maple syrup on top. Collins tore into his burger without waiting. Everyone on the squad knew better than to try to get between Danny Collins and his food.

'We came up through uniform patrol,' Hunter said in answer to Fields's question. 'But not together.'

'You like it? I mean, homicide in the city.'

'Ask me after these cases are done,' Hunter said through his first mouthful of pancake.

'Must have been tough putting Black away and then seeing him walk.'

'It was. But if it turns out he's not our guy then it was the right thing.'

'You're not convinced, are you? Even with what you've got on this DeSanto guy.'

Collins was halfway through his burger already. He paused and looked at his partner.

'I'm not, no. And I can't say why.'

'You handle all the interviews with Black?'

'Yes.'

'He came across as a bad guy?'

'He was wrong,' Collins said, wiping at his mouth with a napkin. 'I sat in after we arrested him and that's how he vibed.'

'He wasn't angry or upset or anything really,' Hunter added. 'An almost complete lack of emotion.'

'I know what you mean,' Fields said. 'I've seen people like that before.'

'I don't think you've met anyone like Chase Black. I mean, he's so smooth and likeable on the surface. A successful businessman by all accounts.'

'A millionaire now with the book,' Collins added.

'But there's something that sits beneath the surface,' Hunter went on. 'It's like he's got a parasite that swarms under his skin.'

'And sometimes that parasite gets out?' Fields asked.

Hunter ran a hand through his hair.

'It sounds crazy when you say it out loud.'

'Nothing that we encounter in this job is sane, Jake. We all know that.'

'True,' Collins said, wolfing down another mouthful of burger.

8

After lunch, Hunter called Detective Sally Kaminski and asked her to e-mail DeSanto's photograph to Fields. When it landed in her inbox, Fields spoke to a civilian administrative assistant about printing off copies.

'How many?' she was asked.

'Start with a hundred.'

Hunter also asked Kaminski to look at Black's history, to see if they could trace where he had been before he came to Denver. And to check the date of birth they had for DeSanto.

'Bowman's pissed at you,' Kaminski told him.

'Tell me something I don't know, Sally. I can't worry about that right now. And anyway, Morris knows I'm here.'

'Still, watch your back with Bowman.'

'He's not going anywhere past sergeant. That makes him not much better than one of us.'

'He's still a boss.'

They agreed to disagree and ended the call with Kaminski saying that she and Choons would make a start on Black and DeSanto as soon as they had finished with the latest city dweller who had been involved in a fatal interface with a bullet.

Fields had identified and got approval for three officers to support their canvass of the town. She gathered them in the incident room – two men and a woman, only one of them older than thirty. They were Patton's cops – the men clean shaven with short haircuts and all three in neatly pressed navy-blue uniforms. Fields had also set up more phones for them to use.

At least they should have the energy to keep going, Hunter thought. Job like this, energy was probably preferable to experience. He wondered if Fields had chosen them deliberately with that in mind.

Hunter and Collins stood in front of the officers. Hunter held up a print of DeSanto's photograph.

'I'm Detective Hunter and this is my partner, Detective Collins. We are with the Denver PD Homicide squad and this man is the primary suspect in the murder of five families. We are here because details in the murder of Kim Dawson lead us to believe that this same man may well be responsible for her death.'

Hunter paused to let the information sink in. 'He may have arrived in Dillon some time in the last five or six months. We know that he used a false identity in Denver. He's likely using another name here so focus on new arrivals and the photograph. He may have sought to change his appearance. Dyed his hair or grown a beard. Be vigilant.'

The three cops nodded, their jaws set firm.

'He is extremely dangerous,' Collins added. 'And skilled at deception. He will have no hesitation in resorting to violence, so don't take any risks, okay? Call for back-up if you have any doubts.'

'We'll do this in pairs,' Hunter said. 'Each of you will pair with me, Detective Collins or Sergeant Fields. We'll let your sergeant determine who works with who. She knows you best.'

Hunter nodded at Fields. It was important in her jurisdiction to give her authority, not walk all over her. She would have to work with these cops when he and Collins were back in Denver.

Hunter looked at his watch. 'Okay,' he said, 'it's ten after two now. We'll hit the phones and the streets until six at the latest and reconvene here for a debriefing. How does that sound?'

They nodded.

'Sergeant Fields has a list of hotels and lodgings,' Collins said. 'We'll divide those up evenly and hit the phones in the first instance. After that, we'll take the businesses in the town and split them geographically.'

Fields took that as her cue and swiftly told the officers whom they would be partnered with. The shorter of the two men walked towards Hunter and extended his hand.

'Officer Ray,' he said as Hunter shook his hand. 'Earl Ray.'

His grip was firm but his eyes betrayed a nervous

disposition, flicking from Hunter's face and away. He was around five-ten and solidly built. His shirt strained only a little at the waist where a few too many beers or burgers or whatever had taken their toll. His face was tanned and his hands rough, as though he enjoyed being outdoors. Hunter thought that maybe he was a sailor.

Collins was paired with the woman – Hope Rodriguez – a light-skinned Latino with dark hair pulled back off her face. She was short at five-four but looked trim and in good shape. That left Fields with the older, taller man – Isaac Foster – as her partner. He was rake thin and looked as though he would break in a strong wind. Hunter thought he might be the difficult one: masking his nerves and slight build with too much testosterone.

They set up at a desk each and started making calls, working through the lists. Hunter left Officer Ray and went downstairs and out into the parking lot to call his wife, Ashley.

'How is it going?' she asked.

'Difficult to say, you know. It's still early. But there are enough things to work on. It feels like we're moving forward.'

'That's got to be good, right?'

'It is.'

'You sound, I don't know, more upbeat. More optimistic.'

'You mean since I stopped obsessing over Chase Black.'

'I suppose. But it's good. Nice to have the old Jake back.'

He grunted.

'You going to be there for the full two nights?'

'Probably. Maybe longer, the way things are looking. I

don't know, but it feels like we'll achieve more here than we will back there.'

'I want you to catch him. And I want you back.'

'The guys still working on the house?'

'What? You think they see the man of the house gone and are gonna take advantage of little old me, is that it?'

'No, I . . .'

She laughed. 'I'm kidding. They're working as hard as ever. It's a good crew.'

'Listen, I need to get back. I'll call later.'

Officer Ray had crossed off six of the names on the list when Hunter got back to the room. He was speaking into the phone animatedly and nodded at Hunter when he saw him.

Ash had been right – he did feel more upbeat. And it felt like something might break here more than in Denver. Maybe he was just glad to be away from the city for a while. He felt like a failure there.

Here, he felt like a cop.

9

Sally Kaminski called Hunter an hour later as they were getting ready to go out and hit the streets. The calls to hotels and lodgings had not thrown up any possible leads and they had gone through all of them – or at least all of them where someone answered the telephone.

'Want an update?' she asked.

'Sure.'

'We're working the date of birth for DeSanto. Like you said, checking the schools that have forensic-type qualifications. We looked at local birth records as well.'

'I thought you had a dead banger to deal with.'

'They're a dime a dozen. I was pulling your chain. This is more important.'

Hunter couldn't remember the last time he'd heard a real person use the phrase 'a dime a dozen'. As opposed to a character on TV. The old ones were the best.

'Nothing on the local records that checks out. If that's his real date of birth, he wasn't born in Denver.'

'Figures. That would have been too easy.'

'We just started on the schools. It's gonna take a while.'

'What's the problem?'

'Believe it or not, but more than half of the schools we spoke to already won't release anything without a warrant. The lawyers stepped in straight away. Seems they're more scared of being sued than letting this guy run free.'

Hunter pinched the bridge of his nose.

'We'll need Federal help on the warrants if they're across State lines,' he said.

'They are.'

'Speak to Morris. Someone should call the FBI.'

'Your profiler?'

'No, he's a good guy but he's too junior. We need someone with authority. Call Dean Graves at Quantico. He knows about this already and he'll kick whoever needs kicking to move it on.'

'I'll do that. How are things there?'

'Ask me tomorrow.'

'Does that mean you got progress?'

'Like I said . . .'

'Tomorrow.'

'What's the plan, boss?' Collins asked when they were assembled in the incident room.

'We've still got some residences. A few apartment buildings and some houses. That's in addition to the businesses.'

'We'll take the residences.'

Hunter looked at Fields who shrugged – *up to you*. 'Fine. You and officer . . .'

Hunter couldn't recall her name. Actually couldn't recall the names of the two he was not paired with.

'Rodriguez,' the woman said. 'Hope Rodriguez.'

'You and Officer Sanchez do that. Give me a call when you're done and we can allocate you some of the businesses.'

Collins nodded. He looked excited. Real police work looming.

'How do you want to split the businesses?' Fields asked.

Hunter looked through the five sheets of paper he held. He took the top two and handed them to Fields. She had already sorted them geographically before printing.

'Easy enough,' she said, taking the paper from Hunter.

'Let's make a move.'

'Daylight's wastin',' Collins said, lowering his voice an octave.

Hunter and Fields stared at him.

'What? It's from a movie. I was just—'

'Let's go.'

10

Friday: FBI Academy, Quantico, Virginia

Dean Graves sat patiently with John Sullivan through a painfully slow conference call with agents at the Houston field office. They were discussing training for the Houston agents and whether it would be paid from the local office budget or from Graves's budget. Graves hated the management stuff that came with being a high-ranking Bureau official. It wasn't his thing, but he knew he had to deal with it.

He walked outside with Sullivan to get some fresh air, looking up at the grey sky. Low cloud swirled overhead. Sullivan complained about the Houston guys trying to stick them with the cost. Graves nodded in agreement. He knew that if it came to it, CIRG would win the argument.

The telephone on Graves's desk was ringing when he returned to his office. He grabbed it before sitting.

'Agent Graves, this is Detective Kaminski. I'm with Denver PD, Homicide.'

'You work with Jake Hunter?'

'That's right.'

Graves wondered why Hunter was not calling; tried not to worry about it. He was already concerned enough about Hunter and what this case was doing to him.

'What can I do for you, detective?'

'I'm running warrants for Jake. We need Federal help with some cross-state stuff.'

'Okay. I thought maybe Jake would have called me himself.'

'He's not in Denver right now. We got a lead off a ViCAP search. A murder over in Dillon.'

'I know about that,' Graves said, sitting down. 'Did Jake go there alone?'

Kaminski explained that Hunter and Collins were assisting the locals. Graves didn't like it much. City cops worked best in the city, where they knew the terrain. Small towns like Dillon were different. The locals often didn't take too well to other cops butting in and in his experience it was easier for the Bureau to cope with that kind of stuff. Everyone resented the Feds, so they could go in and take control without worrying about perceptions.

'Tell me how I can help you?' Graves said, letting his concerns go for now.

Kaminski told him about the trouble getting school records in order to trace DeSanto. Graves asked her to send all that she had and he would make sure that it got top priority.

'Sounds like progress,' he said.

'It's a solid line of inquiry.'

'What's the news from Dillon?'

'They're working it as best they can.'

Didn't sound too hopeful to Graves but he bit his tongue. They finished the call and Graves placed the phone on its base station. He kept his hand on the phone, thinking about calling Hunter. He picked up and called Nick Levine's internal line instead.

'Nick, it's Dean. This thing in Denver. Did you know that Jake Hunter was in Dillon following up on the murder there?'

Levine paused before saying that he knew.

'I'd have appreciated a heads-up.'

'Sorry, sir. But I thought that we weren't going to jump in on this one. Leave it to the cops.'

'Yes. But circumstances change. That decision is not set in stone. I need to know what's going on now that we are officially helping out.'

'I understand.'

Graves ended the call and stood, walking to the window as rain started to spot on the glass. He had to trust his friend. If Hunter wanted help he would ask.

That's what he hoped.

11

Friday: Dillon, Colorado

It was forty minutes later when Collins and Rodriguez stood outside the first of the apartment blocks that they were to check. They had decided that the houses would be best done first. Trouble was, half of them showed no signs of occupation so they would have to go back later. Normal people worked during the day.

Collins checked his watch and saw that it was nearly four. He looked at the low-rise red-brick building. There were three storeys with ten apartments on each floor.

'How many?' he asked Rodriguez.

She ran a finger down the sheet of paper with the addresses until she found the building in front of them.

'Two apartments rented in the last six months, according to the realtor. Both on the second floor. Apartments two-ten and two-oh-three. Single males.'

'Let's do it.'

There was a secure entrance with an intercom system. No video. Collins didn't want to alert their suspect to a police presence – if he was here. He pressed buttons for the first-floor apartments until a woman's voice answered.

'Police, m'am,' he said. 'Can you let us in?'

There was a pause.

'How do I know you're police?'

The woman wasn't being aggressive or defensive, she was simply asking it in a matter-of-fact voice.

'You want to come to the door and we'll show you ID?'

'Who you here to see?'

'Second floor.'

'Why did you buzz me?'

Collins said they were looking for someone and left it at that. Thirty seconds later, a heavy-set black woman came to the door and peered carefully at their identification. When she was satisfied she stepped back to allow them into the building.

'What are you doing all the way over here, Denver?' she asked.

Collins thought it sounded cool that she called him 'Denver'.

'I can't tell you that,' he told her.

She shrugged like it was no big deal.

'Stairs are over there,' she said, pointing to a door to the left of the entrance lobby.

Collins pushed open the door at the top of the stairs leading into a short, carpeted hallway. There were five doors on each side of the hall. They walked to the second apartment on the left – 203.

Collins knocked on the door. He didn't do it hard. Rodriguez stood to his right, turning her head to look down the hall at light spilling in from a window at the end.

There was a peephole in the door. Collins leaned forward and strained to look through it. He jumped back when a dark shadow passed over it.

'Shit,' he whispered.

Rodriguez stifled a laugh.

'Who is it?' a male voice asked from behind the door.

Collins looked at Rodriguez and frowned. Anyone in the apartment would have been able to see her uniform through the peephole.

Rodriguez opened her mouth to speak.

The door splintered, sending wood shards into her face.

Collins fell back, thudding into the opposite wall. He gasped and pulled at his shirt as a red stain spread fast from the bullet wound.

The door splintered again.

The second bullet hit Collins in the neck as he slid down the wall. Flesh and blood sprayed the wallpaper.

Rodriguez froze.

Collins scrabbled with his right hand to find his gun in the holster on his belt. His left hand went to his neck where blood gouted over it. He couldn't coordinate his movements. Couldn't seem to find his gun.

Darkness encroached at the edge of his vision.

The door was pulled open and DeSanto ran out. Rodriguez

snapped out of her shock and put a hand on the butt of her own gun.

DeSanto was quicker, grabbing the wrist of her gun hand. He had a long knife in his other hand.

Collins stared at the scene playing out above him, feeling strength ebb from his body. He tried again to find his gun. Failed.

Rodriguez held her free hand up.

'No!' she screamed.

DeSanto thrust the knife at her face. She got her hand in the way. The blade sliced right through.

DeSanto pulled the blade back and thrust again. This time he missed her hand and embedded the steel in Rodriguez's face. He stabbed her in the face five more times.

She screamed and grabbed at the knife. She caught the blade. DeSanto pulled it free of her grasp, slicing through the tendons of her hand.

A door opened further along the hall and a man stepped out.

'What the hell . . .' he said, stopping when he saw the carnage in front of him.

DeSanto pushed Rodriguez and she fell on to the floor. He turned and ran for the door to the stairs.

Collins found his gun, fell on to his stomach and pulled the trigger while trying to focus his failing vision on the fleeing man.

Plaster misted the air as Collins emptied his magazine and blew chunks out of the walls. The sound roared in the enclosed space.

The door swung shut after DeSanto was gone. Collins

didn't know if he'd hit him. Couldn't see any blood to indicate that he had.

He rolled on to his back and dropped his gun.

'Call it,' he said to Rodriguez, his voice little more than a whisper.

Rodriguez was curled up in a foetal position, cradling her ruined hand to her chest. Collins didn't recognise her face any more.

'Call it,' he said again.

He hoped she would. He could not.

He felt air bubbles gurgling in the wound in his chest.

Hit a lung, he thought. I'm in trouble. In it deep.

Rodriguez made no move to do anything. A sound escaped from her lips that didn't sound human to Collins. He stared at the ceiling as the darkness rolled over him.

12

Hunter felt his phone vibrate and pulled it from his jacket pocket. Officer Earl Ray stopped and turned to look at him.

'It's my wife,' Hunter said. 'Give me a minute.'

He walked a few steps away from Ray as Ray's radio crackled to life. Hunter put the phone to one ear. He was vaguely aware of the voice on Ray's radio sounding slightly off – high pitched and talking in a rush.

'Hey, Ash,' he said. 'What's up?'

'Oh my God, you haven't heard?'

'Heard what?'

He looked back at Ray as the noise from his radio increased. He thought that he heard a siren somewhere close by. Ray's face drained of colour.

Hunter wasn't really listening to his wife any longer.

'What is it?' he asked Ray. 'Tell me.'

'It's Hope. Officer Rodriguez.'

And Danny.

'Jake,' his wife's voice sounded louder in his ear. 'Did you hear what I said?'

'I can't talk, Ash. Something—'

'Chase Black was attacked in London tonight. It's all over the news.'

Hunter struggled to comprehend what anyone was saying. He heard the phrase 'GSW' from Ray's radio: paramedic shorthand for 'Gunshot Wound'.

'What?' Hunter said, not sure if he was talking to Ray or his wife.

'I said Chase Black was attacked. Two people got killed.'

'Was Black one of them?'

'I don't know. They're not saying.'

Ray was speaking into his radio.

'Listen, Ash, I'm in the middle of something here. I can't talk.'

'Call me as soon as you can.'

He said he would and then forgot all about Chase Black.

'What is it?' he asked Ray.

'They must have found him. Hope and your partner.'

'And?'

'Hope got stabbed.'

'Danny?'

Ray shook his head. Hunter turned and ran.

13

Friday: London

Logan stared at the smear of blood on the face of his watch as it ticked on towards midnight. He licked his thumb and wiped at it. His shirt hung loosely at his waist and he grabbed the end of it, rubbing his watch. The blood stained his shirt, blue turning purple.

A door opened down the corridor. He looked up from his seat and saw Carrie walking towards him. There was a bandage on her left forearm and a dark stain on the front of her black T-shirt. The stain continued on to her black trousers. Logan wasn't sure whose blood it was; lost in the confusion.

She reached Logan and sat on the spare seat beside him. A fluorescent strip light buzzed above them, fading then coming on bright again. The green colour of the walls made Logan nauseous. He didn't like hospitals.

'Any news?' he asked.

'He's still in surgery. Which means that he's breathing.'

'That's something.'

She huffed out a humourless laugh.

'Who were those guys anyway?' she asked.

'I don't know,' Logan said, shaking his head. 'No one was talking.'

'They weren't police.'

'No. Something else.'

'You speak to Alex?'

'Yeah. And Becky. And Ellie.'

They fell silent. Logan's mind ran a home movie of what happened in his head: the two men coming out of the car fast and Kate Marlow collapsing like a puppet with cut strings as the bullets hit her.

'Christ, what happened?' Carrie asked, not expecting an answer. 'Who was that on the bike?'

Logan shook his head and thumbed his shirt over his watch again to get rid of the final remnants of the blood.

'A ghost,' he said. 'That's who.'

Carrie reached out and grabbed his hand, squeezing it tightly. He put his other hand over hers and saw tears splash on the floor as she bowed her head.

'I know,' he said. 'I know.'

14

Logan watched one of the surgeons along the corridor. He was with a nurse and scribbled something on the chart that she held on a clipboard. Logan got up and went towards him. Carrie followed, wiping her face and sniffing loudly.

'Can you tell us how he's doing?' Logan asked when he reached the surgeon.

'He's out of surgery now and on his way to the intensive care ward. Beyond that, there's not much to tell you at this time.'

'You'll keep us updated?'

The surgeon looked past Logan and Carrie.

'I'm not sure that I can.'

'What?' Logan said.

Carrie nudged him and nodded along the corridor. Logan looked and saw two men who, judging by the way they carried themselves, could only be in the security service. They were dressed in dark suits with plain ties. They were even close to the same height, only their haircuts identifying them as anything other than clones – one balding and shaven headed, the other with short brown hair.

They stopped when they reached Logan and Carrie, the surgeon already walking away from them down the corridor in the other direction.

'Logan Finch, isn't it?' the bald guy asked. 'And Carrie Richardson?'

Logan nodded.

'You're okay?'

'Other than this,' Carrie said, brandishing her bandaged arm.

Both men glanced down at her, unmoved by the injury and the bloodstains.

'It sucks being me right now,' Carrie said, unprompted. 'But I'll live. You know, in case you were concerned about me.'

The two men remained implacable.

'Concern,' she said, her voice beginning to tighten. 'I mean, you're aware of the concept of human emotion, aren't you?'

Logan put a hand on her forearm and eased it down. She might hit them if he didn't cool her off.

'Who are you?' Logan asked.

'We can't really say much at this stage, sorry,' the dark-haired man said. 'It's not that we don't care. But I need to speak to the medical team.'

Logan felt himself rubbing a finger over the face of his

watch again. He put his hand in the pocket of his trousers to stop from doing that.

'There were two men with concealed weapons,' Logan told them. 'They followed us. Do you know anything about that?'

The man opened his hands.

'I really can't say *anything* at this point.'

'They weren't police,' Carrie said. 'But they weren't bad guys.'

'That's a good summary for now.'

'It's not an answer.'

He sighed. 'We know who you are. The CPO team has a lot of respect in the law enforcement community.'

Logan stared at him, waiting for the next stonewall pronouncement.

'So I'll tell you that those two men were on our side. But that's as far as it goes.'

'Who was the shooter?'

The dark-haired man's face took on a pained expression. He was doing most of the talking now so Logan figured he had seniority.

'You know, don't you?' Carrie said.

'Not exactly, no. But we have a fair idea.'

'You haven't made any arrests?'

'No, but we have brought someone in to answer a few questions.'

Logan frowned.

'What does that mean?'

'Let me speak to the doctor, here,' he said. 'Then we'll talk.'

Carrie stood with Logan watching the men walk to the end of the corridor.

'What the hell was all that about?' she asked.

'I don't know.'

15

Logan went back to people-watching from his chair in the hospital corridor. It was mainly doctors and nurses, though once in every fifteen minutes or so a tearful family member or two would pass by. This was why he hated these places. One tenth joy, nine tenths misery. He wasn't certain if that was statistically accurate, but it was his experience.

Carrie had fallen asleep with her head resting on his shoulder. He felt wide awake.

The dark-haired suit reappeared after an hour. He stopped in front of Logan and leaned back against the opposite wall. Logan waited for him to speak.

'Chase Black is fine,' he said.

'We know that. I mean, he took a pretty good thump on the head when I pushed him into the car. That took, what, five or six stitches?'

'Ten. And a mild concussion.'

'He can leave tonight?'

'No. At least one night as an in-patient to monitor him. Make sure there's no more serious damage.'

'I guess that means I should set up camp here.'

The man looked along the corridor as a woman in a pale grey suit came out of a door and walked past them. She had a hospital ID card pinned to her jacket – looked like a manager-type, rather than a clinician.

'How is *your* man doing now that he's out of surgery?' Logan asked when the woman had gone.

'He's stable. That's about as good as it gets right now.'

'I'm sorry that you lost someone. That's hard.'

'Sounds like you know something about that.'

'I've lost people close to me. Close enough for it to still hurt.'

The man nodded. He looked along the corridor again, seemed to come to a decision in his mind, then stepped away from the wall and held out his hand. Logan shook it.

'My name's Simon Eden.'

'Nice to meet you, Simon.'

Carrie shifted in her seat but stayed asleep.

'I'm with M-I-Five.'

'You're a spy.'

Eden smiled. 'That's the popular perception.'

'And what's the official term?'

'Intelligence officer.'

'So, what's a spy doing here? And what were your fellow officers doing following us?'

'We're not really spies. Or, at least, not in the sense that you mean it. We're responsible for assessing threats to national security and undertaking investigations into such threats.'

'Was Chase Black considered a threat?'

'No. I mean, not really. He was low on our radar.'

'Not enough to justify a two-man tail?'

'Correct.'

'I'm not sure I understand what's going on.'

'We were following Mr Black because we had credible information that he was at risk. And we categorised that risk as being a possible threat to our national security.'

'Someone was trying to kill him?'

'Yes.'

Logan tried to think, his head still fogged from the day's events.

'And for M-I-Five to be interested, that someone was a foreign national?'

Eden's head inclined from side to side.

'Not necessarily,' he said.

Logan put his head back against the wall. The light above them flickered off and on again. A thought occurred to him and he took his head off the wall to look at Eden.

'You said before that you had taken someone in for questioning?'

'Yes.'

'I'm guessing you guys don't undertake questioning lightly. This person is of serious interest in this?'

'Also correct. You've got a good deductive brain.'

'Can you tell me who it is?'

'No. But if we're right about what's going on, it'll come out soon enough.'

Carrie lifted her head and looked drowsily from Logan to Eden and back. She frowned, like her mind was having trouble completely waking up, then went back to sleep.

'Why don't you tell me what happened today?' Eden said.

'How much do you want to know?'

'Everything. I'll decide what's important and what's not.'

Logan told him everything.

16

Friday Morning: London

The day started serenely, the sky warm and clear. Logan was again surprised, as they went from one event to the next, at how popular Chase Black was proving to be. There were very few negative attitudes. Mostly people were there to buy his book, get it signed and shake the man's hand. By far the majority of those people were women. Black had charisma, of that there was no doubt. Logan hadn't really found anything to dislike about him.

They had to close one of the events early after the store ran out of stock of Black's book. When Logan asked how many copies they had sold since its release, the manager told him it was in excess of two thousand. That was one store in less than one week.

Black was relaxed and seemed to be enjoying himself. Logan watched him carefully when he did not have to concentrate on the crowds. The man gave off no sense of danger or threat. He and Marlow were comfortable together and Black was not tactile. If anything, it was the other way around. Marlow draped herself over him any chance she could get.

Cops made mistakes. God knows Logan was aware of that. Not too long ago he'd had to go to extreme lengths to get Cahill out of Scotland's most notorious prison – Barlinnie. It seemed that when cops had a suspect in mind and enough of the evidence fitted, they got tunnel vision.

He didn't know Jake Hunter very well, but he seemed like a straight guy and a good cop. That didn't mean he wasn't human and prone to the same kind of behaviour as anyone else. From what Logan had observed of Chase Black so far, he was inclined to believe that the correct outcome had been achieved by the appeal that set him free.

Logan turned to Black in the back of their car as they travelled towards the fourth event that day.

'Can I ask you something?' he said to Black.

Black smiled, his usual relaxed self.

'Sure. Go ahead.'

'You know what I'm going to ask?'

'Everyone wants the answer to that question.'

'Did you kill those people?'

Marlow sat forward.

'Don't answer that,' she said, putting an arm across Black's chest.

Logan was intrigued by the defensive move she had made. Carrie turned around to look at Black.

'Do you know how many people have asked me that question since I was released?'

Logan shook his head. Marlow's face flushed, angry at being ignored.

'Just you.'

Carrie laughed.

'I mean, they ask other questions that skirt around the subject. I know that's what most of them want to ask. So I respect your honesty.'

Logan waited for an answer.

'You used to be a lawyer, right?' Black asked him.

'Technically, I'm still a lawyer.'

'A trial lawyer.'

'I've done some.'

'So you've interviewed witnesses? Cross-examined them in court?'

Logan nodded.

'I'm curious, how do you spot the liars?'

Logan thought about it, aware that Black had deflected the question aimed at him. He had conducted maybe twenty trials before he moved into corporate law. And interviewed witnesses in another thirty cases. He felt that he had a good sense of when people were being honest.

'Everyone is different,' he told Black. 'Some of them can't hide the physical symptoms, you know. They blush or their neck and chest area flushes red.'

'Sounds like you've had experience,' Marlow said.

'We all have,' Logan told her. 'Show me someone who claims not to have lied, and I'll show you a liar.'

Black laughed. Marlow sat back in her seat and folded her arms across her chest.

'The more complex and far from the actual truth you make

the lie,' Logan went on, 'the easier it is to break it down.'

'Because other people will tell different versions of the same events?' Black asked.

'Correct. And usually there's a neutral – an outsider with no axe to grind. I always focused on finding that person and then built my strategy from there.'

'And you think Detective Hunter is that person? I mean, so far as my case is concerned.'

Logan held Black's gaze.

'You know the detective, don't you?'

Very few people were aware of Logan's involvement in the events in Denver. The resident FBI chief, Randall Webb, had seen to that. Logan wondered how Black knew.

'I do know him, yes. But I never look at the police as being neutral. That goes for Jake too.'

'So who is the neutral?'

'I don't know enough about your case to answer that.'

'You haven't answered Logan's question,' Carrie said. 'Did you do it?'

Black looked from Logan to Carrie and back again.

'No,' he said eventually. 'I did not kill all those people.'

Logan listened for any tone or inflection in Black's voice. He found none. Marlow looked at Black without turning her head.

'What do you think, Logan?' Carrie asked. 'Is he telling the truth?'

'That's an interesting way of putting it,' Black said.

'What do you mean?'

'What he means,' Logan said, 'is that you didn't ask me if I thought he was lying.'

Carrie frowned. 'Same difference.'

'No, it's not. You asked if he was telling the truth. Which means that you think he is. If you had asked me if he was lying, that would have shown that you didn't believe his answer.'

'I'm impressed,' Black said. 'Have you studied this?'

'A little.'

'Now it's your turn to answer a question, Logan. Am I telling the truth?'

Logan didn't hesitate. 'Yes. I think you are.'

17

Logan first noticed the car after the fourth signing event. He was standing by the open door of their vehicle as Black got in, followed by Marlow, when he saw the silver saloon parked at the kerb around fifty yards behind them. Two men in suits sat in the front seats.

He waited until Marlow was in the car and closed the door, leading Carrie around to the front window on the passenger side of their vehicle. The driver turned his head to look at them and Logan motioned with his hand for him to lower the window. When it was down, Logan leaned on the door frame with his elbows.

'There's a silver car about fifty yards back,' he said, looking at the driver but speaking loud enough for Carrie to hear as she stood behind him. 'Keep an eye on it for me, will you?'

The driver nodded.

'What are you thinking?' Carrie asked as Logan straightened up and the driver buzzed the window closed.

'I don't know. Two guys in suits.'

'Sounds like police to me.'

Logan nodded. 'Why are they following our man?' he asked.

'At a wild guess, keeping the country safe from a convicted serial killer.'

Logan gave her a reproachful look.

On the drive to the next venue, Logan turned around to talk to Black and Marlow on three separate occasions. What he was really doing was quickly checking to see if the silver car was following them.

It was.

He told Carrie at the next stop – asked her to step outside before they got Black seated at the signing desk and give the impression that she was having a quick break to stretch and get some air.

'Still there,' she said when she came back into the venue. 'We've officially got a tail.'

Logan nodded.

'Do we tell Black or Marlow?' she asked.

'I don't think so. Not yet, anyway. If they are cops, there's no threat and no need to let them know.'

'Want me to call around? Find out if any of our contacts knows what's going on?'

'Yeah, do that when we get back to the hotel.'

The silver car stayed with them for the final two events of the day and on the drive back to the hotel in Mayfair.

After Black and Marlow were in their rooms and getting ready for the dinner, Logan left Carrie in their own room to make the calls and went back down to their car to speak to the driver, who was leaning against the car smoking a cigarette.

'Did they follow us all the way in?' Logan asked, looking along the street but not seeing the other car.

The driver nodded.

'Funny thing,' he said. 'I was watching them as we came along the street and they pulled in to the side of the road before I had even indicated that I was going to do the same.'

'So they knew you were about to stop?'

'Must have. They obviously had information that this was our hotel.'

'Where are they now?'

'They drove past a few minutes ago and turned the corner at the end of the street. Want me to go down and see if they are waiting down there?'

Logan said yes and waited while the driver sauntered to the end of the street and disappeared around the corner. He reappeared after less than a minute and again took his time walking back to the car.

'Yep,' he said. 'They're about twenty feet from the corner.'

'What are they doing?'

'Just sitting there.'

Logan went back to his room and told Carrie that the car was still there.

'I called a few people,' she said. 'Nobody knew anything.'

'Or they weren't telling you.'

'Could be. What do you want to do now?'

'Let's keep an eye on them. But I'm pretty sure they're some sort of police.'

'Yeah, too conspicuous for the bad guys. The cops are always so obvious. Do they have a special training course where they learn how to tail people with maximum visibility?'

'It seems that they do.'

Carrie went into the bathroom to get ready for the dinner, claiming that she was actually going to put some make-up on. Logan told her not to change the habits of a lifetime.

He sat by the window and sipped from a bottle of water, disturbed by the tail that they had but not sure why. He wondered what it was that the police were hoping to achieve.

18

When it happened, it happened fast.

They arrived at One Marylebone, the venue for the party that Black's publishers had set up, at seven-thirty. The ever so slightly over-the-top flaming torches burned dimly in the early evening light. The publishers had laid on an ostentatious show for the photographers who lined the pavement outside the converted church. A red carpet led from the road over the pavement and up the steps into the cavernous interior of the domed building. The light system inside switched in slow, dreamlike fades from lilac, to red, to blue and back again. Music leaked out of the open doors.

There was a small gathering of people who could only have been fans there for a glimpse of the notorious Chase Black. A solitary protestor walked along the pavement in front of the building with a sorry-looking home-made placard that read: 'Not In Our Country – Black out'. It looked half-hearted to Logan as they drew up at the kerb.

Two large men in black suits stood at the entrance gate and another two further back, at the top of the steps into the building.

Logan got out of the car with Carrie, telling Black and Marlow to stay put. He turned to look in the direction they had come from and saw the silver car go by. The man in the passenger seat looked directly at Logan and held his gaze until they were out of sight. There was no tell-tale red light as the brakes were applied. Maybe they were done for the night, Logan thought.

He walked to the gates and spoke briefly to one of the security guys, asking if everything was okay, checking that there was nothing out of the ordinary. He got confirmation in the affirmative. That was the kind of language the guy used. Like he was in a movie or something.

Logan turned back to the car where Carrie stood in front of the closed rear door. He saw a motorbike pull up to his left but thought nothing of it. The rider was dressed like a courier with a fluorescent yellow safety vest over black leathers. There was a company name and insignia on the vest. The rider kept the helmet on with the darkened visor closed.

As he walked forward, the silver car reappeared, pulling past the building and stopping around the corner.

Carrie's head turned to look at the car. Logan told her it was okay.

The motorcycle courier went to the back of the bike and opened the storage box strapped there.

Logan opened the car door and slid it back. He stepped

out of the way to allow Marlow and Black to get out. Marlow had gone all out for glamour in a short, shimmering silver dress. Black looked cool and handsome in narrow grey trousers and a white shirt.

Some of the photographers moved in to get a close-up, Marlow posing for all she was worth. Logan thought she looked a little bit desperate.

'Would you get a load of that skank,' was Carrie's subtle appraisal of the performance.

Logan was moving his head, scanning the surrounding area when he became aware of movement from the silver car. Then it all went fast forward.

The passenger of the silver car came up out of his seat, already pulling his sidearm from a holster on his belt. The driver did the same on the far side of the car.

Logan shouted 'Gun!' and grabbed Black's arm.

The passenger from the silver car was pointing to something behind Logan.

A woman in the crowd saw the gun, screamed and ran out into the road causing a taxi to swerve and crunch into a car in the outside lane. After that it was bedlam.

Photographers started snapping in a frenzy, their flashes strobing in the dusk.

Marlow was three steps ahead of Black. She turned as Carrie reached for her.

Logan turned to look at what was behind them – where the passenger from the silver car was pointing.

The bike courier had pulled two handguns from the box strapped to the rear of the bike. Walking forward, less than ten feet from Black, the rider opened up.

Logan spun, pulling Black and heaving him towards the open rear door. There was an audible 'thunk' as Black's head cracked into the door frame and he slumped on to the rear seat with a line of blood quickly forming on his forehead.

Logan felt bullets fizzing around his head. He turned back to help Carrie.

Marlow took two bullets high on her head and fell straight to the ground. She was dead before she hit the concrete.

Carrie shouted and turned away from the bike rider, grabbing at her arm and crouching to avoid any more bullets.

The passenger from the silver car started firing at the bike rider while on the run. His aim was way off. Bullets crunched into the pavement and one shattered the window of the crashed taxi.

The bike rider stopped walking forward and took careful aim at the man. Logan ducked into the car, shouting at Carrie to get in.

The bike rider fired at the passenger from the silver car.

He went down in a mist of red.

His partner from the silver car, the driver, stopped when he saw his partner fall. He dropped into a classic firing stance and started to bring his weapon up. He never got it all the way as the bike rider fired again.

Carrie fell into the car and Logan shouted at the driver to punch it.

He did as he was told.

They screeched out into the road, leaving plenty of rubber behind. The rear window shattered as the bike rider fired at the car.

Then they were safe.

19

Friday: London
Now

Simon Eden listened intently as Logan told his story. His face took on a pained expression when he heard about his colleagues being shot.

'What happened to the shooter?' Logan asked. 'We lit out of there and never saw what happened.'

'Disappeared.'

'Just like that?' Carrie asked.

Logan had not been aware of her waking up.

Eden shrugged.

'There were no police on site. Our two officers were out of commission and the on-site security was no better than nightclub bouncers. From what we can glean from the witnesses who have talked so far, the courier dropped the guns when you guys were gone, got on the bike and drove off.'

'Easy as that?'

'The civilians scattered. The bouncers ran inside the building to get out of the line of fire.'

'What about the bike?' Logan asked. 'You must have caught it on traffic cameras. I mean, do you have the registration number?'

'Better than that. We have the bike. It was abandoned and torched.'

'Let me guess,' Logan said. 'You haven't been able to trace the rider from there?'

Eden smiled ruefully and nodded.

'Funny thing, though,' he said. 'A couple of the witnesses swear blind it was a woman. What do you think of that?'

Logan closed his eyes, trying to recall the rider from memory.

'I don't know. I suppose it's possible. Certainly whoever it was had a slight build. The leathers and the vest bulked her out.'

'I didn't really see her,' Carrie said.

Eden's colleague appeared at the end of the corridor and gestured for him to follow. Eden excused himself and walked away.

'He *knows* that it was a woman,' Logan told Carrie.

'What?'

'Don't you remember? He said before that they had brought someone in for questioning.'

'Yeah, you're right. I forgot.'

Carrie stood and stretched, wincing a little and grabbing her arm.

'You need to take it easy,' Logan told her.

'But we're going home now, right? We're done here.'

'Our client is injured and whoever attacked him is still out there. The press are all over this and there have been reports on TV already that this hospital is where he was taken.'

Carrie's shoulders slumped.

'It was a bike courier last time . . .' Logan started.

'Next time it might be a nurse in scrubs,' Carrie finished for him.

Part Six
Monsters

Memorandum

From: Franck Zimmer

To: Section Chief

Re: Project Eden

Interpol Ref: 735F-27

Sir,

I regret to advise that one MI5 officer was killed by gunfire and another seriously wounded in operations this evening. A civilian woman was also killed. Subject 'Night' survived with what appear to be minor injuries.

The working assumption is that subject 'Eve' was responsible for the attack. Some witness corroboration is available that it was a woman.

We are in contact with MI5. They have subject 'Mamba' in custody ostensibly for questioning. It is unlikely that subject 'Mamba' will have useful intelligence on subject 'Eve' – her whereabouts or her plans. He has already confessed to engaging subject 'Eve' and that subject 'Night' was indeed the target of the engagement.

A further attack on subject 'Night' is anticipated. Subject 'Eve' is not known to have left any prior engagement incomplete.

Reports to follow.

1

Friday: Dillon

Jake Hunter sat quietly in the front passenger seat of Sutton Fields's police SUV. They were on County Highway 9, heading for the nearest trauma unit at St Anthony Summit Medical Center in Frisco. It was seven miles south of Dillon in Frisco Bay at the other end of the lake.

The in-car radio crackled to life sporadically as the cops back in Dillon continued their search for DeSanto. It sounded like so much white noise to Hunter. DeSanto would have to wait. Danny came first.

'What have you heard?' Hunter asked Fields. 'About Danny.'

She glanced at him as the needle on the speedometer crept above sixty.

'He's in a bad way. He wasn't breathing when they got to him at the apartment block.'

Hunter closed his eyes.

'But they revived him, stabilised him as best they could and got him in the ambulance.'

'As best they could . . .' Hunter repeated, trailing off.

'Hope will pull through,' Fields said. 'But she'll need a lot of reconstructive work on her face. Bastard cut her up.'

She slammed a hand against the steering wheel.

'He's our guy,' Hunter said. 'I don't think there can be any doubt of that now. He probably recognised Danny and decided that he had to come out fighting.'

'Hope got lucky,' Fields said. 'I mean, why didn't he shoot her too? Why use a knife?'

'It's what he likes,' Hunter said, turning his head to look at Fields. 'You saw the crime scene photographs from Denver. And what he did to Kim Dawson.'

Fields slowed and made the turn into the hospital grounds. It was a modern facility in two different shades of brick with darkened windows. Trees were dotted around the parking lot which was sparsely populated. She pulled the SUV into a parking bay close to the entrance. They got out and ran into the main reception area.

Inside was probably the nicest hospital Hunter had seen – still fresh and new in various pastel shades of blue and green. There were some small trees and shrubs in an indoor garden, no doubt intended to help add to a calming environment. He'd been in worse hotels.

They were directed to the ER on the ground floor and found Chief Patton at the nurses' station leaning on the desk talking to a middle-aged woman in blue scrubs. Patton turned when he heard their footsteps.

'Frank,' Fields said, using the abbreviated form of his first name.

It was, Hunter thought, the first real sign of any informality he had seen with the chief. Maybe he wasn't such a strait-laced type after all.

'Any news on Danny?' Hunter asked.

'They're still working on him. That's all they'll tell me.'

'Have you seen Hope yet?' Fields asked.

Patton gently took Fields by the arm and steered her away from the desk. Hunter followed after them.

'She's gone into surgery,' Patton told them. 'But they say she'll be okay.'

'They didn't say the same about Danny,' Hunter said, not asking.

Patton's lips stretched into a thin line and he shook his head.

'Do we know what happened yet?' Fields asked.

'Not much to it so far as we can tell,' Patton told her. 'They went to the apartment, knocked on the door and that was it.'

'Did we find anything useful in the apartment?'

'Not really, no. Seems the guy travels light.'

Hunter ran his hands up over his head and sat in a chair. There was a row of five of them fixed to the floor against the wall. The other four chairs were empty. Patton and Fields walked down the corridor, talking. Hunter couldn't remember having ever felt so alone in a building full of people. He looked at the nurse and she smiled at him.

'I'll let you know as soon as there's any update,' she said.

He told her that he appreciated that, but couldn't muster a smile. He took his cell phone out and started to dial home.

'You'll have to go outside to use that,' the nurse said. 'Sorry.'

Hunter called out to Fields and pointed at his phone when she turned around. She nodded that she understood.

He stood under the canopy outside the main reception area and listened to the phone ring. He thought that it would all be okay when he heard his wife's voice. Instead, he choked back a cough when she said hello, his eyes brimming. He sucked in a breath before he spoke, but still heard the tremor in his voice.

'It's me, Ash.'

'What's wrong?'

She recognised the fear in him; her medical background meant that she'd experienced it on many occasions.

'It's Danny.'

'What happened, Jake?'

The fear was contagious. Danny was a friend as well as his partner. A friend to both of them.

'We found the guy. The killer. Danny did.'

He spoke in short sentences, not trusting himself to hold it together enough to talk at length.

'Oh no, Jake. Tell me. Just tell me.'

'Danny got shot. It's bad.'

He heard a sharp intake of breath.

'One of the local cops got cut up too. They think she'll be okay. But he messed up her face real bad.'

'Did they catch him? At least tell me they did that.'

Hunter shook his head, kicked at a small stone by his feet.

'He's still loose. But we'll get him. It's a matter of time now that he's on the run.'

Hunter walked along the path until he got to the end of the building. Two nurses were standing around the corner smoking and laughing; talking about something that had happened earlier in the day. They stopped laughing when they saw Hunter. He turned and went back towards the main entrance.

'You hear any more about Chase Black?' he asked his wife, trying to take his mind off what had happened to Danny.

'He's in hospital. But they don't think it's serious.'

'Who got killed?' Hunter asked, stopping.

'They're not saying.'

Hunter wondered if it was Logan Finch.

Sutton Fields appeared inside the glass doors and motioned for Hunter to come inside.

'I gotta go, Ash.'

'Call me when you can.'

He told her that he would and put his phone in his pocket. As he walked towards Fields he heard voices from where the nurses had been smoking. He turned his head and thought for an instant that he saw Danny. But there was no one there.

Hunter stepped into the interior of the building. Fields put a hand to her mouth and shook her head as he approached her. He stopped.

'Say it,' he told her. 'Tell me.'

'He's dead. Danny's dead.'

2

Hunter listened to the ER physician telling him what he'd heard many times before. That they did all they could, but his injuries were too severe. The man's tunic was stained with blood. The smell of it was thick in Hunter's nostrils.

'I want to see him,' he said, interrupting the doctor.

Fields put a hand on his shoulder.

'Do you think that's a good idea, Jake? I mean, do you want to see him like that? All tore up.'

He said that he did.

The doctor led them past the nurses' station and down a short hallway. It was quiet, the only sound the squeak of their shoes on the non-slip floor covering. The doctor stopped and pushed at a heavy door. Hunter looked at the metal plate on the door that read 'Trauma Room T-10'.

Inside, Danny lay on a treatment table in the middle of the room. Above him was an array of lights trained on the table and shining so brightly that they bleached the colour from his skin.

There were three nurses in the room: two of them peeling the various monitoring pads from Danny's skin and the other working on a computer terminal at the back of the room. They stopped working and looked up as Hunter and Fields came through the door.

'Do you want time alone?' the doctor asked, still holding the door open.

'No,' Hunter said. 'You can keep working. I just want to . . .' He trailed off and walked to the table.

Fields stood where she was, not wanting to intrude on Hunter's private moment with his partner.

Hunter stopped by the table and looked at Danny's face. It was streaked and speckled with blood, the gunshot wound in his neck a ragged, gaping hole. He put his hand on one of Danny's arms and felt it still warm, the last trace of what had been his life still lingering.

Hunter felt his chin tremble and he sniffed hard.

There was a dressing on the chest wound and the skin around it discoloured where iodine solution had been used.

'Did he ever regain consciousness?' Hunter asked, still looking at his friend.

'No,' the doctor said.

That's what it was like in real life. You got shot, you died. There was no big, emotional scene with the dying cop telling his partner to get the guy. Do it for me.

It didn't happen.

Hunter turned and left. He stopped at the door and shook the doctor's hand.

'Thanks for trying,' he said.

The doctor nodded but said nothing.

Patton was waiting for Hunter and Fields at the end of the hall, beside the nurses' station.

'Are you okay?' he asked Hunter.

'Not really, no.'

Patton shook his head, admonishing himself for asking such a stupid question.

'Of course,' he said.

Fields pulled Hunter over to the same row of chairs he had been sitting in earlier and pushed him on to one of them.

'I'll get you something to drink then I'm taking you to your hotel.'

Hunter felt all his energy drain away and he slumped back against the chair. There was no fight left in him. No desire to tell Fields 'no' – to hell with how he felt and that he would join the search in Dillon for Danny's killer.

That's what DeSanto was now. Not a serial killer. Not a threat to anyone who came into contact with him. Not someone who needed to be taken off the streets and punished for those families he had ripped apart.

He was Danny's killer.

That was all that mattered.

3

Hunter stared out the window of the SUV as Fields drove back towards Dillon. Sun slanted through the trees along the road, shadows flickering across his face. He remembered standing in the cold winter sun the day Black was released from prison. He had been so sure that Black was guilty; thought that he could read people so well. Thought that he could divine evil from good.

What was it they said came before a fall?

His phone rang and he answered it without checking who was calling.

'Jake, it's Nick Levine. I had a look at the bindings issue for you.'

'Tell me what you have.'

'You said that the killer used bindings found in the house of the victim in Dillon. That he didn't bring them to the house. Which was different from his MO in Denver.'

'Yes.'

'Well, you'll remember that my initial thinking was that it might be a different killer in Dillon.'

Hunter waited.

'I think I was wrong about that. I mean, there's another possible explanation.'

'What's that, Nick?'

'It could be that he went to that house not intending to kill the victim. Which is why he didn't have his kit with him. His tools.'

Hunter sat up in the seat, his mind starting to wake.

'It could still be the same man?'

'Yes. The question for the profile then becomes, why did he go to that particular house?'

'Maybe he was scoping it out and got disturbed.'

Fields heard the change in Hunter's tone and looked at him. He mouthed 'FBI' at her.

'Unlikely. Like I said before, the Denver killings indicate a killer at the top of his game, if you'll pardon the expression. Someone who had developed his skill at killing to a high degree.'

'So if he didn't get caught checking out his victims in Denver it's unlikely he would suddenly get worse at that aspect of it?'

'Correct.'

'Where are you going with this?'

'I checked our database to see if I could find anything similar. And there is a kind of pattern, though the sample on the use of bindings is perhaps too small to provide any firm conclusion. No more than a handful of cases.'

'Anything would be useful at this point.'

'Okay, here's the thing. What the database tells me is that when a killer uses bindings found in the victim's home it's almost always the first killing. Not all the time, but enough for it to be considered a kind of pattern.'

'Meaning the killer went unprepared?'

'Yes. Or perhaps went with no immediate intention of killing the victim.'

Hunter frowned. 'Why is that important?' he asked.

'Why does someone go to the house of another person? Ignore the fact that this person is a potential killer.'

Hunter started to see it.

'It's not just that the killer goes to the house of anyone, is it?'

'Now you're getting it.'

'He goes to a house where he is allowed inside.'

'Correct.'

'And not because he's there to deliver anything or do work in the house. I'm right, aren't I? That's what your research shows.'

'You've got it, Jake.'

'The victim knows the killer. Or met him before. And that's how he gets into the house with no force.'

'Yes.'

Hunter thanked him and was about to end the call when Levine spoke again.

'I updated SAC Graves earlier today. He didn't know you were in Dillon. He seemed a little . . . annoyed about it. I mean, that you hadn't told him directly.'

Hunter wondered how Graves would feel now, if he knew about Collins.

'You still there, Jake?'

'Tell him I'll speak to him later. Thanks, Nick.'

He ended the call without waiting for Levine.

'What is it?' Fields asked.

'That was the profiler at Quantico.'

Fields turned to look at him. 'I gathered as much. Does he think Kim Dawson knew our guy?'

'That's the theory,' Hunter said. 'She might well have known who DeSanto really is.'

'Which means the husband might know him too.'

Hunter nodded.

'We're close,' she said. 'Can you feel it?'

Hunter turned to look out the window. He wasn't sure he knew what he felt any more.

4

They went back to the police station in Dillon. Fields told Hunter to wait for her in the incident room while she checked on the husband's whereabouts. Hunter went up the stairs, passing an officer on the way. They exchanged sombre looks and nods of sympathy. Sometimes you didn't need words.

Sometimes words were no good.

He called Ash and told her about Danny's death. They spoke quietly for a few minutes. Doing that thing where the dead are remembered fondly in anecdotes. It eases the pain.

'What about his family?' Ash asked. 'Who will tell them?'

'I don't think there's anyone to tell. His mother's in a nursing home. Late stage Alzheimer's. His dad died a few years back.'

'No brothers or sisters?'

'No.'

'That's sad. That there's no one to tell.'

'I want to take care of the funeral, Ash.'

'Won't the department pay for it?'

'Yes. I mean that I want to make all the arrangements. See that it gets done right.'

'Of course.'

Hunter closed his eyes, fighting fatigue. He had lost all sense of time.

'I need to go work, Ash. We've got a chance to get this guy.'

Fields came into the room and told him that the husband had checked out of his hotel. She had tried his cell phone but got the answer machine.

'Maybe he went home,' Hunter said.

'You want to drive out there to see?'

'Okay. But let me make a couple of calls first.'

Hunter's boss, Lieutenant Art Morris, was quiet after Hunter told him about Danny.

'I'm sorry, Jake,' he said after a moment. 'I really am.'

'Yeah.'

'Does this mean that he's our killer? This DeSanto?'

'That's the way it looks right now.'

'Where is he?'

'We don't know. The local cops are out on the streets right now. So far as they can tell he didn't have a car or any other type of transport. All the vehicles at the apartment block have been accounted for. We reckon he must be on foot.'

'It's always hard when one of your own goes down.'

'Yes, sir.'

'Do you need any extra resource? I mean, we're up to our necks in it here, but this takes priority.'

'Maybe, if we don't have the guy by this time tomorrow. I want to let the local cops do their thing now that it's a search rather than an investigation.'

'It's up to you. Anyway, Molly August was looking for you earlier.'

'Can you put me through to her?'

'Sure. Call me if you need anything.'

Hunter said that he would then waited on the line until he heard August's voice. There had been a long enough pause for Morris to have told her what had happened to Danny. Hunter had the conversation again, growing weary of the emotion that washed over him each time; wanting to do his job right now. Grieving would come later. When he had time for it.

'Morris said you were looking for me,' Hunter said.

'Uh, yes. I spoke to the FBI lab. The hair they have from the Dillon scene matches ours.'

'We got all three then. Our scene, DeSanto's house and now here.'

'Looks like a slam dunk. Especially with . . .'

'Uh-huh. Listen, Molly, call me if anything else turns up.'

Fields's phone rang as Hunter finished his call. She spoke briefly and ended by telling the caller that she would 'Meet you there'.

'The husband?' Hunter asked.

She nodded.

'He's at the house. Said he couldn't stand being away from it any longer. That it was his home.'

'Place will never be the same again for him. He'll find that out soon enough.'

5

Kim Dawson's husband, Jamie, looked hollowed out in person. He stepped back from the door and allowed Hunter and Fields into the house, closing the door and leading them to the kitchen area at the back of the house. He started fussing with a coffee machine. Hunter didn't want a drink right now but he knew that the physical activity would take Dawson's mind off the unthinkable.

'We've made progress,' Fields said after she introduced Hunter.

'How's that?' Dawson asked, not sounding convinced.

Fields looked at Hunter who shook his head: *Don't tell him about Danny.*

'Let's just say that we're closer to Kimmy's . . .'

Dawson looked at Fields, his face crumpling as the structures beneath it struggled to contain the hurt.

'. . . the man we're looking for,' Fields corrected herself.

Dawson turned from them and sniffed, wiping a hand at his eyes.

'We think that your wife may have known this man. Or met him at some point.'

Dawson turned, confusion in his face.

'What are you saying? That my wife was . . .'

'We're not suggesting that it was anything untoward,' Hunter said, interrupting him. 'Most likely it was someone she had met only casually.'

He wasn't certain that was correct, but saw no reason to add to this man's pain when they had nothing much to go on except some incomplete FBI research.

'What makes you say that?' Dawson asked.

'There was no sign of forced entry here,' Fields said. 'We think Kimmy may have let him in.'

Hunter couldn't read the emotion that passed across Dawson's face. It looked equal parts anger and confusion. Hunter took DeSanto's photo from his jacket pocket and unfolded it before handing it to Dawson.

'Do you know this man?' he asked.

Dawson looked at the photo and then at Fields.

'Is this him? I mean, did he kill Kimmy?'

She nodded.

'I don't know him,' Dawson said, looking at the photo again. 'This is Kimmy's home town.'

'You're not from here?' Hunter asked.

'No. I'm from the east coast. Washington. We met at college.'

'Why come back here? I mean, it's such a small town.'

'Kimmy wanted to be near her parents. They're getting old. Her dad doesn't keep well.'

'You were okay with that?'

'Sure. I love Kimmy. I'd do anything for her.'

He dropped the photo and covered his face with both hands. His chest heaved as the tears came. It overcame him suddenly and with such force that it took Hunter by surprise. He held Dawson's elbow and led him to a chair.

'Take it easy, Mr Dawson.'

Fields poured him a glass of water from the tap and handed it to him when he was composed enough to hold it. He took a long drink and his breathing returned to something approaching normal.

'So,' Hunter said, 'Kimmy must have known a lot of the locals.'

'Yeah.'

'Did she mention seeing anyone she knew recently? I mean, in the last couple of months. Someone she hadn't seen for a while.'

Dawson thought for a moment and then shook his head.

'I don't think so,' he said. 'Not that I can remember.'

Hunter motioned with his head for them to leave.

'Look, Jamie,' Fields said, 'if you do remember anything Kimmy might have said, give me a call.'

He nodded, though Hunter was not certain that he was really listening any more.

'You know,' Hunter said when they were back in the car, 'if we're right about this and Kim Dawson did know DeSanto, it's most likely from when they were younger. Like at high school.'

'We can check school records here to see when she was

at school. Get yearbooks and check photographs. Compare them with that picture of him that you have.'

'It would be too easy to find him like that. After all we've been through.'

'Sometimes that's how a case breaks.'

'I know. But not this one.'

'Keep the faith, Jake.'

He wasn't sure that he could.

6

Saturday Morning: London

Logan told Carrie that he would take the first shift outside Chase Black's hospital room. She protested, but he wouldn't listen.

'Go back to the hotel,' he told her. 'Get changed out of those clothes and freshen up. You can relieve me in four hours.'

He looked at his watch, surprised to see that it was now after three in the morning.

'Make it three hours,' he said.

Logan walked with Carrie to the ground floor where they found the MI5 officer, Eden, at the end of the hall in the main waiting area for the accident and emergency unit. There was the usual early weekend collection of drunks and brawlers with two uniformed police officers trying to keep the peace between two bloodied and determined men, both of whom were clearly inebriated.

'Can we talk?' Logan asked Eden.

He nodded and led Logan and Carrie through the waiting area and into another hallway.

'What is it?' he asked.

'Chase Black is our client,' Logan said. 'And it's our job to look after him.'

'You're saying that you want to take him away from here?'

'No, not if that would be against the advice of the doctor.'

'Then what?'

'We set up outside his room. I mean, you're not going to do that, are you?'

'We lost one man today. And maybe another. On what was supposed to be routine surveillance.'

'Your main concern is catching the shooter,' Carrie added. 'Isn't that right?'

'It would be unfortunate if another US citizen was to be killed on our shores,' Eden said. 'Particularly after an attempt has already been made on his life. Wouldn't look good for our special relationship.' He smiled. Logan detected a hint of sarcasm.

'That's not an answer,' Carrie said.

Eden looked down at her, drawing himself up to his full height of around six-three.

'I've seen bigger,' Carrie told him.

Logan laughed. She had a way of deflating a man's ego.

Eden smiled at Carrie. 'If you want to watch over him, that's fine with me. And you're right. That's not my main concern.'

Hunter nodded. 'Fair enough. Can you take us to Black's room and smooth over our presence with the hospital?'

'We'd appreciate it,' Carrie said.

Eden stared at her before nodding and telling them to follow him.

Black was in a private room on the second floor. The man who had accompanied Eden earlier was standing at the nurses' station immediately outside the bank of three lifts. Eden nodded at him as they stepped out of the lift and went directly to the desk at the station. A young Asian man was sitting there typing on a computer keyboard and looking at the screen in front of him. Eden showed the man his identification and explained that Logan and Carrie would be responsible for Chase Black's security. Eden did not explain who they were, leaving the nurse with the impression that both of them were on Eden's team.

It was smart on Eden's part — avoiding an unnecessary argument with hospital managers. Logan told him he appreciated it as they walked along the corridor behind the desk. Eden waved a hand — *don't mention it.*

Eden pushed at the last door on the left and walked in ahead of Logan and Carrie. Black was sitting up in bed watching a TV mounted high on the wall. Logan had expected to see a news channel, but instead Black was watching an old John Wayne Western.

'You like cowboys?' Hunter asked.

Black looked at him and shrugged.

'Better than the news,' he said. 'It's always full of death and violence, you know.'

He didn't smile and Logan was unsure if he was joking.

'We spoke earlier, Mr Black,' Eden said.

His voice had taken on a different tone and timbre – deeper and more formal in its pronunciation. Becky Irvine would have called it his 'phone voice' in a derisory manner and the thought made Logan smile.

'Your protection detail are going to look after you from here.'

'No official presence?'

Eden shook his head and left without saying anything else. It seemed unduly brusque to Logan.

Black looked from Carrie to Logan, his face devoid of any recognisable emotion. He lifted the TV remote from the table beside his bed and pressed a button to mute the sound.

'He told me earlier that they picked up Jay Drayton. And that he confessed to paying someone to kill me. Can you believe that? A hitman. It seems so . . .' He looked to the ceiling, searching for the right word. 'Absurd.'

'Jay Drayton,' Logan said. 'His family was killed in Denver?'

'Yes. He tried to attack me at my trial. I guess this time he wanted it done right.'

Logan thought that was an odd way of expressing it. A little callous. He couldn't really blame Black after what had happened.

'You know more than we do,' Carrie told him, rubbing at the bandage on her arm.

Black looked at her injury and then at her face.

'We were lucky, you and I,' he said. 'People died today.'

'I know that.'

'We're going to stay here to make sure no one else dies,' Logan said.

'You think this . . . killer will try again? Even with Drayton in custody?'

'I think it would be sensible to be cautious.'

'Will you get paid? I mean, won't my publisher consider the job to be complete?'

'We don't share that view if that is what they think. Leave any arguments over fees to us.'

Black's eyes narrowed as he looked at Logan.

'A man with real principles. Do you have true grit, sir?'

Logan couldn't help but laugh at the Western reference.

'It's never been put that way before,' Logan said. 'But I like it.'

7

Logan waited with Carrie at the lifts, Eden and his sidekick nowhere to be seen.

'Those M-I-Five guys made a sharp exit,' Carrie said as she pressed the button to call a lift.

'They're not renowned for their bedside manner.'

The elevator machinery clanked and whirred behind the heavy metal outer doors, the nurse still typing on the keyboard behind them.

'You like him, don't you?' Carrie asked. 'Black, I mean.'

'Difficult to judge the guy from our limited interaction with him.'

'But—'

'Yeah. He seems like an all right guy.'

'Doesn't mean he's not a killer.'

Someone coughed behind them and they turned to see Black leaning on the desk in his hospital-issue gown. He looked pale under the fluorescent strip lights.

'I was just—' Carrie started.

Black waved a hand at her. 'I'm used to it. Don't sweat it.'

The nurse stood and told Black that he should get back to his room. He walked around the desk and took Black by the elbow, turning him to go down the corridor.

'Did he follow us to eavesdrop?' Carrie whispered when they were out of sight.

'Kind of looks like it,' Logan said.

'He's a little . . . weird. Even if he is innocent.'

'I didn't say he was innocent. Just that I liked him.'

'Deep.'

Carrie nudged Logan in the ribs. The lift pinged to announce its arrival and the middle set of doors slid open. She turned and embraced him firmly, holding on for a few seconds. When she released him, she wiped a line of tears from both eyes. Logan squeezed her hand and nodded.

'We made it through,' he said.

'So far,' she said, backing into the lift. 'You be careful.'

She held his eyes with hers until the doors closed all the way.

Hunter walked down the corridor heading for Black's room. He passed the nurse on the way and heard the sound of the TV behind the door. He pushed at the door and went in to get a chair to sit on.

'I'll be out here if you need me,' he told Black as he lifted the chair from beside the bed.

Black looked at him blankly and back at the TV, turning the volume up.

Logan went into the corridor and closed the door. He sat

on the chair, facing along the corridor. He'd always wondered about the cops in movies who sat facing the wall opposite the room when they were guarding someone. It never seemed likely that any threat would come crashing through a wall.

There were metal detectors at all of the hospital entrances and Logan hoped that would be enough of a deterrent for Black's attacker to leave her guns behind. There wasn't much he could do about that anyway. He swallowed hard and put those thoughts out of his head.

The talk with Black about Jay Drayton had made him think of Jake Hunter. He checked his watch again and calculated that it would be somewhere around eight at night in Colorado. He took out his phone and dialled Hunter's number. It was answered on the second ring.

'Jake, it's Logan Finch. How are you doing?'

Logan heard a heavy sigh.

'Not too good, man,' Hunter said. 'Rough day, you know.'

'Tell me about it.'

'Of course, I heard what happened. How are you?'

'I'm good. Listen, they think Jay Drayton hired someone to kill Chase Black.'

'Jesus. Really?'

'Was what I heard.'

'What a world.'

'What's up with you, Jake?'

Logan sat in silence as Hunter explained what had happened. The walls of the corridor seemed to shrink around him.

'I don't know what to say,' Logan said when Hunter finished. 'I'm sorry. Danny seemed like one of the good ones.'

'He was. Impetuous and a pain in the ass sometimes.'

'Which of us isn't that, right?'

Hunter snuffed out a laugh.

'This guy,' Logan said. 'The one who killed Danny. Do you think he's the one?'

'Yes.'

'Does this mean for sure that Black is innocent of those murders?'

Hunter did not answer immediately.

'That's how it looks.'

'You don't sound convinced.'

'I don't know what I think any more. Listen, I'm going to have to book. We've still got a bad guy to catch.'

They promised to catch up again soon.

Logan stared at the floor and tried to comprehend what had happened in a single day thousands of miles apart. So much violence and anguish seemed to flow in the wake of this case. And it was innocents like Kate Marlow and Danny Collins who had been swamped by the waves.

8

Friday: Dillon

Hunter put his phone in his pocket and rested his forehead on his hands, splayed across his desk in the Dillon incident room.

'Maybe you should go to your hotel and get some sleep, Jake,' Frank Patton said, leaning against the door frame.

There was no one else in the room. Hunter remembered that Fields had been in the room when he was talking to Logan Finch and wondered if he'd fallen asleep for a few minutes. He sat up and rubbed his hands over his face.

Patton was still immaculately dressed in his full uniform. Hunter grabbed his tie and pushed it up to his neck, the top button of his shirt still undone.

'Sergeant Fields and every available cop on this force is on it,' Patton said. 'We're getting the local school caretaker to open the place up tonight so that we can go through their old yearbooks. We're still pounding concrete too. And the State highway patrol has been alerted. Guy can't have gone far. Won't get anywhere if I have anything to do with it.' Patton's face looked hard in the artificial light of the room. 'Except maybe into the ground.'

Hunter knew the feeling. 'Best keep your people on an even keel,' he said. 'I know how it feels, believe me. But we need to do this right.'

Patton stood away from the door frame.

'Far as I'm concerned, dead *is* right.'

He turned and left the room. It sounded as if Patton wanted to make this into a war. But they weren't at war. They were cops and that meant due process.

It sounded weak in his head. But he believed in it. Even after bending the rules and breaking the chain of command: it was a huge leap from that to having a shoot-on-sight policy in an investigation. That was no better than vigilantism.

Fields came into the room and handed Hunter a coffee.

'Looks like you could use this,' she said.

Hunter said thanks and sipped at the hot liquid. It coursed through him and into his stomach, burning all the way. It felt like the caffeine had been injected directly into a vein.

'The Chief was just here,' he told Fields.

'That man is hungry for some action,' she said.

'I know the type.'

Fields told him to take it easy and left again. He felt isolated. All of these people were out there looking to get the man who had injured their colleague. But his partner had died; had been murdered. It made him want to scream.

He finished his coffee and sat staring at the blank computer screen in front of him. He wondered if this was getting out of hand. He didn't really know the locals here. Fields seemed more than competent, but the more he saw of Patton, the more he seemed like he was wound a little too tight. And he was all alone in command. The cliché was true – being in charge was lonely at times like this. Maybe Patton had taken on too much and it was time to call in some support. It felt like things were teetering on the edge of being out of control.

Hunter got his phone and scrolled through his contacts. He paused when he found Dean Graves.

He pressed the button after a few seconds and waited for Graves to answer.

'Jake. What's up?'

'This is official now, right? I mean, the FBI's involvement in this case. My case.'

'It's official.'

'So if I need your help, need you here, all I have to do is ask?'

'You're making me worried.'

Hunter told him about Danny, and his concerns about Patton.

Graves was quiet for a while. Hunter did not fill the silence.

'Say the word and I'll be there,' Graves said eventually. 'It's not weakness to ask for help when you need it.'

'How soon could you be here?'

'Long as it takes to get wheels up and down again. Be there by dawn tomorrow, if you want. Say the word and I'll make it happen.'

Hunter wasn't so sure any more – wondered if maybe fatigue and grief were affecting his judgement. Had it really got *that* bad?

'Jake?'

'I'm tired, Dean. Let me think about it when I'm in better shape.'

'Don't leave it too long.'

Hunter ended the call and walked into the hall. He heard raised voices from Patton's room and walked towards it. As he neared the door, it was pulled open quickly. Patton came out followed by Fields. Hunter could see that Patton's anger had now morphed into something close to fury.

'Frank,' Fields said. 'Take it easy.'

She saw Hunter and stopped.

'What?' Hunter said.

'The foot patrols found a body. Woman got cut up.'

Hunter looked at Fields.

'DeSanto?' he said.

'Who the fuck else would it be?' Patton roared. 'I want that bastard taken down before he tears my whole town apart.'

Hunter saw that Patton had put on his gun belt. He had not seen him wearing it around the office before.

'Chief,' Hunter said. 'I think we need help.'

Patton turned on him, his face inches away.

'More city cops? How's that working out for us so far?'

Hunter wanted more than anything to lay Patton out right there. Fields saw it in his face and stepped between the two men.

How did it fall apart so fast? Hunter thought. Kimmy

Dawson, Danny and now another one. All in the space of a week.

Two dead in the space of a few hours. One of them a cop – his partner.

'He didn't mean it, Jake,' Fields said, pushing the two men apart with a hand on each of their chests.

Hunter took a breath. 'I'm calling in the FBI,' he said. 'They can be here in the morning.'

Patton stared at him.

Hunter turned away without waiting for any further response, taking his phone from his pocket and pressing 'redial'.

'I'm saying the word,' he told Dean Graves.

'We're moving now.'

9

Friday: Andrews Air Force Base, Maryland

Graves stood on the tarmac at Andrews Air Force Base, fifty miles north of Quantico, with the wind strong in his face and the sound of jet engines roaring in his ears. It had been nearly three hours since the call from Hunter and in that time he had hand-picked a small team of three men from the ranks of the Hostage Rescue Team and set in motion the official mount-out operation now taking place at Andrews.

Graves knew the HRT's reputation had suffered in the past from operations gone bad; that they were gung-ho soldier types with short fuses. And while it was true that the team had some veterans, they were also drawn from the ranks of the FBI field agents. The candidates went through a rigorous and exhausting training course and not everyone made it. They were the elite of the Bureau.

A man of average height with wide shoulders and short dark hair approached from behind Graves as he stood watching the ground crew checking the Gulfstream G-5 jet and topping up its fuel.

'Wheels up in ten, sir,' John Sullivan told him.

'Thanks, John. How's it going?'

'The boys are here and the gear stowed in the plane. We're waiting for the word from the pilot that he's ready to go.'

Sullivan was a long-serving member of the team and Graves's preferred second in command. He was, like the other men Graves had picked, a former field agent. Graves did not want soldiers on this trip. They were going to a small town to assist the local police force and there was no hostage situation to deal with.

Two other men walked around from the far side of the plane and nodded to Graves that they were all squared away and ready to go.

Jeff Seale was the shortest of the men at five feet ten. He was a marathon runner and had that long, lean look that made him appear taller than he actually was. His fair hair was thinning rapidly and it waved in the light wind. He was, in Graves's view, the best pure investigator on the team.

The last man, Doug Warner, had experience as a hostage negotiator and Graves knew that in situations like this – with a desperate man on the run and the body count rising – that the chances of the suspect holing up somewhere with hostages was high. Warner was a quiet man and a qualified HRT sniper. Graves always felt when he talked to Warner that he was being sized up through the highly magnified scope of his rifle. Warner held himself still and watched. If he hadn't known the man so well, Graves might have tagged him as a serial killer in waiting. He was, Graves had to admit, a little bit creepy.

'We short-handed or something, sir?' Seale said as he and Warner reached Graves and Sullivan. 'I mean, isn't this a light load for an HRT operation? We're looking at a cop killer, you know.'

Graves looked over the tarmac at the Gulfstream, the jet's wing lights glowing in the twilight gloom.

'I want to keep it as quiet as possible,' Graves said. 'Once we have the chance to assess the situation on the ground in Colorado we can always call in help from the local field office in Denver if we need to. The station head's a good man.'

Seale squinted at him in the wind, unconvinced.

'I picked you guys for a reason,' Graves told him. 'At this stage it's a low-level manhunt. One man on his own. I don't want to rumble into a small town with an army.'

'We do that,' Sullivan added, 'and the guy ends up dead? We'll take the heat for it. We've seen it happen.'

The men nodded.

The door of the Gulfstream opened and the pilot descended the short flight of stairs. He spoke to the head of the ground crew, though Graves could not hear what was being said over the rumble of the idling jet's engines.

This was the part that Graves loved: the start of an operation when they were in control and driving forward at their own pace. Being on the tarmac with the smell of jet fuel in his nostrils reminded him of his past, when he flew fighters off carriers.

The pilot came over to them and said that they were ready to go. He was an air force captain from the base's host Wing – the District of Washington's 11th Wing. Graves nodded in thanks and motioned for the men to board. They were wearing street clothes with blue FBI windcheaters. Ballistic vests and helmets were stored in the hold along with their weapons. They had handguns and H&K MP5 automatic rifles: short-barrelled weapons for close-quarters work. Warner had insisted on bringing his rifle too. Graves's sincere hope was that none of them would have to fire a single shot.

Graves looked across the airfield and saw an army transport plane on the far side of the base being loaded.

'What's your estimate for the flight time?' Graves asked the pilot as they walked together towards the Gulfstream, almost shouting now to be heard over the rising noise as the co-pilot started take-off procedures inside the cockpit.

'Five hours or so.'

'Gives us some time to review and plan for what's going on over there.'

'Yes, sir.'

Graves walked to the foot of the Gulfstream's steps and shook hands with the pilot, allowing him to mount the steps first. Graves went into the passenger cabin and sat next to John Sullivan. Doug Warner already had earphones on and was listening to some godawful heavy metal band. He remained motionless, not even tapping a single finger in time with the music.

'We all set?' Sullivan asked.

'Yes.'

'Try to get some sleep. Tomorrow could be a long day.'

Graves closed his eyes and remembered the first time he had met Jake Hunter. He still felt responsible for the bullet wound that scarred Hunter's right forearm. He could not forget Hunter's sense of duty or his courage – rushing into the dark, smoky interior of that bank on a crisp winter morning in Denver as a gun battle raged between Graves's FBI team and a small group of violent and committed bank robbers they had been tracking for six months. His memory of the events was fading now after more than ten years, but their friendship remained strong.

Graves sometimes wondered what would have happened if Hunter had not come running that day. His first action had been to shoot and kill the gang leader – who had Graves pinned down with automatic weapons fire.

In his darkest moments, he wondered if he would still be alive today had it not been for Jake Hunter.

10

Friday: Dillon

'We may have something on DeSanto,' Sally Kaminski told
Hunter over the phone.

Hunter turned his back on Sutton Fields who banged on
the side of the ambulance carrying the body of the last
victim. The ambulance engine rumbled to life and the vehicle
pulled around in a slow semi-circle and left the scene. There
was no need for the driver to activate the lights or siren. No
rush with a lifeless body in the back.

Hunter looked out over the still, black expanse of Lake
Dillon and walked away from the small amphitheatre with
its shallow bank of concrete steps sloping up and away from
the canopy of the stage. The steps doubled as seats. It was
typical of so many small town open-air theatres, except for
its idyllic location at the edge of the lake. Hunter could smell

the sharp odour of pine sap from a thin patch of trees that lined the ground next to the theatre's steps.

Two police vehicles were parked at either side of the rear entrance to the stage where the young woman's body had been found. She had been identified as a volunteer at the local amateur theatre company and had gone to the theatre to pick up some stage props left behind after a performance last week. As best they could figure it, DeSanto must have been hiding out in the backstage area and she disturbed him.

'What is it?' Hunter asked Kaminski, unable to muster any enthusiasm right now.

'We have a hit on the date of birth for a forensic programme at a community college in Boulder. It's small, but has a decent reputation.'

'It said on his application papers that he went to another school?'

'Penn State.'

'Nobody checked it with the school?'

'No.'

Hunter sighed.

'How in hell did this guy get past Steve Ames and Molly August? They're usually so precise.'

'I spoke to Molly earlier today when we were still running this lead down. See if she could remember anything else about the guy. Maybe something he had said at the interview for the job.'

'And?'

'She didn't interview him. Neither did Ames.'

'So how did he get hired?'

'You remember that gang turf war, when the bangers were taking each other out almost nightly?'

Hunter did. The whole department had been slammed, with no time off for almost a month.

'Well,' Kaminski went on, 'the lab was just as busy as we were so Ames delegated hiring two new technicians down the line.'

Hunter watched a speedboat cut through the water at the edge of the lake and thought that the owner was mad to be out at this time and in such poor light.

'They took who they could,' Kaminski said.

'Which is how DeSanto slipped through the usual filters.'

'So it seems. Anyway, we're looking into the individual with the same DOB who graduated out of Boulder.'

'How far have you gotten?'

'We have a name. Kurt Singer.'

Hunter repeated the name, rolling it around his tongue. It didn't seem any more, or less, sinister than Joel DeSanto. But it was usually after the event that names took on the weight of their crimes. He was willing to bet that Ted Bundy, Charles Manson and Ed Gein were all once considered normal names. Not any more.

Maybe Kurt Singer was the next one to be added to the roll call; the next name to be forever associated with the brutal murder of so many people.

'Is that his real name?' Hunter asked.

'We don't know. Not yet anyway.'

'Why not?'

'His academic records before he got to the Boulder school are sealed.'

'Why?'

'I don't know. Probably to maintain some kind of confidentiality. Like he was adopted or something. Anyway, we need another warrant to get access to those records.'

'Look at all records in the care system. Adoption, foster records and anything else that you can think of.'

'I will.'

'Didn't he have a home address registered with the college?'

'Yeah, but it was a local place in Boulder. A student residence. No prior home address was listed.'

'Jesus. How much red tape do we have to cut through to find this guy?'

'I spoke to Angel over at the DA's office already. We'll get the warrant worked up and have access to the records tomorrow. The net's closing, Jake.'

'Not fast enough. Did you hear that we have another body in Dillon?'

'We did.'

'I called in the FBI.'

'What? Why, Jake?'

Hunter turned away from the lake and looked back at the crime scene. Fields was kneeling beside the wide pool of blood where the victim had fallen. She was wearing protective plastic covers on her shoes and latex gloves while she leaned down and looked for clues in the blood. Another deputy did the same at the far side of the pool while two more taped off the area with yellow crime scene tape.

'I don't know,' Hunter told Kaminski. 'It just felt right.'

'Listen, take care of yourself. Don't push it if you don't have to. I'm on it and by this time tomorrow we'll have this Singer in cuffs.'

Hunter ended the call and walked towards Fields. A police cruiser pulled into the area behind the theatre and stopped. Chief Patton got out, taking the time to close the door gently and put his hat on. He walked over to Hunter.

'I got a call from your man at the FBI,' Patton said. 'Special Agent Graves.'

'Why was he calling?'

'He wanted to check with me that it was okay for him to be coming here.'

'That was good of him.'

Patton looked at the pool of congealed blood.

'Given he was calling me from an airplane en route to Denver, it didn't seem to me like I had much choice in the matter.'

That sounded to Hunter like something Graves would do. Patton continued staring at the ground.

'Are we square on this, chief?' Hunter asked. 'Because, you know, if I tell Agent Graves to turn back, he will.'

Fields stopped what she was doing and looked back at Patton and Hunter. She wiped a sleeve across her forehead, staining it with sweat. Flies buzzed around the lights of the police vehicles and in a cloud over the surface of the blood.

Patton turned his body to face Hunter.

'No,' he said. 'You were right to call in help.'

Hunter nodded.

'I just didn't like the way that you did it,' Patton said.

Hunter extended a hand to Patton.

'We're square, detective,' Patton said, gripping Hunter's hand firmly and shaking it once before letting go.

Fields joined Hunter and Patton and the three of them walked down to the lake's edge away from the deputies. Hunter brought them up to speed on Kaminski's call.

'The name Kurt Singer come up on anything you've looked at so far?' he asked Fields.

She shook her head. 'Don't think so.'

'I never heard it,' Patton said.

'If he did know Kim Dawson and he came to see her here, chances are he's been in this town before. Lived here, in fact. We need to check that name.'

'If you're finished here, detective,' Patton said, 'I'll drive you to your hotel tonight and we can make a start on checking the local records tomorrow. You need some rest and we won't get anything tonight. Don't worry. My deputies will be looking for this guy until the cavalry arrives in the morning.'

Hunter ignored the cavalry jibe and went with Patton to his car. He watched from the passenger seat as they reversed away from the crime scene and Fields went back to picking through the blood.

11

Saturday: London

It was a struggle for Logan to stay awake. He shifted in the chair at the end of the corridor, walked to the nurses' station and back and even did some exercises: push-ups and squats. It kept his blood flowing enough to stave off sleep at least for the first two hours. But he could feel his body shutting down.

He got up and walked to the nurses' station again, looking for a vending machine. There were none. He went to the desk and caught the attention of the male nurse.

'Where's the nearest coffee machine?' he asked.

'Ground-floor waiting room.'

Logan looked back down the corridor. He didn't want to leave Black alone.

'You got some back there?' Logan asked, nodding at the room behind the desk.

The nurse turned his head slowly to look behind him, as though he didn't know what he would find there.

'I'll make it myself,' Logan added.

The nurse looked at him again.

'We're not supposed to.'

'Or you can make it. I don't mind.'

Logan smiled, telling the nurse he was only a little serious. This guy was hard work.

'Sure, why not?' the nurse said after thinking about it a little further.

'Just milk,' Logan said as the nurse stood.

The man looked at Logan then turned and went into the room. Logan leaned against the desk and waited. He watched the floor indicators above the bank of lifts move up and down, heard the lift mechanisms grinding away. It was almost hypnotic.

He took a mug of coffee from the nurse when he came back and said thanks. It was pretty good for what was probably instant stuff and he sipped at it as he walked back to his chair. He set his mug down on the floor and felt his phone vibrate. He took it from his pocket and saw that it was Carrie calling.

'Can't sleep?' Logan asked her when he answered.

'Not really. I got maybe an hour on and off. How about you?'

'I could have slept.'

'You holding up okay? I mean, I can be there now if you want.'

'I'll be okay. The friendly neighbourhood nurse made me a decent cup of coffee.'

'If you're sure?'

'I am.'

He told her to grab another short nap before they switched in around an hour and then ended the call.

Logan heard footsteps and saw the nurse walking towards him. The man held a hand behind his back and Logan felt his muscles stiffen. The hand swung into view holding a packet of biscuits.

'Want one?' the nurse asked.

Logan's shoulders slumped as he relaxed again. He nodded and reached out to take a biscuit from the top of the packet. The nurse made no move to return to his desk. Logan took a bite and crunched through a mouthful of biscuit.

'It's good, thanks.'

The nurse nodded.

'How long you been doing this?' he asked. 'Being a body-guard, I mean.'

'Not long, really.'

'You got to train for a while?'

'Yeah. Couple of years before you get allowed out in public.'

One of the lifts started to move. Logan could hear the mechanism. He looked past the nurse and saw the floor indicator count down past them to the ground floor.

'What kind of training?' the nurse asked.

'You know, hand-to-hand combat. How to recognise danger and stop it before anything happens. That sort of thing.'

The lifts were all on the ground floor according to the digital displays above the doors.

'Any weapons? Knives or guns or anything?'

'A little of that, sure. But the key for us is to avoid trouble, not get into it.'

'Of course.'

The nurse nodded animatedly. Logan thought that the mention of weapons seemed to excite him more than it should.

'I'm into karate,' he said.

'Oh, yeah. How's that working for you?'

'It's great, you know. I love the full contact stuff.'

The nurse made a move, swirling his hands. The biscuits went flying.

'Shit,' he said, dropping to his knees to pick up the packet.

A ping sounded and Logan looked up to see a woman step out of one of the lifts. She held a bloodstained cotton pad to her head. Blood smeared her face and dripped on to the floor. She looked up and saw Logan, started walking towards him.

Logan thought she looked familiar, couldn't quite think where from.

The nurse stood and looked back at the woman.

'You're in the wrong place,' he said to her.

She kept walking down the corridor.

12

The nurse walked forward to meet the woman.

Logan's mind started to process everything. She moved purposefully and with full strides. The blood that had been dripping on to the floor when she had stepped from the lift did not now seem to be flowing down her face. And it looked overly bright, like it was *too* red.

'Where do I need to go?' the woman asked the nurse as he approached her with his hands held up, palms out.

What Logan thought was: the A & E department was hard to miss when you came into the hospital grounds – big signposts showed you the way. And if the woman was really lost, she would look more uncertain of her surroundings. She wouldn't stride down the corridor past the desk the way she had done just now.

He processed this in the space of a few seconds.

She walked right up to the nurse, dropped the cotton pad

to the floor and slammed her elbow into his throat with an audible cracking sound.

The nurse fell, his hands grasping at his throat, unable to get any air in through his damaged windpipe.

Logan turned quickly, shouted Black's name and grabbed the chair behind him. He swung the chair around and released it without pause. The woman tried to dodge it and threw her arms up to protect her face. The body of the chair was hard plastic but the legs were metal and it thudded into her, one leg catching her below the left eye and tearing open a two-inch cut.

She shouted out and fell sideways on to the wall, staying on her feet and reaching behind her. She brought the hand back around and Logan saw a thin knife. He wondered how she had got it past the metal detectors he had seen downstairs.

Probably ceramic, he thought.

She knows what she's doing.

Logan went backwards quickly and grabbed for the handle to Black's door, never taking his eyes off the woman. She drew an arm across the cut beneath her eye, this time real blood streaking her face.

Logan remembered her now; the woman from the club that night.

'Is he worth it?' she asked, her voice calm and even.

The nurse coughed on the floor behind her and rasped in a few breaths, the air feeling like razors in his throat.

'What?' Logan said.

The woman took a step, eight feet away now.

'That murderer,' she said. 'Chase Black. Are you ready to die for him?'

Her face remained calm despite the anger in her words.

'He's innocent,' Logan said, unsure if engaging with her would make any difference, but willing to give it a try. 'The cops in the States have another suspect now. I know.'

She took another step.

'*I* know his kind,' she said. 'I can smell it on them. Saw it in him at that club.'

Blood poured from the gash on her cheek, drops of it splashing on the floor at her feet. The nurse got on to his knees and gasped in some more air.

So much for karate, Logan thought.

The woman held the knife out in front of her, pointing it at Logan. He turned the handle of the door to Black's room and pushed it open an inch. He was sure that Black would have heard the noise and hoped he was calling the police right now from his mobile.

'This is wrong,' Logan said. 'You can walk away now and disappear. You're good at that, right?'

She shook her head, more blood spotting the floor. Logan stared at the centre of her chest, aware that any movement would start there. Not in her eyes.

'You ready for me?' she asked.

'Anytime you are.'

She moved fast, bringing the knife up and jabbing it towards Logan's throat. He pushed at the door and moved sideways through it, the blade slicing through the air behind him.

13

Logan slammed the door behind him and moved towards the bed. He glanced at the bed and saw that it was empty.

The door burst open.

The woman came into the room without pausing, moving at Logan in a straight line. He backed up until he was against the wall beside the bed. He reached out and picked up a glass of water from the table beside the bed, tossing the contents at the woman and smashing the glass on the table edge. He held the ragged edge of the glass out.

She stopped four feet from Logan and looked at the bed. A frown creased her forehead when she saw that it was empty.

Black burst out of the bathroom behind the woman. She turned at the noise but he was too quick for her, grabbing the hand that held the knife and twisting it sharply. She shouted in pain and dropped the knife as the wrist bone broke.

Black did not hesitate. He grabbed the woman's head and pushed it down as he brought his knee up, shattering her nose.

'Chase,' Logan said.

The woman's head snapped back and she fell to the floor, her eyelids fluttering on the edge of unconsciousness. Her arms were stiff and her hands spasmed as her brain tried to function.

Black knelt beside her and lifted the knife.

'No!' Logan shouted.

Black ignored him and slid the knife into the woman's chest, piercing her heart. She gasped and her hands flapped ineffectively at the knife embedded in her chest. She writhed on the floor for a moment and then her body grew still, her arms falling to her sides.

Black stood and stepped back from her, watching as she sighed out a final breath.

Logan stared at the body on the floor, blood pooling quickly around her.

'Jesus, Chase,' Logan said. 'Why?'

Black looked at Logan, his eyes flat in the half-light from the lamp on the table beside his bed.

'What do you mean?' Black said. 'She was trying to kill both of us.'

'But . . .'

'Now she's dead. Didn't quite work out for her, did it?'

Black went to the bed and sat on it, wiping blood from his hands on to the bed covers. Logan knelt beside the woman and felt the absence of a pulse.

'I was defending us,' Black said behind him.

Logan looked at him.

'There's no story here,' he said. 'I'll tell it like it happened, Chase. After that it's up to the police.'

Black shrugged.

'It's like I said. She attacked us. I killed her to protect myself.'

Logan stepped over the woman's body and went into the hall. The nurse was sitting with his back against the wall, his face pale and his breath coming in short gasps.

14

'It happened how it looks,' Black told Simon Eden, the MI5 chief.

They were standing at the mouth of the corridor while the police crime scene team worked at the end of the corridor and in Black's room. Logan sat on the edge of the desk at the nurses' station. Carrie paced back and forth in front of the lift doors, chewing at a loose fingernail.

Logan could see blood staining the floor of the corridor where the woman had bled from the cut on her cheek. He'd asked how the nurse was doing but beyond a terse 'he'll live' from Eden, hadn't been told much of anything.

Eden looked from Black to Logan.

'Is that right?' Eden asked Logan.

'What? That it happened how it looks?'

Eden nodded. Logan couldn't read his face; didn't know if he wanted anything more than confirmation. If Eden's reticence about the dead woman in Black's room was anything to go by, she was forever going to be known as 'the woman'. Logan understood from his previous conversation with Eden that MI5 had some idea of who she was. For all he knew, they were happy that she was dead and would be delighted for it to be confirmed as self-defence.

Black watched Logan impassively. His hands were still streaked with blood. There had been time for him to get cleaned up so Logan figured he'd been told not to by the crime scene people until they had examined him. How else to explain that he had not washed?

'It happened how it looks,' Logan said, finally.

Eden scratched the back of his head and looked down the corridor.

'Are you in control of this scene?' Black asked. 'I mean, isn't that something for the police?'

'The security services work together, Mr Black. I'm sure it's the same in your country. Common goals and all that, you know.'

Black rubbed his hands together and Logan saw flakes of dried blood flutter to the tiled floor like crimson snow. Logan thought that Black might try to rationalise the killing more than he had. That's what any normal person would have done – sought to exonerate themselves by giving elaborate details. Not Black. His version of events amounted to no more than – 'She attacked that nurse, tried to kill Logan and would have killed me.'

'The only security service here tonight', Black said, 'consisted of Logan. Nobody else.'

Eden stared at Black.

'My men were downstairs,' he said, sounding defensive for the first time.

Black shrugged, but said nothing.

Carrie finished pacing the floor and came over to stand by Logan.

'When can we get out of here?' she asked Eden. 'I mean, we're all exhausted and I know I could use some sleep.'

'What about Mr Black?'

'What about him?' Carrie said, frowning.

'Well, aren't you supposed to be looking after him while he's here?'

'I think that threat has been neutralised, Mr Eden,' Black said. 'Don't you?'

Eden looked uncomfortable, caught between Carrie and Black. He wasn't a man used to dealing with the public much – or explaining his actions to anyone but his superiors.

'You know I can't say anything about that.'

'I'm not asking you to surrender state secrets. I want to know if I'm safe or if I still have to look over my shoulder.'

'That would be useful information to have,' Logan added.

Eden could walk away without responding, he knew. That's what Logan expected of him. Outside of CPO, he did not have much experience of the intelligence community, but he suspected their reputation for secrecy was both essential and well deserved.

'There's no other threat to you that we are aware of,' Eden said, stuffing his hands in his trouser pockets like a schoolboy forced to make a confession.

'So I'm free to leave whenever I want?' Black asked.

'You've always been free to leave this country, Mr Black.

That's never been in any doubt. You'll have to ask the medical staff about leaving their care. That's not my decision.'

'Far as I'm aware, it is my decision. I'll sign whatever waiver of liability they want.'

Logan couldn't blame Black for wanting to get the hell out of that place. Or the country, for that matter. So far, it had not been a great experience for him.

'We'll stick with you if you want,' Logan told Black.

Eden turned and walked away without excusing himself. Logan watched him go.

'I think I've had about enough of British hospitality,' Black said, smiling thinly.

'Can't argue with that assessment,' Logan said.

'Can you stay till I get checked out of here, take me back to the hotel to pack and then drive me to the nearest airport?'

'Be expensive booking a ticket to travel on the same day,' Carrie said. 'If you can even find a spare seat.'

'I'll pay whatever it takes. Didn't you hear? I'm a rich man now.'

15

Saturday: Dillon

Hunter watched from the door of the police station as the black Chevy Suburban turned into the parking lot in front of the station. He smiled, knowing that Special Agent Dean Graves enjoyed playing up to the image most people had of the FBI – though he was far from conventional. Sutton Fields stood beside him and shifted her weight from foot to foot.

The big SUV bumped over the low kerb and swung into a spare parking bay, light from the morning sun reflecting off the flawless paintwork.

Dean Graves was first out of the car, stepping down from the front passenger seat and putting on a pair of aviator glasses as he walked towards Hunter. Three other men got out behind him and moved to the back of the car to unload their kit.

Hunter met Graves halfway where they embraced briefly. Graves had not been a regular field agent for many years and did not need to wear the Bureau regulation suit and tie. He wore a dark T-shirt over light-coloured chinos. Logan saw the USS *Eisenhower* tattoo half showing on his big right arm, peeking out from the sleeve of his T-shirt.

'You had a haircut since last time I saw you?' Hunter asked, looking up at Graves who had three inches on him.

Graves ran a meaty hand over the grey stubble on his head.

'Thought I'd go for something a bit more butch.'

'I think it's safe to say you achieved that.'

Graves stepped back and looked Hunter up and down.

'You look like crap, Jake. But it's good to see you.'

Hunter nodded.

'Good to see you too, Dean.'

'How are you holding up? I mean, after what happened.'

Hunter squinted in the sunlight.

'I'm fine, you know.'

Fields walked over and held out her hand to Graves. He shook it and they introduced themselves.

'It's good to meet you, sergeant,' Graves said. 'We don't have much time to waste, I guess, so I suggest we get inside and you can bring us up to speed.'

Fields nodded and told Graves that Chief Patton was waiting for them in the station. Graves looked back at the three agents who now had canvas equipment bags on the ground behind the Suburban.

'Can you have someone help my guys bring their gear inside while we all meet the Chief?'

'Sure, leave it with me.'

'I don't mean to be brusque. Just making the best use of our time.'

'Don't worry about it,' Fields told him. 'We've got a job to do and we're all professionals.'

Fields led them up to the incident room where Chief Patton was waiting. Graves introduced the members of his team and explained the expertise that each one brought to the operation. He was efficient and economical, Hunter realising that he had never really seen him at work like this. His immediate command of the room was impressive.

'What's the current position?' Graves asked.

Hunter shifted in his seat and glanced at Fields.

'We've had two-man patrols out all night,' she said. 'Where we have the spare manpower. But we're stretched for sure.'

'How so?' Graves asked.

Fields told him about the last murder the previous night.

'Plus the officers here don't have the experience to deal with this kind of thing. Some of them have never seen a dead body, never mind been involved in a murder investigation.'

Graves nodded.

'So far as you're aware, the killer is still in town?'

'That's our working assumption,' Hunter said. 'I mean, he fled the scene on foot and was hiding out at the amphitheatre when he killed his last victim. So it appears he had nowhere to go and no means of transport.'

'No reports of stolen vehicles?'

'No,' Fields said.

'His clothes will be heavily bloodstained,' Hunter added.

'This isn't really a murder investigation, is it?' Jeff Seale asked.

'What do you mean?' Patton asked.

Seale looked at him.

'It's a manhunt.'

16

'What do we know about this guy?' Graves asked after Seale's statement had sunk in around the room. 'I mean, apart from the fact that he likes to kill people?'

'Based on what your profiler, Nick Levine, told me,' Hunter said, 'we think he knew the first victim here in town. A woman named Kim Dawson.'

'She's a local?'

'Moved away to go to college. But yeah, this is her home-town.'

'You think he's from here?'

Fields nodded. 'Or at least that he's lived here at some point in his life.'

'So he must know someone else here,' Doug Warner said. 'I mean, you don't live in a town this size for any length of time and not know anyone, right?'

'I guess . . .' Fields said. 'But we think he was hiding at an open-air theatre.'

'Why do that if he knows someone local?'

'I don't know.'

'You think he might be getting help now?' Patton asked, his voice moving up in pitch. 'I find that hard to believe.'

'You been in this game long enough, you believe anything,' Graves said.

'I've been a cop for longer than anyone in this room.' Patton bristled. 'Including you, Agent Graves.'

Graves held a hand up.

'So we understand each other, chief, I'm not in the business of insulting anyone or questioning their abilities.'

Patton's face had flushed a little.

'But this kind of thing is what the FBI does. I know that the murder rate here is almost non-existent. So I'm not denigrating you. Merely stating facts.'

Patton's face lost some of its red sheen.

'I speak plainly, chief. And I know sometimes that rankles.'

Hunter got up from his chair and walked to the window. He looked out at the town and wondered where DeSanto/Singer was. The sun was higher in the sky and the town looked like every other one he'd ever been in.

'We think that our guy, Singer, might have been in the care system as a kid,' Hunter said. 'Denver PD is looking into it. Trying to get a warrant to get deeper access to the records. But he's used different names before so we may not find that name in those records.'

'A parent would protect a child,' Warner said. 'Can we check who the registered foster parents are in town?'

'Good idea, Doug,' Graves said.

'I'll get them to look at that in Denver,' Hunter said.

'This is good,' Graves said. 'This is what teamwork can do. Keep thinking and talking. No idea is too stupid to say out loud.'

'You're saying the foot patrols are probably no good?' Fields asked. 'Should we pull them?'

'If your people are tired and there's been no result, I'd say yes. Better focusing their efforts elsewhere.'

'We could interview teachers from the local schools,' Hunter said. 'Retired ones, I mean. They might remember kids who were in the care system.'

'Not a bad idea,' Patton said. 'Classes are small enough that they might remember.'

'Social services too,' Fields added.

'Good,' Graves said. 'Get your people back in off the streets and start working on those inquiries.'

Hunter felt the energy in the room rise. It had been a long day and night but Graves and his team had lifted everyone. It was what they had needed, a fresh perspective. No doubt they would have got to the same point, but they might have lost valuable time in the process.

'Let's get to it,' he said.

17

'Do you really think all of that is necessary?' Patton asked Graves as his officers brought the canvas bags into the incident room a few minutes later. 'I mean, it's just one man.'

'We like to work with our own equipment,' Graves said. 'Plus, I didn't know what your resources are like.'

'We don't have anything like that,' Patton said, pointing to the sniper rifle that Warner lifted from the longest of the bags.

Doug Warner walked over to Graves and Patton. Hunter and Fields were working the phones – Hunter speaking to Sally Kaminski in Denver to progress what they had discussed moments ago.

'It's tough dealing with even one person if they're in a house,' Warner said to Patton. 'It's the kind of thing I used to do. Talk them out, I mean.'

Patton stared at John Sullivan who was checking the short-barrelled machine guns and the loaded magazines.

'Unless you're really lucky,' Warner went on, 'you don't know the exact layout of the interior of the house. Even if you have plans, it might have been altered during a renovation project. And you can't be sure what kind of weapons the person might have.'

'We assume the worst,' Graves added. 'And hope for the best.'

'Correct,' Warner said. 'If you make the call to send a breach entry team in, you give them maximum protection and firepower. If they don't need it, great. If they do . . .'

He shrugged, the message clear enough.

Patton tilted his head back and rolled his shoulders, trying to release the tension in his muscles.

'I know that, of course,' he said. 'But this is a quiet town. It feels like the army rolled in on us.'

He tried to smile, and made a decent go of it.

'I understand your position, chief,' Graves said. 'Don't get me wrong, I try to be sensitive to local law enforcement. But I need to be able to run my operation the way I want if that's what it comes down to.'

Patton rested his right hand on the butt of his handgun which was still holstered on his belt. It seemed to Graves that Patton did not recognise the irony in the gesture, given his apparent dislike of the FBI's weaponry.

Sutton Fields ended her call and approached the group of men.

'Would you and your men like a quick tour of the town? Get a feel for the place.'

'That would be good,' Graves said. 'Let us get everything unpacked and we'll be good to go.'

* * *

Hunter nodded at Graves as he and his men left the room with Fields fifteen minutes later. Fields had left officers Earl Ray and Isaac Foster with instructions to locate and interview teachers who might be able to recall foster children they had taught. It was a long shot, but both men had been shaken by the attack on Danny Collins and Hope Rodriguez. They were more than willing to do anything to help.

Hunter knew from his call with Kaminski that they had the warrant to access social services records on Kurt Singer but were still trying to run the name down.

'They treat these records very carefully,' Kaminski had told him. 'To protect the kids. They're usually some of the most vulnerable in society.'

Hunter knew that there were sound reasons for such protection, but still felt incredibly frustrated.

'Would it help if you went down to wherever these things are held and kicked over a few tables?' Hunter had asked her.

Kaminski hadn't laughed.

'Don't think I haven't thought about it,' she said.

Officer Ray, who had been with Hunter when they got the news about Collins and Rodriguez, finished another call. He looked at Hunter.

'Anything new?' Ray asked.

Hunter shook his head, recounting the call with Kaminski.

'You hear anything about Officer Rodriguez?' Hunter asked.

Ray looked down at the pad on his desk where he had scribbled notes from the various calls he had made. The other officer, Foster, glanced at Hunter still holding the phone to his ear.

'Me and Isaac, Officer Foster, went to see her,' Ray said, still looking at his notes.

That was all he said. Hunter had heard what had happened to her and could understand the effect it would have on these men.

'Is this what it's like?' Ray asked after a moment.

Hunter frowned, not certain what he was being asked.

'What do you mean?'

'In homicide. Being murder police personnel.'

'What we're doing now is mostly what it's like, yes. Phone calls and the like.'

'What about those FBI agents?'

Hunter looked at the open door of the room. Recalled another open door he had walked through a long time ago.

'No, they're a breed apart. I mean, we get to go out on scene and pick over corpses but nine times out of ten it's either gang related or a domestic. We know who did it and it's pretty straightforward. Not many actual whodunits.'

'I thought maybe it would be exciting, you know.'

Hunter nodded.

'It is, but only sometimes. Mostly it's mundane.'

Ray turned in his seat to face Hunter.

'But it's good at the end, right?' he said. 'When you catch them.'

'It is.'

'Makes it all worthwhile?'

Hunter thought about Danny Collins and his ruined, empty body lying on an operating table.

'Not all of it,' he told Ray. 'Not by a long way.'

18

Graves and his men returned to the station in Dillon after two hours with still no further progress from any of the lines of inquiry that had been identified. The energy of the morning dissipated and the phones were quiet.

Patton came into the incident room when he heard the FBI team return. Hunter noticed that he no longer wore his gun belt.

'Slow progress?' Graves asked.

'That would be putting a positive spin on it,' Hunter replied.

'That's the way it goes.'

Hunter nodded.

Graves liked to be active. His days of being a pure investigator were long behind him and so staking out phones while others ran down warrants was not his notion of being productive.

'Chief,' he said to Patton, 'did you call your foot patrols back to the station?'

'Yes. Like you said.'

'Detective Hunter and the rest of your people have this stuff covered, so maybe my men could resume the foot patrols.'

Patton shrugged.

'Fine.'

'I'll come too,' Fields said. 'If that's okay, chief.'

Patton said it was, appearing resigned now to having lost most of his authority in the matter.

'Are you boys suiting up?' Fields asked Graves. 'I mean, your vests and the heavy weaponry.'

'The vests and sidearms, yes. The other stuff we'll load back up in our car so that we're ready to roll at short notice.'

The radio on Fields's belt crackled to life and she keyed the button on the mike fixed to her shirt.

'Sergeant Fields.'

Graves directed his team to prepare for their patrol while Fields listened to her radio. Hunter heard something about a complaint from a resident on Derby Street but didn't pay much attention to it.

Fields acknowledged the message she had received.

'What is it?' Patton asked her.

'Sounds like a domestic. Woman on Derby heard an argument in her friend's house. Said it got pretty loud and maybe physical from the noises she heard.'

Patton rubbed at his forehead like he was trying to suppress a headache.

'Want me to take it?'

'No, sergeant. You stay here. Ray, Foster, get the address from dispatch and head over there.'

The two men stood and headed out of the room.

'Be careful,' Fields told them before they left. 'Treat all calls with caution. We don't know where our man is.'

19

Saturday: London

It was quiet on the drive to Heathrow Airport. Chase Black sat beside Logan in the seats behind their driver, neither of them in the mood for small talk. Carrie had gone back to the hotel with Black while Logan stayed at the hospital and closed things off with Simon Eden and Black's publisher. One of the senior directors had arrived at the hospital as Black was getting ready to leave, checking on their investment.

Carrie had not been in the car when it returned to the hospital to collect Logan.

'Where's Carrie?' he had asked as he got in the car.

The driver shrugged.

'Said she wanted to pack,' Black said, looking straight ahead. 'Told me to come get you.'

Logan frowned. Their job wasn't quite done yet, not till Black was through security at the airport and beyond their control. It wasn't like Carrie to give up on anything. She stuck it out to the end.

'Did she say anything else?' he asked.

'Nope. She was real quiet, in fact.'

Logan took out his phone and called Carrie as the car moved away from the hospital entrance. There was no answer and it clicked on to voicemail.

'She's not answering her phone.'

'Probably catching up on some sleep,' Black said.

Logan wasn't happy, but there was nothing he could do about it now. He would find out her reasons later.

They approached Terminal 5 at the airport an hour later. The driver pulled Black's case from the rear of the car while he and Logan waited on the pavement. A mixture of holidaymakers and business travellers came and went from taxis, minibuses and private-hire cars. Logan saw a police armed response vehicle at the far end of the drop-off point. Two policemen with ballistic vests and automatic rifles slung across their chests walked along the pavement in front of the terminal.

Black took his case from the driver and rolled it into the building through sliding glass doors. Logan followed him. Inside, the ceiling stretched high above them. Black stopped under a bank of screens listing departures.

'You get booked on a flight home?' Logan asked.

'Yeah. Got a couple of hours or so before boarding.'

'You want to grab a drink or anything?'

Black set his case upright on the floor and turned to Logan.

'I think we've shared enough over the last few days, don't you?'

'It's up to you.'

Black glanced back at the departure screen and rubbed his chin with the back of his hand.

'No, let's call an end to this adventure now.'

'Okay.'

'I don't mean to be rude, Logan. But I want to get out of here.'

'Sure,' Logan said.

Black laughed.

'You think I'm full of shit, don't you?'

'Honestly, Chase. I don't think I know you at all.'

Black narrowed his eyes and smiled.

'Do you want to? Get to know me, I mean.'

'What would I find out?'

Black put his hand on the suitcase.

'I'll tell you one thing,' he said. 'Whatever happens from here, you're the reason I'm still alive. That I'm still in this world.'

It was Logan's turn to squint at Black.

'I don't think that's true. I mean, I'm not the one who killed that woman.'

'You got me in the car and out of the line of fire the first time. And you slowed her down in the hospital. Warned me that something was happening.'

'I suppose . . .'

'That's how it happened.'

Black grabbed Logan's hand and shook it firmly. Logan

looked at Black's hand gripping his and recalled how Black
had delayed washing his hands after killing his attacker. He
saw a line of red at one of Black's fingernails.

'You missed a bit,' he said as he let go of Black's hand,
pointing to the finger.

Black held the finger up and looked at it. He opened his
mouth, put the finger in and sucked at it. When he was done,
he examined it to make sure it was clean and dropped it to
his side.

Logan stared at Black as he turned and walked away
towards the security screening at the far end of the building.

Logan's phone rang in the car ten minutes after they had
pulled away from the terminal.

'I forgot to tell you,' Black said when Logan answered
the call. 'I left something for you back in your hotel room.
I think you'll like it.'

'Thanks,' was all Logan could think to say.

'See you around, Logan.'

Logan pressed the end call button. He wasn't so sure any
more that he wanted to see Chase Black again.

He dialled Carrie's number. There was still no reply.

20

Saturday: Dillon

Officers Ray and Foster arrived at the north end of Derby Street ten minutes after they left the police station. They saw a small house with cracked white stucco walls and a red tile roof. A beat-up old Sebring was parked at the kerb outside the house and all the curtains were drawn.

'What do you think?' Ray asked.

Foster shrugged.

'We go knock on the door and see what's what.'

Ray shifted uncomfortably in his seat. He knew what had happened when Hope Rodriguez had knocked on the door with Detective Collins. He wanted to tell Foster that it didn't feel right, but Foster was ten years older and Ray respected his partner's experience. He didn't know that Foster felt the same discomfort but was trying to act all nonchalant to show Ray what a tough, seasoned veteran cop he was.

They got out of the car together and approached the door at the front of the house.

Ray thought that he saw the curtains move to his right and jerked his head in that direction. The drapes were closed.

Foster moved ahead of him, stepped up on to the narrow porch and knocked heavily on the wooden door. It was such a loud sound in the quiet street that Ray almost jumped. He was still looking at the window.

'Jesus,' Ray said. 'Gimme a heart attack, why don't you.'

Foster turned to look at Ray.

The door exploded and Foster was thrown back off the porch and on to the wet pathway.

The blood soaking his partner's jacket didn't register immediately with Ray. He was momentarily deaf from being so close to the door when Singer had fired the shotgun behind it.

Foster pulled in a loud, ragged breath and tried to get his weapon from the holster on his belt. He looked wide-eyed and Ray realised that he was dying.

Ray pulled his weapon and half raised it before the remainder of the door shattered as another round from the shotgun ripped through it.

Ray fell sideways on to the lawn at the front of the house. He felt wood splinters from the door in his hand, raised his weapon and fired blind at the doorway. He was vaguely aware of someone shouting from inside the house. He raised his weapon again and emptied the clip at the door.

21

'Got a name and an address for you,' Sally Kaminski told Hunter.

Hunter was only half listening while watching Doug Warner take extreme care to pack his sniper rifle away. It was a thing of dark beauty.

'What?' Hunter asked.

'Got a hit. You were right to look at him being in foster care. We think Singer was a foster child and we got access to the records.'

'That was fast.'

'What can I say, I'm such a sweet talker. And ADA Angel is a difficult man to say no to when he really wants something. He came through with the warrants.'

'That's his real name? Singer, I mean.'

'No. We got three kids with that DOB. But, get this, one of them was placed with a family in Dillon.'

'You got a different name again?'

'If it's our boy, yes.'

'Give me the details.'

'Okay, the name this time is John Brown. The couple he was with from age four to age fourteen in Dillon, Colorado is called Reich. Amelia Reich and her second husband Gunther. Address is eighty-two Derby Street. The husband died, but the woman still lives at the same house as she did back then.'

Hunter turned to Sutton Fields.

'This must be him,' Kaminski went on. 'Would explain how he knew the Dawson woman if he lived in the town back then.'

'What was the address Ray and Foster went to?' Hunter asked Fields. 'The domestic.'

'Derby Street.'

Hunter felt a shard of ice slice down through his spine.

'Jake, you there?' Kaminski asked.

He ignored her. Asked Fields the number of the house on Derby Street.

'Eighty-two?' Fields said.

Hunter dropped the phone to the table. Everyone in the room turned to look at him.

22

Foster managed to pull his weapon free as Singer stepped out on to the porch, lifted the shotgun and shot him in the face.

Ray watched his partner die as he fumbled at his belt for a fresh clip. He looked up at Singer and shouted for him please not to kill him.

Singer turned his head slowly and looked down at Ray desperately pulling a clip from his belt and trying to smack it into the handle of his weapon. Singer cocked his head to one side and shot Ray in the stomach.

Ray felt his guts burn up and looked at the red mess that used to be Foster's face. He heard Singer step down off the porch and walk towards him, his footsteps soft on the grass.

Singer looked down at the bullet wound in his side where one of Ray's rounds had caught him.

When Singer looked at Ray again he realised he'd waited

too long and that Ray had his weapon reloaded. Singer raised the shotgun and fired at the same time as Ray pulled the trigger of his Glock.

Ray had his free hand raised in front of his face and it took most of the buckshot from the shell. Two of his fingers disappeared in a red mist. He dropped his gun and grabbed his hand, trying to stem the flow of blood from the stumps where his fingers used to be.

Singer dropped to his knees and let the shotgun fall at his side. A tendril of smoke wafted out of the fresh wound in his chest. He smelled cordite and the coppery aroma of his own blood.

Ray passed out, his hands falling on to his chest. Blood soaked his uniform shirt.

The neighbour from across the street who had called in the noise from the house earlier walked down her lawn to the edge of the road, trying to work out what all this new noise was about. She had been in the toilet when the shooting started.

Singer picked up the shotgun and fired two wild rounds at the neighbour. He didn't wait to see if he hit her and slowly crawled back into the house through the ruined front door.

23

Hunter was in the front of the Chevy with Graves driving and the three other FBI men crammed together in the back seat. They were following Chief Patton's car and skidded to a sharp halt behind him at the north end of Derby Street. Hunter saw the police car sitting at the kerb about fifty feet away. The bodies of Ray and Foster were visible on the lawn of number eighty-two.

The south end of the street was blocked off by two police cars – one driven by Fields. Three other cops with shotguns were crouched behind the tyres of the patrol cars. They looked young and scared.

Patton got out of his car alone and stood staring at the bodies of his men.

'Chief,' Graves shouted to Patton as he climbed down from the Chevy. 'You might want to get behind your vehicle for cover.'

Patton looked back at him and nodded before doing as he was told. He peered over the bonnet of his car from a crouching position with his gun drawn.

Graves had stopped the Chevy so that it was side-on to the street. The four FBI men and Hunter went around to the far side of the car out of sight of the house. They wore ballistic vests and the FBI men had their short-barrelled automatic rifles slung across their backs on nylon straps.

Hunter saw tension in Patton's face and realised then that he was really no more than a politician and didn't have the experience to handle anything on this scale.

He looked past Patton at the red splashes on the path and lawn of the house and heard Fields's voice on Patton's radio. Patton told her to sit tight.

'Nobody in this town is going to have enough reason to shoot and kill two cops,' Hunter said. 'This is our guy.'

'We don't know that they're dead,' Patton said without any real conviction.

Graves took a long breath.

'You're right, Jake.'

'So we're going in?'

Graves looked to Doug Warner.

'Time for negotiation is long past,' Warner said. 'Believe me, I've learned it from hard experience.'

'There may be a woman in there,' Hunter said.

'Chances are she's dead already.'

'If not,' John Sullivan said, 'we're the best hope she has to make it out of there.'

'What about the floor plan?' Hunter asked. 'I mean, we need to know what the interior layout is.'

'Best guess only at short notice. But the Chief may know these houses pretty well so I'd be happy to take his word based on what we have.'

Graves called Patton over. The Chief walked in a crouch from behind his car to the Chevy before he stood up. He explained that the house was probably pretty basic. A central hallway with a kitchen at the back and three or four other rooms off it. He wasn't sure, but thought that maybe the hallway finished in an 'L' shape, leading to the bathroom.

'We're going in now, chief,' Graves told him. 'Is that okay with you?'

Patton nodded.

'You and Detective Hunter stay here. My team will handle the breach.'

'No,' Hunter said.

Graves stared at him.

'This is my case, Dean, and I'm going to see it through to the end.'

'I have control of the scene,' Graves said.

'I know.'

Graves popped a knuckle on his left hand and looked at his second in command, Sullivan.

'Your call, sir,' Sullivan said. 'But if he'd taken down one of our men, I'd want to be in there too.'

Graves thought for a second then nodded. He told Warner to stay with Patton.

'Jake, you follow me down the street staying tight to the walls of the neighbouring houses. He shouldn't be able to see us because his house is recessed back from the others. I'm going in the door first with you at my back. John and

Jeff will take the back door. Put him down if you have to. You have my authority on that.'

Hunter nodded and sweat ran out of his hair and down his face. His shirt was plastered to his skin and he still felt colder than he ever had. Patton got on the radio and told Fields the plan. When he was finished, Graves walked out from the Chevy with Hunter behind him and started down the street.

The density of the air changed and seemed to thicken, making it hard for Hunter to breathe. Graves moved quickly at a fast walk with his rifle firmly against his shoulder, pointing straight ahead ready to engage any target.

Sullivan and Seale moved off to the left and went behind the row of houses.

This is it, Hunter thought.

24

Saturday: London

Logan called Carrie three more times from the car. He had been stuck in a slow-moving traffic jam for more than an hour – the result of an accident closing one lane of the motorway. There was no answer on her mobile or the phone in their room.

He didn't know what it meant, but it made him uneasy.

He thought of Chase Black's last words – something about him leaving a present for him back in the room.

That meant that Black had been in the room.

With Carrie.

What was going on?

25

Saturday: Dillon

Graves turned smoothly up the path at Singer's house without pausing. Hunter looked down and saw blood on the path and then he was at the door behind Graves. It was half blown away and hanging off its hinges. Graves put his hand on what was left of the door when they heard a moan behind them. Hunter turned sharply and saw Officer Ray's hands slip from his chest on to the grass. He moaned again.

Graves pointed at Patton and then at Ray. He gave a thumbs-up sign to Patton, hoping the chief would understand what he meant. Ray needed immediate medical attention if he was to have any hope of surviving his injuries.

Graves didn't wait for Patton to react. He pushed the door open and went into the house quietly. Hunter followed.

The house smelled stale, like a retirement home. As they

moved up the hall, Hunter felt the place close around him. The paint in the hall was cracked and flaking.

Graves pushed a door on the right wall and it opened into a cramped living room. The room was empty.

There was noise behind the door at the far end of the hall. It sounded like someone trying to speak through pain but they couldn't make out any of the words. Graves looked back at Hunter and motioned forward with his hand. Hunter slipped past Graves in the hallway and Graves trained his weapon on the door that the noise had come from.

Hunter put his hand on the door to open it and felt it pulse warm and moist under his palm. He pulled his hand away and looked at the door. It was just a plain door and when he put his hand on it again he felt only cracked paint and dry wood. He pushed the door open and moved inside the room, his gun pointing directly ahead.

A man was slumped on a wooden chair in the kitchen. The sink overflowed with rancid water and a bare bulb in the ceiling bathed the room in weak yellow light. The man was slicked red with his own blood that pooled around his feet and spread like a great lake to the edges of the room. His skin was bleached of colour. Hunter couldn't believe he was still alive.

Behind him was the body of an older woman slumped on the kitchen table on top of what looked like a large book.

The only thing preventing Singer from slipping off the chair and on to the floor was a pump-action shotgun propped under his chin. The butt of the gun rested on the floor and the index finger of his right hand was wrapped around the trigger.

Graves went into the room behind Hunter. They moved apart, keeping their weapons trained on Singer. Graves saw Sullivan and Seale at the back windows behind Singer and held a hand up telling them to maintain their position. The last thing he wanted was two more high-powered weapons in that small space.

Singer lifted his head and blinked the slack skin of his eyelids. His eyes were the only part of him that looked alive. They were black in the weak light, but it was only the reflection of his blood on the floor. His body looked empty and his face had the gaunt look of someone waiting to die. The effort of looking up seemed to exhaust him and he wheezed in a shallow breath and grunted it out before resting his weight back on the barrel of the shotgun.

Hunter stepped forward. The floor was slick underfoot, a mixture of Singer's blood and water from the overflowing sink. The cold electric current of his evil felt like a living thing, infecting the house and everything in it.

'I'm dying,' he said. 'One of those cocksuckers shot me.'

'What do you want from us?' Hunter asked.

'I want to die.'

His voice was surprisingly strong and deep now, echoing off the bare walls and floors.

'He made me in his image,' Singer said. 'After what she did to us. He helped me become strong again. Helped me survive.'

Hunter frowned, feeling sweat soaking his back under the vest. The gun felt heavy in his hands.

Graves moved slowly towards the body of the woman. He checked her for signs of life. There were none.

'He said you would know him,' Singer said.

'I don't know what you're talking about.'

Singer made a noise that must have been intended as a laugh of sorts.

Then his face disappeared. Hunter reeled back against the door frame, the flash and the noise of the shotgun going off in the small space, the sudden utter violence of it, like a bomb exploding. Singer pulled the trigger, taking his face and half of the front of his head with it.

His body slumped wetly to the floor.

Sullivan and Seale burst in through the rear door, Sullivan slipping on Singer's blood and landing in the puddle on his side. He slipped twice before getting upright again.

'What happened?' he asked.

'Guy blew his head off,' Graves said.

Even he sounded shocked by what had happened.

'Jesus,' Seale said, looking down at what was left of Singer's head.

'John,' Graves said, walking around the body to the door into the hall, 'go tell the Chief what happened.'

Hunter holstered his gun and went to the table where the woman's body was. He pulled the book out from under her and saw that it was a photo album, open at a page where the date had been written in black ink. The photographs there were more than twenty years old.

He wiped a hand across the page to clear some of the blood spatter and looked at the largest of the photographs that was fixed at the centre of the page. It showed two boys sitting on the lap of a woman. Hunter guessed that it must have been the dead woman.

There was a caption under the photograph that read: 'John and James – One Year Anniversary'.

The smaller of the two boys was obviously Singer. He looked painfully thin, his face a mask of misery.

Hunter was drawn to the other boy. He was older and much bigger. He sat upright with a look of defiance on his face. His green eyes almost shone. Maybe it was a trick of the light or Hunter's imagination, but that's how he would remember first seeing that photograph.

Seeing Chase Black and his foster brother Kurt Singer.

The portrait of a family of killers.

26

Hunter went outside into the daylight and gulped in a lungful of clean air. Patton was kneeling on the grass beside Ray. An ambulance came on to the street, its lights pulsing and the siren wailing. It stopped at the kerb and the siren faded. Two paramedics jumped out and ran to Ray. Patton stood and backed away to let them work on him.

Hunter fumbled in a pocket for his phone and dialled Logan Finch's number. He was redirected to voicemail. He tried again with the same result, leaving a message for Logan to call him immediately.

He sat on the top step leading up to the porch and rested his elbows on his knees, watching the paramedics. It all made sense now: the mistakes with the evidence and why Singer had not been more careful at the last scene.

Singer didn't want Black convicted of the murders. He wanted the evidence, Black's blood recovered at the last scene, tainted so that Black would be acquitted. It had been deliberate. He had put himself at the heart of the investigation and the recovery of evidence so that he would be beyond suspicion. And so that he could do the same for his brother if he needed to.

He was free to tamper with and taint evidence as it suited him. As it suited both of them.

But Hunter couldn't figure out one thing – why Black and Singer had stayed quiet about the tainted blood evidence at trial and allowed Black to be convicted. Was it part of a plan to make money somehow from Black's notoriety? Use the tainted evidence to get free on appeal? Hunter didn't know if Black was insane enough to try that gambit, but it had worked out one way or another with his book deal giving him all the money he could want or need.

He wondered if it was abuse suffered at the hands of his foster mother that had made Singer into the man he had become. Was that what he had said at the end – *'after what she did to us'*? It was such a familiar story, such a heartbreaking one.

Abuse breeds abuse. Breeds murder.

But Chase Black was a different kind of monster. Hunter was convinced of that now more than ever. Black was the strong one. Had obviously used his brother's weakness, vulnerability and terror to create him in his own image.

Made him a killer.

Graves came out of the house on to the porch and handed Hunter a cotton wipe. Hunter scrubbed at his face to get rid of the blood that was already beginning to dry and crust. Graves put a hand on Hunter's shoulder briefly and told him they would get Black, that it was only a matter of time. He walked away from Hunter towards the Chevy.

Hunter's phone rang. It was Logan.

'Where's Chase Black?' Hunter asked without any introduction.

'What?'

'Where's Black?'

'Probably on his way back to Denver. I left him at the airport.'

Hunter closed his eyes and rubbed at them. Maybe this would all turn out all right after all. Pick Black up at the airport and put him back in jail, hopefully to stay there this time until he died.

'He did it, Logan. He killed all those people.'

Logan was quiet for a while. Hunter thought he had lost the signal before he spoke again.

'You're sure of that?'

'No doubt about it this time. He had a partner. The other guy we've been looking for. His brother'

'Did you catch him?'

'Yes.'

'Look, Jake, I have to go.'

Hunter said goodbye without recognising the fear starting to shake Logan's voice. He walked to Graves and told him that Black was on a flight to the US.

'He's coming home,' Hunter said.

'I'll call the Denver field office to pick him up off the plane. Give him the welcome he deserves.'

'I want to be there. To snap the cuffs on him myself.'

'You will be.'

Sullivan came out of the house and shouted Graves over.

'Stay strong, Jake,' Graves told him as he went back to the house.

Hunter opened the door of the Chevy and sat sideways on the runner. His phone rang again and he answered the call from Kaminski.

'I found something else,' Kaminski said.

Hunter tried to cut her off, but she spoke in a rush.

'Those foster records for Singer. The family had a second kid at the same time. Another boy. Get this, his DOB matches Black's. I mean, Singer and Black are brothers. Jake . . .'

'I know.'

'What?'

'We got Singer. He was at the house. He killed himself.'

'But . . .'

'There are photographs of him with Black. Back when they were kids. He as much as confessed, for him and Black, before he blew his head off with a shotgun.'

'We have to get Black.'

'We will. He's on his way back from London. The FBI will arrange to get him at the airport.'

'What do we charge him with?'

'Conspiracy. If we can show that he planned it all with Singer, we can charge him separately with conspiracy to commit murder. Can use the same evidence.'

'We've got him.'

'Yeah, and this time I want to make sure he goes away for good.'

Hunter hung up and placed the phone on the seat behind him. He lifted his face to the sun and tried to smile.

27

Saturday: London

It took Logan an hour to reach the hotel after the call from Hunter. He ran past the line of tourists waiting at the lifts and burst through the door to the stairway, taking the stairs two and three at a time.

He knew that he had to keep moving, that if he stopped he might never get there. He had not been able to reach Carrie since the airport more than two hours ago and that image of Black sucking the blood from his finger was burned on to his retina.

The corridor where their room was situated seemed to stretch out ahead of him, the room getting further away the faster he ran. His legs were past their physical tolerance limit.

I left something for you back in your hotel room. I think you'll like it.

That's what Black had told him.

Logan dropped the credit card-style key to the room and grabbed at it when it fell to the floor. He banged on the door and shouted Carrie's name. There was no answer.

He pushed the card into the slot above the handle and the light turned green. He flung the door back against the wall and ran in. The book on his bed did not register for a moment. The room was clean and the beds made up.

Logan went into the bathroom. There was nothing.

He stood there for a moment, feeling his legs tremble from the effort.

Back in the room, he sat heavily on his bed, not even noticing that the door out into the hall was still open. He felt something at his back and reached around to find a copy of Black's book. He opened it to the title page.

Carrie walked into the room with a gym bag slung over her shoulder, her hair tousled and damp.

'Hey, stranger,' she said, smiling.

Logan looked up and her smile faltered.

'Where were you?' he asked, his voice little more than a whisper.

'I went to the spa. Had a sauna and then a lovely girly massage. Why?'

Logan stared at the book open in his lap and at the inscription in Chase Black's handwriting above his signature:

For Logan
You're the reason that I'm still alive.

'What is it?' Carrie asked, sensing Logan's unease.

He handed her the book and waited while she read the inscription.

'I don't get it.' Carrie frowned. 'What's it mean?'

Logan went to the window and looked down at the street below, at all the people going about their ordinary lives. All of them potential targets for a man like Chase Black.

'I got a call from the police in Denver,' he said, turning to face Carrie. 'They've got new evidence. Black *is* a killer. He had a partner to help him.'

Carrie looked at the inscription on the book again.

'He's taunting you,' she said.

Logan nodded.

'It's over for him anyway. I left him to board a flight home. Back to Denver. They'll arrest him straight off the plane, is my guess. He's not going anywhere except jail.'

'That's good.'

'He's right about one thing. Black, I mean. He'd be dead if it wasn't for us.'

'We did our job, Logan. They told us he was innocent.'

He turned to the window again, thinking of Becky and his daughter and Black's last words at the airport – *see you around*.

Now it seemed less like a friendly parting.

More like a threat.

Carrie came up beside him.

'He's trash,' she said. 'He'll get what he deserves.'

Logan knew she was right. But he wanted to hear his daughter's voice anyway. He took out his phone and called her. She answered before the second ring.

'Hey, Dad.'
Dad.
He liked that.

Memorandum

From: Franck Zimmer
To: Section Chief
Re: Project Dawn – Intial Report

Interpol Ref: 8159A – 1

Sir,

We have confirmation from the US authorities that Subject 'Night' is officially wanted in connection with several deaths in the United States. As you are aware, subject 'Night' was acquitted of murder charges on appeal and cannot be tried again on those same charges. Prosecutors in the US advise that they will now charge him with the separate crime of conspiracy to commit murder in relation to the same victims. It's an excellent strategy.

Regretfully, MI5 surveillance in the UK of Subject 'Night' ceased upon the death of Subject 'Eve' – who was the target of our initial inquiries. Her sponsor, Subject 'Mamba', is in custody and will face charges in connection with the murder by Subject 'Eve' of the US citizen Kate Marlow and one MI5 intelligence officer.

Subject 'Night' was booked on a flight out of London Heathrow to Denver, Colorado. FBI agents and local law enforcement waiting in Denver secured the aircraft upon landing.

Subject 'Night' was not located on board. It is suspected that he left the UK on a flight to another destination under a different name. MI5 are searching CCTV records at London Heathrow in an attempt to identify which flight he boarded.

He is listed on the FBI's most wanted list at number six – ahead of some Al Qaeda members still known to be at large. That is a measure of the seriousness with which his crimes are viewed.

Financial records obtained from subject 'Night's' publisher disclose that he has been paid more than $1 million. The money was sent to a Swiss account. As is standard practice in that jurisdiction, we have been denied information and access.

Subject 'Night' is now believed to be at large in continental Europe and considered highly dangerous. He has substantial means available and we have deployed major resources to assist in the hunt for him.

Reports to follow.